"Whateve bappens to me."

She saw the loyalty in his eyes, the pure stubbornness, and understood that he intended to stand by her. Despite the risk, despite what had happened between them last night, he didn't want her to leave.

His protectiveness soothed her battered emotions. Looking up, she managed a small smile. "You don't have to do this."

He searched her eyes for a long second. "I do, Jenna. I do."

Reflexively she reached up and caught his hand on her shoulder. His hand folded around hers, warm and solid and strong.

Jenna tightened her grip, needing the connection, the steady feel of his support and presence. She'd forgotten what strength a simple bond like this could bring, forgotten that solid intimate connection with another person. A man.

With Linc.

Dear Reader,

Have you noticed our special look this month? I hope so, because it's in honor of something pretty exciting: Intimate Moments' 15th Anniversary. I've been here from the beginning, and it's been a pretty exciting ride, so I hope you'll join us for three months' worth of celebratory reading. And any month that starts out with a new book by Marie Ferrarella has to be good. Pick up *Angus's Lost Lady;* you won't be disappointed. Take one beautiful amnesiac (the lost lady), introduce her to one hunky private detective who also happens to be a single dad (Angus), and you've got the recipe for one great romance. Don't miss it.

Maggie Shayne continues her superselling miniseries THE TEXAS BRAND with *The Husband She Couldn't Remember.* Ben Brand had just gotten over the loss of his wife and started to rebuild his life when…there she was! She wasn't dead at all. Unfortunately, their problems were just beginning. Pat Warren's *Stand-In Father* is a deeply emotional look at a man whose brush with death forces him to reconsider the way he approaches life— and deals with women. Carla Cassidy completes her SISTERS duet with *Reluctant Dad,* while Desire author Eileen Wilks makes the move into Intimate Moments this month with *The Virgin and the Outlaw.* Run, don't walk, to your bookstore in search of this terrific debut. Finally, Debra Cowan's back with *The Rescue of Jenna West,* her second book for the line.

Enjoy them all, and be sure to come back again next month for more of the best romantic reading around—right here in Silhouette Intimate Moments.

Yours,

Leslie J. Wainger

Leslie J. Wainger
Senior Editor and Editorial Coordinator

Please address questions and book requests to:
Silhouette Reader Service
U.S.: 3010 Walden Ave., P.O. Box 1325, Buffalo, NY 14269
Canadian: P.O. Box 609, Fort Erie, Ont. L2A 5X3

THE RESCUE OF JENNA WEST

DEBRA COWAN

Silhouette®
INTIMATE™MOMENTS®

Published by Silhouette Books

America's Publisher of Contemporary Romance

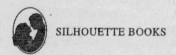

SILHOUETTE BOOKS

ISBN 0-373-07858-7

THE RESCUE OF JENNA WEST

This edition published by arrangement with Harlequin Books S.A.

® and TM are trademarks of Harlequin Books S.A., used under license. Trademarks indicated with ® are registered in the United States Patent and Trademark Office, the Canadian Trade Marks Office and in other countries.

Printed in U.S.A.

Books by Debra Cowan

Silhouette Intimate Moments

Dare To Remember #774
The Rescue of Jenna West #858

DEBRA COWAN

Like many writers, Debra Cowan made up stories in her head as a child. Her B.A. in English was obtained with the intention of following family tradition and becoming a schoolteacher, but after she wrote her first novel, there was no looking back. She recently quit her job at an oil company to devote her full time to writing both historical and contemporary romances. An avid history buff, Debra enjoys traveling. She has visited places as diverse as Europe and Honduras, where she and her husband served as part of a medical mission team. Born in the foothills of the Kiamichi Mountains, Debra still lives in her native Oklahoma with her husband and their two beagles, Maggie and Domino. She would love to hear from you.

SASE for reply: Debra Cowan, P.O. Box 5323, Edmond, OK 73083-5323.

To those with the courage to shed the darkness of the
past and reach for the light.

Prologue

He wasn't drunk enough.

He still knew where he was—his barn, slumped against the back stall door.

And the pain still burned through him like a jolt of bad drugs—disabling, numbing, weakening.

Even the familiar, often comforting scents of hay and oats and horseflesh couldn't dim the pain. The reality.

Michelle had left him for another man. And she'd also—

Enraged, Linc Garrett closed his mind against the thought.

He drained his beer, hurled the bottle at the barn wall, then crumpled back against the stall door. Getting out of the house—Michelle's house—hadn't helped.

He'd thought the liquor would blunt the edge of agony. Instead it had sharpened, burning deeper into his soul. Every time he moved, every time he thought her name, he sliced himself on another memory of Michelle. Damn her!

He groped beside him for another long-neck, guzzled the beer and slammed the bottle into the door beside him, breaking it off at the neck. The sharp *crack* and splinter satisfied him. He needed the sound to drown out the scream of agony that welled inside him.

Staring vacantly at the broken bottle piece clutched in his hand, he brought it closer to his face. Closer. He turned the ragged edges this way and that, wondering if he would even feel the pain of a cut.

He couldn't imagine feeling anything else on top of this searing brutal pulse of his senses. She'd cheated on him with a friend, but that wasn't the worst of it. Today, he'd learned that she'd taken his—

"Dr. Garrett?"

He started, the jagged piece of broken glass grazing his cheek. Peering into the hazy light that filtered into the barn, he squinted up. "Who is it?"

"Jenna West. The vet. I came to check Dixie's sprained fetlock."

"Don't need a vet. Go away." He barely recalled his mare's injury. His blurry gaze focused on the slender, jean-clad legs in front of him then climbed over a denim shirt with cuffed sleeves, and up to a smooth sweep of auburn hair. She knelt until her eyes met his.

She smelled like flowers and hot sin. Gently, she pulled the piece of broken glass out of his hand. "I want to help you get to the house."

"Don't need your help. Don't like women. Hate 'em."

"I'm a doctor," she said reasonably. "Like you."

"You're pretty." He'd noticed her before, all those times she'd come to check his dogs or the horses. Noticed the way her jeans cupped her shapely rear, noticed the aqua of her eyes. She had incredible eyes. Eyes that now gazed at him warmly. She wasn't Michelle. She wouldn't treat him the way Michelle had.

Jenna leaned closer, reaching for him.

She had nice lips, not too full and they were soft looking.

She wanted to help him. She could make him feel better. He grabbed her forearm and pulled her toward him, wanting to kiss her, wanting to feel the hot slide of her tongue against his. Wanting to forget.

"No!" She wrenched away from him, so hard and fast that she nearly fell. She caught herself, her nails digging into the dirt floor.

Linc blinked. What was wrong with her! All he wanted was a kiss. She'd said she wanted to help.

"Come back," he said hoarsely. Frustration burned through him. And then the sense that something was wrong. *But what?*

Her chest rose and fell rapidly. Tension lashed her lithe body, but it was her eyes that captured his attention. They were dark now, with fear. And revulsion.

Fear. She was afraid of *him.*

No one had ever looked at him like that, as if he disgusted them. As if he scared them to death.

The realization crashed over him like a frigid wave.

Beneath the alcohol, beneath the pain, guilt welled. He leaned his head back against the post that supported him and closed his eyes. "I won't hurt you," he whispered, sickened at putting that look on her face. "I won't."

"Don't you want to go inside?"

He opened one eye, surprised at her question, surprised she was still there.

"In the house? Don't you want to go in the house?"

She was afraid of him, but she hadn't left. He wondered why, but his tongue was too thick to form the question. Grateful now, he nodded.

With soft words and persistence, she coaxed him to his feet. Keeping his gaze on her, careful to keep his hands to himself, he staggered toward her. She backed out of the barn and he followed, struggling to stay upright.

Nausea rolled in his gut; sweat prickled his neck and back. Still he followed her.

They reached his sprawling gray stone house and she persuaded him to the front door. He fumbled with the knob, still haunted by the look of sheer terror in Jenna's eyes. He'd done that to her. *Him.* He was as big a jerk as Michelle had always said.

Hearing the retreating scuff of Jenna's boots, he turned. She moved gracefully down the shallow porch steps and toward her white Jeep.

He'd scared her to death. His stunned mind seemed capable of only that thought as he watched her walk away from him.

He gripped the doorknob, balancing himself. "I'm sorry," he rasped, hating himself for frightening her. "I'm sorry. Didn't mean...to scare you."

She never turned around, just kept on walking.

Chapter 1

Four years later

Sirens screamed. Noise exploded in a burst of shouted orders and the rush of thundering footsteps. Inside the emergency room of Oklahoma City's Mercy Hospital, doors popped open and the sirens' wail foghorned through the busy sterile corridors. A blast of August heat cut through the cool interior.

Linc scribbled a prescription for the ten-year-old boy on the bed in front of him and shoved it at the boy's mother.

"These are for pain. Just take the script to your pharmacy." He turned away, barely registering the paper whiteness of the woman's face.

She grabbed his elbow, turning him slightly. "Thank you, Dr.—" her gaze dipped to his name tag "—Garrett."

He nodded brusquely, giving a vague smile as he walked out of exam room number three. Signing off on the boy's chart, Linc stepped into the hallway and ran into Bridget Farrell.

"Farrell, bandage that kid's sutures and send him home."

The pretty blond nurse took the chart from him, scanning his orders. "Which kid?"

Linc motioned to the cubicle he'd just left. "Number three."

"Don't you want to dismiss him?" She turned, backing into the exam room.

Linc shook his head. "Already did. And tell him to stay clear of handsaws in the future."

She aimed a look of disgust at him, her attractive features flattened. Shaking her head, she turned away from him to enter the exam room.

The sirens whined to a stop at the emergency room doors and Tracy Bartlett ran past him. "Assault victim. Are you staying?"

"No." Linc had been on for thirty-six hours without sleep and though he had nothing to go home to, he was craving a cheeseburger.

He shouldered his way inside the doctor's lounge and shucked his coat, scrubs and hospital shoes.

He dressed in worn jeans and the same red knit polo he'd worn to work thirty-six hours ago then pulled on his snake-skin boots. He had staff privileges at other hospitals, but he'd started working this emergency room shift about two months ago and liked it. Palming his keys, he pushed through the door and headed out the exit.

The EMTs were wheeling in a trauma and Linc sidestepped a nurse who sprinted past him to ready exam room one. Dr. John Clive, a third year resident, walked up beside Linc.

"You taking off?"

"Yeah." Linc edged closer to the wall to give the other doctor more room to pass on his way to the stretcher.

"Multiple contusions, possible broken arm," one EMT called to Tracy Bartlett.

Nurses clustered around the new arrival like grannies over

a new baby and Linc gave a deep sigh of fatigue. Maybe he would forget the cheeseburger and grab some sleep after all.

He neared the door, stepping out of the path of the oncoming stretcher and glanced over at the patient.

His heart slammed to a stop. "Jenna?"

He couldn't remember the last time he'd *known* a patient.

Shock burned through him and he stepped toward the gurney, pushing between Tracy and Dr. Clive. "Jenna, can you hear me?"

Tracy shot him a look of surprised curiosity and Dr. Clive stepped back.

Jenna West turned her head toward him and Linc's gut clenched. The combination of sculpted cheekbones and square jaw that gave her features such strength were now bloodied and swollen. Always so self-contained, she now looked fragile. Vulnerable.

Her dark auburn hair was stark against the pale marble of her skin. A gash seeped blood above her right eyebrow; her right arm rested carefully across her stomach and her generous lips were busted. Angry red marks ringed her throat like a cruel chain, foretelling of bruises tomorrow. Blood streaked her smooth tanned skin and he noted blood under her fingernails, too.

Blue-green eyes, glazed with pain, sought his, then focused in recognition. "Dr. Garrett?" she managed to whisper through puffy lips.

He nodded, leaning in closer. "What happened?"

Her left hand reached for his, grasping, clutching, her nails digging weakly into his skin. "Wilbur. Where's Wilbur?"

Linc blinked, wondering who Wilbur was, wondering how much of her was operating on shock. She trembled and beneath her golden tan, her skin was waxy. He glanced toward the EMTs and noted a uniformed cop striding through the emergency room doors.

Johnson, a veteran EMT, nodded at Linc. "We did find an old guy at her office. He's DOA."

The patrol cop, robust and bald, stepped up. "What we figure is the old guy saw the assault, called 911 and headed out the door to help her. He distracted the assailant long enough for us to get there, but it was too late for the old man. The assailant ran off when he heard us coming. She's lucky. She could've been worse."

Linc thought she looked bad enough. "Did you get a look at the guy?"

"No. We searched the whole area, but haven't turned up anything yet."

"What about Wilbur?" Jenna's words sounded as if they were scraped out of her throat. "What about the animals? Someone has to take care of the animals, the clinic."

The officer eased closer to the gurney, light bouncing from his badge. "I'm Officer Sikes. I need to talk to this lady."

"Not right now," Linc snapped.

Jenna's hand tightened on his. "Where is Wilbur?"

"We're going to take care of you," he soothed automatically as he had so many times to other patients, but this time it sounded hollow, less than reassuring. A strange feeling pressed at his chest, as if his heart had just cracked open.

What had happened to her? Who would want to do such a thing to Jenna West? She was a veterinarian, for crying out loud! *His* veterinarian. He'd seen her last week coming out of his barn, though they hadn't spoken.

Guilt pricked at that, then Linc felt an unfamiliar, unwelcome rage rise up inside him. Try as he might, he couldn't dismiss it. Compassion stirred and something deeper, a concern he hadn't allowed himself to feel toward a woman for four long years. Since Michelle had left. It scared the hell out of him.

He motioned Dr. Clive forward. "Jenna, this is Dr. Clive. He's going to take care of you."

"No." Her lashes fluttered and her eyes, cloudy with pain, met his. "You. I know you."

Panic arrowed through him and his instincts screamed for

him to get out of this while he could still do so without investing emotionally. He'd been dog-drunk in his barn, and she'd helped him.

How could he turn his back on her? Besides, he knew if he left, he'd wonder about her all night. Something else he never did.

That night in the barn he'd made a drunken pass at her, but he hadn't been so plastered that the revulsion in her eyes didn't register. Revulsion, directed at him.

Now there was no disgust in her jewel-colored eyes, only a plea. Linc found himself allowing his emotions, as unwanted as they were, to control his actions, cloud his judgment. He *could* help her, not only as an apology for that drunken pass, but also to return the favor she'd done him that night. She'd most probably saved his life; she had definitely saved his career, had prevented him from cutting his hands to shreds with those broken beer bottles.

"My patients," she moaned. "Someone needs to take care of them."

"Shhh. They'll be fine." Compelled to help in a way he hadn't been in years, Linc realized his decision had been made. He waved Clive away. "I'll take it."

Moving with the gurney into exam room one, he snapped to Bridget, "Get X-ray down here."

But she was already running down the hall, anticipating his orders before he could voice them.

The police officer followed, planting himself in the doorway. "I'll need to talk to her as soon as you're finished. If she says anything—"

"I'll let you know." Linc slammed the door in his face.

Across the gurney from him, Tracy leaned down to Jenna, asking quietly, "Miss West, who should we notify?"

"My—" Tears welled up in her eyes, seeped onto the raw-looking scrape at her cheekbone. "My parents. Dave and Barbara. On Gleneagle."

Tracy glanced at Linc on her way out. "I'll call them."

"And Steve—" Jenna inhaled sharply as Linc touched her arm.

He didn't know who Steve was and Jenna didn't—or couldn't—say anything further at the moment. Linc focused his attention on her dilated pupils, gently examining her arm. In a distant, detached way, he realized she was beautiful. But as he worked, tamping down emotions that had roared to unsuspecting life inside him, he was uncomfortably aware that he had just allowed himself to become emotionally involved with a patient.

And he had a distinct sense of foreboding that he might not be able to walk away this time.

Rage crested inside him. He'd had her, right in his hands where he'd visualized her for the last eight years. And she'd gotten away.

Deke Ramsey stood in a phone booth outside a convenience store a few miles from her clinic. The August night, thick and steamy, clung to him and sweat trickled down his temple. Gripped in his hand were the hospital listings he'd ripped from the phone book. He shook violently, grinding the receiver into his ear.

Only a couple of hours ago, Deke's hands had closed around her soft throat. He could still see the desperation and fear in her eyes, feel the sharp, but useless kicks she'd aimed at his legs and crotch.

Night after night, he'd lain rotting in that cell, planning his revenge, imagining his body ramming into hers over and over as she begged him to stop.

And she'd gotten away.

The old man who'd raced to her rescue had paid, though.

With his life. At that thought, Deke's lips twisted in grim satisfaction. The fury rose up again, hazing his vision, triggering a loud buzz in his ears. So far he'd had no luck finding her, but he was far from finished.

He shoved another quarter in the slot and jabbed in the number.

"Mercy Hospital," answered a cheerful, feminine voice. "Emergency."

Deke's fists clenched, the paper in his hand crackling. He schooled his voice to convey just the right amount of concern and anxiety, leashing the black rage that clawed through him. "Yes, I'm trying to find a friend. I'm not sure if I have the right hospital."

"What's the name, sir?"

"Jenna West."

"Just a moment."

He'd already called the several hospitals ahead of this one as he worked his way alphabetically down the list. In the background, he could hear the staccato clicking of a computer keyboard.

Not allowing thoughts of failure, his gaze fixed intently on the old man's blood speckling his arm. Anticipation filtered through his hatred. This was it. He'd find her now.

"I'm sorry, sir. We have no one here by that name."

Deke slammed down the phone, cursing violently, the rage straining at his lungs. It didn't matter. This was only the first play of the game. He would call every hospital in this city and if he didn't find her, he'd start over. But one way or another, he'd find her.

Waves of pain ebbed through her. Red and black and blue tangled, circling viciously inside her. Images flashed through her mind. Wilbur's face crumpled in pain and disbelief as he fell to the ground. Linc Garrett's gray eyes, distant and remote, stared through her. Someone else—someone she didn't want to see—leered at her.

A soothing voice reached out to her with gentle strokes and she latched on to it, pulling herself to consciousness.

She came awake with a start, but had no energy to open

her eyes. Slowly she peeled them open, pain shooting behind her temple.

The voice was gone, silent now. In its place was an insistent memory and the fear—nagging, mushrooming.

Cool air swirled around her. Groggily she registered the quiet sterile room, the flimsy hospital gown, the heavy cast on her right arm.

A monitor hummed quietly beside her. It hurt to swallow, to breathe. Her throat was raw. Her chest and torso ached as if she'd been trampled by a horse.

Then she remembered. In a hazy surge, she recalled heavy hands on her, brutal, punishing, uninvited. But she didn't want to remember that. She had felt other hands, gentle and soothing. Whose hands were those?

Pressure pushed against her ribs and she tried to take a deep breath. Fear swelled in her chest, squeezing, crushing. She moved, trying to escape the fear, but it spread, locking her in a merciless grip.

It gnawed at her confidence, erased the determination with which she'd rebuilt her life. No, she wouldn't allow it, she thought groggily, overwhelmed by a black tide of tension she couldn't escape.

She was alone. But she was safe, for now.

She held on to that thought with the last remnant of her strength. Her breathing eased and tears burned her eyes. Her gaze dragged slowly around the room. Her mouth felt thick and dry, but the razor-edge of pain was gone. Her IV beeped, dispensing more medicine through the needle in the back of her hand.

Then she saw Linc Garrett. He sat beside the bed, his arms folded on the side rail, his head resting on his arms. She remembered then *his* hands moving gently over her, *his* voice soothing.

She shifted and his head came up. Smoky eyes locked on hers, concerned, searching.

He looked tired. He'd stayed. She could barely register the thoughts.

He leaned closer. "You're all right."

"No, I should—" She was swept by a sudden need to tell someone about the fear, about the man who'd assaulted her, but she felt her eyes closing. "Steve."

"It's okay," Linc murmured. "I'll stay with you."

She felt herself slipping, losing control and rational thought. Her thoughts tumbled through a mass of shock and buried pain. She didn't want to remember. She couldn't afford not to. She wouldn't allow Deke Ramsey to destroy her life again. She wouldn't.

It was her last conscious thought before the drugs claimed her.

Linc stared down at the woman in the bed, shaking with rage. The violent marks around her throat were dusky purple in the artificial light that ran in tracks around the ceiling. Who would do such a thing to her? And why?

Since the night Jenna had found him in the barn, he'd seen her less than a dozen times. He'd never thanked her for what she did for him. At first because he was embarrassed for making that drunken pass at her. And the real reason—harder to admit—because he couldn't forget the horror in her eyes.

He didn't blame her. Even he had been sickened by his behavior that night. Well, he hadn't had a drink since then. Not that Jenna West knew. Or cared. He stifled the impulse to tell her, as if telling her would magically heal the battering her body had taken.

Seeing Jenna on that gurney tonight had resurrected, violently, those long-ago memories. That night in the barn was a blur of anguish and hate and a small taste of comfort. Ignoring his curses and drunken attempts to retrieve the bottle, she'd somehow gotten him into the house.

Without once touching him, he now realized.

Now, sitting here in the darkened room with her, he realized she'd never mentioned the incident, either. No doubt due to his behavior that night.

Nurse Karen Jameson walked silently inside and stopped short at the sight of Linc beside the bed.

Annoyed at her obvious astonishment over finding him there, he waved her impatiently toward Jenna. "Do what you need to," he said in a curt whisper.

Curiosity burned in Karen's dark eyes, but she stepped toward her patient. After a quick check of Jenna's blood pressure and temperature, and a small adjustment to the IV drip, she turned for the door.

She glanced over her shoulder at Linc. "Are you working another shift?"

"No," he replied, dismissing her abruptly. "I'll be right here."

Karen's gaze darted to Jenna and speculation crossed her features.

"Good night," he said coolly.

She eyed him curiously and disappeared out the door.

Linc leaned forward, resting his forearms against the bed's metal railing. Jenna slept peacefully. Her smooth wide brow was unfurrowed, her breathing steadier now, yet her skin was chalky beneath her tan, making the bruises appear black.

He could've left, and probably should have. But Tracy had been unable to reach Jenna's parents and Linc didn't want to leave her alone. He wouldn't, even though he was probably the last person on earth she'd want here.

"I've got to talk to her, Linc."

"I said no. She's not even awake!"

Jenna had been conscious for a few seconds, struggling to sort out the distant echoes she now recognized as voices in her room.

She was still groggy, but not disoriented. Daylight filtered into the room, proof that she'd made it through the night. And though she wished to be waking from a bad dream, the ache in her body and the nausea in her stomach told her that her confrontation had been all too real. Having rested, Jenna could no longer dodge the memory of what had happened last night.

Deke Ramsey was out of prison. And he'd found her.

Now she could determine that the hushed masculine whispers just inside her door belonged to Linc Garrett and another man. With her left hand, she awkwardly fingered the bandage above her right eye.

Her right arm lay at her waist in a heavy cast. Her throat burned and her lips felt as large as melons. For an instant, she wished she had a mirror then decided it was best she didn't. Heaven only knew what she looked like. Her face felt like a football that had been kicked flat.

"The longer we wait, the more headway the bastard will make." That from the man Jenna couldn't see.

"Well, you can't talk to her if she's unconscious, can you?" Linc said sharply.

The other man paused then added quietly, "She might've fought him. Scratched his face or bloodied his lip, something we can look for."

"Too bad she couldn't have killed the son of a—"

"Dr. Garrett?" Jenna's throat was tight and his name croaked out.

She wasn't certain he heard her, but then his head peeked around the wall extension.

"Jenna." Relief shaded his voice and he walked toward her. "Glad you're awake."

The other man stepped into full view and she frowned at his resemblance to Linc. "Hi, Dr. West. I'm—"

"This is my brother, Mace. He's a detective, which makes him a natural nuisance," Linc interrupted dryly then frowned at Jenna.

"He needs to ask you some questions, but only if you say so."

She nodded, feeling as if she were weaving in and out of

consciousness. Her body throbbed and her mouth was thick from the medication.

Mace Garrett stood about an inch shorter than Linc and where Linc's hair was a sandy brown, Detective Garrett's was sable dark. Linc's eyes were gray and sharp; his brother's were blue, direct yet warm.

He rolled a small stool next to Jenna's bed and eased down onto it. His eyes were kind. "I hope you're up to this, Doctor."

"I'll try," she rasped. "I want to catch him, too."

Linc leaned threateningly toward his brother. "Don't bully her. You only get a few minutes. Three."

Mace stared oddly at Linc then turned to Jenna. "Now, could you—"

"What about Wilbur?" Jenna's breath lodged painfully in her chest.

Mace's blue eyes softened with compassion and before he said the words, Jenna knew. "I'm sorry. Dr. Hanley didn't make it."

Deke had killed Wilbur. She took a deep breath, wincing at the sharp pain in her side as the memories flooded in. "He was trying to help me."

A tear seeped out of the corner of her eye and Jenna lifted a shaking hand to wipe it away.

"I'm sorry," Detective Garrett said softly. "I take it he was a friend of yours?"

She nodded, anger melding with the nausea, the fear.

I'll get you, bitch. I'll get you.

Deke's words circled viciously in her head. He'd killed Wilbur, who'd never done a thing to him. She had no doubt Deke Ramsey would make good on his threats to her.

A new fear stung her. "What about my parents?"

"We're still trying to get in touch with them," Detective Garrett said kindly.

Panic slashed at her, cutting her breath. "What if he—"

"Let's not think the worst, Dr. West. Perhaps they've been out of town or—"

"Yes." Relief slid through her and she closed her eyes on another surge of exhaustion. "Yes, they're at Laurel's. I'd forgotten."

"Laurel?" the detective probed.

"Laurel Chevlan." Jenna struggled to open her eyes. "My sister. She lives in Tulsa."

"Can you stay with me for a few more minutes? I need as much information as you can give me."

"I'll try." She longed to slip into the black void that beckoned, but forced her eyes to stay open. "I was through for the day, walking to my Jeep and he just grabbed me. By the hair. He shoved me against the truck and started saying—"

Her bruised stomach muscles tightened painfully. She struggled to breathe past the horror of retelling the story. She refused to repeat his exact words. "He started threatening me. He hit me and I hit back. I just kept hitting him. I wasn't going to let him…"

"What, Dr. West? You weren't going to let him what?" Mace urged.

"Mace," Linc warned, hovering over her.

"I wasn't going to let him…" She was so tired. And her head hurt. "Hurt me anymore."

"Can you give me a description, Jenna? Anything. I know it was dark, but as much as you can remember. *Anything*."

"I can do better than that." The words scraped her tender throat like glass. "I can give you his name."

Linc frowned and stepped closer to the bed.

Surprise flared in Detective Garrett's eyes and he nodded, pen poised above a small notebook.

She closed her eyes, licking lips that were dry and split.

"It's…Ramsey. Deke Ramsey."

Mace scribbled the name, frowning. "I know that name."

Linc moved to Jenna's other side. "She's fading, Mace. Isn't that enough for now?"

"I can do more, if you need it." She struggled with the words, feeling as if she were being sucked into a dark void, completely at the mercy of her drug-induced lethargy.

She had no energy, no strength. She couldn't focus on the detective, but she felt him rise to his feet. Then she heard other voices, familiar voices.

A gentle hand touched her face and her father's deep voice settled over her. "Jenna, doll?"

"Dad?" She fought to open her eyes, wanting to see him.

He stroked her hair away from her eyes. "Mom's with me. We're right here."

Jenna fought against another swell of lethargy. She opened her eyes and looked into her mother's green ones, bright with tears, her father's blue ones glimmering.

"Oh, I'm so glad you're here." They were all right. Ramsey hadn't gotten to them. With the relief came a trickle of strength.

"We came as soon as we returned from Laurel's." Her mother edged around her dad and placed a kiss on Jenna's head.

She was so tired, so sore. She wanted to rest, but something niggled at her. "Mom, the animals. Will you take care of the animals? And Puppy."

"Yes, honey. Don't worry about that."

There was something else, something important. "Oh, Detective. Did you...more questions?"

"Only a couple."

She nodded, her head heavy and throbbing.

Linc spoke from the foot of her bed. "Mace, she's had enough for now."

"It's...okay," she managed to say through swollen lips. "Just get it finished."

She tried to focus on the detective next to her bed, but it was too much effort and pain crashed through her skull.

"This Deke Ramsey, Dr. West. How do you know him?"

Her mother gasped and her hand tightened on Jenna's.

Her father tensed as well. "Honey, you don't have to do this."

"I do, Dad." She struggled to open her eyes, to meet Detective Garrett's shrewd gaze. "I knew him when I was in vet school. He went to the university. Oklahoma State."

The detective scribbled something in his small notebook. "You were friends? Or maybe you dated him?"

Tension webbed the room, crisscrossed in sharp prickling patterns between her and her parents that even Jenna, groggy on drugs, could feel. They hated for her to talk about it, but they knew it was sometimes necessary.

"No, Detective." Peaceful sleep pulled at her, but she lifted her gaze to his, struggling to hold on to consciousness. "He raped me."

She was aware of Linc's strangled curse then nothing.

Chapter 2

*R*ape? Shock and horror sliced through him, crowned quickly by a compassion that wrenched at Linc's heart. He could see things now, things that before he'd attributed to the revulsion he'd seen in her eyes that night in the barn. Why she hadn't pursued even friendship with him after rescuing him from the barn, why she never stayed to chat, why she often checked the animals when he was gone.

No wonder Linc had repulsed her. Now as he stood outside her door with Mace and his partner, Reid O'Kelly, the too familiar scents of soap and antiseptic were suddenly choking. *What a jackass he'd been.*

A page sounded over the loudspeaker and an orderly walked past, steering a man in a wheelchair.

O'Kelly glanced at Mace. "I'll run the scumbag NCIC."

As O'Kelly hurried off to run a check through the National Crime Information Center, Mace turned to Linc. "It looks like revenge. A brutal attack and now I see why."

"What are you going to do to help her?" Linc snapped, suddenly wanting to hit something, someone.

Mild curiosity gleamed in his brother's eyes, then he scratched his head. "Well, we've got to get her somewhere safe in case this guy comes after her again."

Linc froze. "Do you think he will?"

"Very possible. We'll have a better idea after O'Kelly gets back."

Just then Mace's partner strode up, dodging an orderly and a nurse. O'Kelly's face was grim. "Nurse Farrell said a call about Dr. West came in last night."

Mace's lips flattened. "So, he's already looking for her."

This was the closest Linc had ever been to Mace's work. Besides having a sense of stepping out of reality, Linc felt totally inept.

O'Kelly edged closer. "Ramsey finished his time, but he got out of the penitentiary at McAlester two weeks ago."

"Damn," Mace said.

Linc kept his voice down, not wanting to alarm the Wests or their daughter. "Are you saying this Ramsey knew exactly where to find Jenna?"

O'Kelly shrugged. "Well, it didn't take him long."

Nausea rolled through him.

Mace shoved a hand through his hair, his gaze flicking to his partner. "What's the story?"

O'Kelly didn't even glance at the notebook he held. "She testified in a rape case against him and they put him away for eight years. He played football for OSU and—"

"I remember." Mace snapped his fingers. "He was all set to sign a letter of intent to go pro when they handed down his sentence."

O'Kelly nodded.

Linc felt as if he were spinning into a cone of fury.

"This guy played football for Oklahoma State University?"

"If you didn't work so much, you'd remember," Mace said dryly. "It was her testimony that convicted him. After she came forward, so did several other women."

"That was Jenna?" Maybe everyone in Stillwater knew the particulars, but not in a city the size of Oklahoma City. Linc felt a surge of admiration. He shook his head, astonished at the secret pain this woman hid.

He noted that Mace wore his gun, strapped in a shoulder holster and he wondered if Jenna had been at all intimidated by the cops in her room. Sadly he realized she was probably used to them.

O'Kelly lowered his voice. "Look, Mace, this guy wants her bad. He knew where she was. He's already killed one man who tried to help her. What are we going to do with her until we find him?"

"First, put out a radiogram on his whereabouts."

"Done."

O'Kelly and Mace efficiently and briskly put together a plan of action while Linc stood by feeling as useless as he had his first year of med school. He kept seeing the vicious bruises on her throat, the blood under her fingernails attesting to the fight she'd waged against her attacker.

Mace braced one arm on the wall. "We need to find somewhere for her to stay."

"What about her parents?" Linc offered.

Mace looked doubtful. "Not a good idea. If he could find *her* that easily—"

"Detective?" Mr. West stepped outside Jenna's room and closed the door. "Could I speak with you a minute?"

"Certainly." Mace shifted toward the older gentleman, who looked to be in his midfifties, just at six feet tall, robust with a thick head of gray hair.

Linc observed absently that Jenna got her cheekbones from her mother, but she had definitely inherited her determined jaw from Dave West. And her eyes were a perfect combination of her father's blue eyes and her mother's green.

The older man glanced hesitantly at Linc and O'Kelly.

"It's all right, Mr. West," Mace reassured gently. "We're all working on this together."

Once again Linc marveled at the way his brother firmly, yet kindly handled the people he dealt with. Linc himself felt as if he were about to disintegrate into a wild sweeping rage.

"Barbara and I thought you should see this. We found it in our morning paper today, just before we got the message about Jenna."

He reached into his trouser pocket and pulled out a piece of paper, handing it to Mace.

As Mace read, his face tightened with concern. He handed it to O'Kelly and turned back to Mr. West. "Has your daughter received any others?"

"Not that we know of, but you should ask her."

Mace nodded. "You did the right thing by showing this to us. We're going to put your daughter somewhere safe, but I'm afraid it can't be with you."

"That's why I thought you should know."

Linc's nerves stretched taut and he leaned toward O'Kelly, reading the short handwritten note addressed to Jenna.

D - E - A - D
Dead is what you're gonna be.

The floor seemed to tilt beneath him. Had Jenna seen this? How was she handling it?

Resistance rose up, fierce and abrupt. He didn't want to get involved. But wasn't he already? Something about Jenna West, or perhaps it was her circumstances, pulled at him deep inside, where he hadn't allowed himself to feel anything for a long time.

He could tell himself he wasn't involved, but the truth was he had become involved that long-ago night in the barn when she'd rescued him.

Mace and O'Kelly talked with Mr. West, trying to figure out a place for Jenna to stay.

"She won't go far," warned her father in a low voice. "She won't let Ramsey control her life again."

"But she needs to stay clear until we can get our hands on him." Mace's voice was hushed as well.

"I agree," said Dave West. "But you'll have a hard time convincing her. Especially if you try to get her to give up her work."

"You said her sister lives in Tulsa?"

The older man nodded. "But she won't go there. She'll say it's too far to drive if she needs to get to her patients."

"We'll find a safe house for her." Mace exchanged a look with O'Kelly. "Assign police protection—"

"She can stay with me." Linc couldn't believe he'd said the words. He'd meant only to consider it, not to offer.

Mace, O'Kelly and Mr. West all turned to him, astonishment on their faces.

"What!" Mace exclaimed.

"I said—"

"I heard you. I think."

"That's a great idea," O'Kelly agreed, looking relieved.

Mace eyed him speculatively. "That means you'll have to take some time away from the sacred halls of medicine."

Linc shifted, uneasy with the pointed speculation of the three men in front of him. "I have some time coming."

"Yeah, about twelve years' worth," his brother drawled.

Linc ignored him.

"That would be very kind of you, Doctor." Dave West studied Linc warily, his sun-weathered features concerned. "I don't mean to sound ungrateful, but why?"

The same question was in Mace's eyes and O'Kelly's, too.

Linc saw no reason to go into specific detail. "Your daughter is my veterinarian and she helped me out once. A long time ago."

"That's my Jenna." Her dad's face softened and love glowed in his eyes so brightly that Linc's chest hurt.

"Well, then it's settled. Now, we have to figure out a way to get her out of here." Mace's tone was strictly business, but he considered Linc as if trying to figure a code.

Linc still felt as if he'd been broadsided. He couldn't imagine what Jenna had gone through last night. In addition to being brutally assaulted, she had to have relived what Deke Ramsey had done to her eight years ago.

"After seeing this note, there's no doubt he's serious," Mace said carefully, glancing at Dave West.

"He wants to kill her. He's said it often enough." The older man's voice was flat, yet it shook.

Mace said gently, "I'm afraid it looks that way, Mr. West."

Linc's stomach rolled, much as it had the first time he'd cut into a cadaver. "Man, what has she been through?"

"More than anyone should have to," her father said tightly.

Mace turned to Linc. "How's her condition?"

"She's stable, but she'll need to take it easy for a few days. Just to make sure she's all right internally." Linc wondered if his voice always sounded so clinical, so detached. He didn't like it much.

"We don't have that kind of time. We need to move her, now."

"You can't do that!" Linc clenched his fists. "She needs to remain stable for at least twenty-four hours."

"The guy's already called the hospital, Linc. We can't leave her here."

"Look, bro, in the precinct you can call the shots, but not here on my turf."

"You can supervise the move, but I'm serious." Mace stared grimly into his eyes. "She can't stay."

"I think we should talk to Jenna." Mr. West's quiet suggestion served to remind them all that they were talking about her as if she didn't exist.

Ashamed, Linc nodded. "You're right. We should."

"All right," Mace said briskly.

The four of them walked back inside the hospital room and Linc listened as Mr. West calmly explained to his daughter what had happened. When he showed her the note he'd found in the morning paper, fear crested her swollen features.

She paled beneath the bruises, but she nodded and said softly, "I think Detective Garrett is right. I shouldn't stay with Mom and Dad."

Linc tried to summon a reassuring smile though he was still numbed by all he'd learned about this woman today.

"Have you gotten any other notes like this, Dr. West?" Mace asked.

She hesitated, then nodded. "A couple. And some weird phone calls."

"Did you report it?" Mace's voice sharpened.

"No. I thought I was refusing to allow him to intimidate me. I see now, he was just warming up." The bitterness in her voice was directed at herself.

Linc's heart went out to her.

Mace considered her for a moment, as if he would reprimand her. When he spoke, he said only, "Do you still have the notes?"

"Yes."

"I'll need them."

"They're at my house—"

"We'll find them. You don't need to go there."

She nodded, turning to her mom. Pain shunted through her at the motion. "My Jeep is still at the clinic. Could you and Dad pick it up for me?"

"Don't worry, doll." Her dad gently rubbed the back of her hand. "We'll take care of it."

Linc turned to his brother. "So, how are you going to get her out of here without anyone seeing?"

"You leave that to me." Mace turned to Jenna, visibly relieved at her agreement. "There are some options. We can put you in a safe house. Or a rehabilitation center out of town. Or you can stay with my brother."

"Your—" Jenna's gaze sliced to Linc. "Oh, no. I don't think so."

Her mother gasped and her father frowned, but Jenna focused on Linc Garrett's smoky eyes. There was no hurt there, simply an expectancy and a remoteness. Always that remoteness.

Last night his eyes hadn't been so distant, had they? She recalled warmth, concern in those crystal eyes, but her memory was probably distorted by the drugs she was taking.

A sudden resentment crowded through her. Was he always so detached from everyone and everything? Realizing he was waiting for an explanation for her blunt refusal, she sighed, feeling the pain carve through her.

"Why?" she asked flatly. "Why would you offer such a thing?"

"Jenna—" Her mother began.

"It's all right, Mrs. West." Linc edged closer to the bed. "Don't you know?"

"No." She tried to focus on him. Though still groggy, this news had zinged through her like a shot of adrenaline. "I don't understand. Why are you doing this?"

"You helped me once, a long time ago," he said quietly, still cool, still aloof. "Do you remember?"

"Oh, that." Of course she remembered, but taking care of her would be more than a one-night ordeal. She tried to push herself up on her good elbow, but weakness washed through her, incapacitating, annoying. She could barely summon the energy for a fight, but she didn't want to be alone with him, even though she knew how large his home was. "I need to be close to my animals. With Wilbur gone—"

She broke off, her head throbbing, her heart hurting.

Linc said quietly, "I can help with the animals. I can check your messages. Or help you with procedures. You certainly can't drive. I can do that, too."

"Steve can help me take care of the animals."

"Steve?" Linc recalled she had mentioned a Steve in the emergency room. "Is he your boyfriend?"

"He's her *best* friend. He's a vet, too," Barbara West put in.

Linc nodded. "Well, that's fine, but he can't take care of you. You need a doctor for that."

She stared at him, wanting to refuse, but remembering the note her parents had found, the anonymous phone call to the hospital about her.

"I don't need a baby-sitter."

"Trust me, I'm not one of those."

"I don't think it's a good idea. This guy tried to kill me. If he finds you—"

"He has to find me first." He flashed a rare smile.

"This isn't a joke, Dr. Garrett. He killed Wilbur—" Her voice cracked and she searched for anger, something to give her strength. "He wouldn't hesitate to do it again. Trust me on that."

"He won't find us," Linc insisted, grave now, his eyes dark as shattered glass. "I live north of the city limits. There's no real connection between us. There's no reason he would ever suspect that you would be with me."

"If something happened to you... There's no reason for you to get involved. And you *will* be *involved.*"

She didn't know him well, but she knew Dr. Linc Garrett didn't like to be involved, not with patients, not with women, not with anything.

Surprise flashed across his features, as if she'd discovered some kind of secret. Then his eyes crinkled at the corners and she realized he was smiling. Smiling! These drugs must definitely be getting to her.

"My house isn't Shangri-la, but it's comfortable."

Since that night in the barn she'd been careful not to think about Linc Garrett. Something about him drew her, something that made her wonder what it would have been like if he'd kissed her. She didn't want to be drawn to him, didn't want to wonder about him or any man.

But right now she didn't have the luxury of *want to.* Deke

Ramsey was after her and she needed a place to stay, a safe place near her animals. That place seemed to be Linc Garrett's house.

She nodded, her eyes burning with fatigue and tears. "Thank you, Doctor. I do appreciate it. I just hope you don't come to regret it."

She hoped she didn't, either. Something about Linc Garrett threatened her carefully erected defenses, the sense of control she'd clawed tooth and nail to build after the rape.

She wouldn't give that up to anyone, ever again. Certainly not to a handsome man, even if he did have haunted gray eyes and gentle hands.

"I won't get in your way," she said in a rush. "You'll hardly know I'm around."

His gaze swerved to hers, deliberate, probing, promising nothing.

Frustrated at his remoteness, she nearly snarled, "What I meant was, I'll keep my distance. And you can keep yours."

Beside the bed, her mother gasped and squeezed her hand, but Jenna kept her attention on Linc Garrett.

Finally, he gave a curt nod. "Good idea."

His words were far from a promise, but Jenna sensed they were the best she would get. She gritted her teeth and determined to ignore him as much as possible.

Linc had every intention of abiding by Jenna's wishes. He had no desire to get any closer to her than he did anyone else.

What on earth had possessed him to sign on as a baby-sitter? Especially for a leggy redhead with eyes the perfect blue-green of Caribbean waters?

As they stepped into his house early that evening, Linc's pulse kicked into overdrive. Muscles knotted in his shoulders, spasmed down his spine. He flipped on the lights in the spacious living room and stood aside as Detective O'Kelly double-checked the interior, then the exterior of the house. Mace had said he would try to stop by later.

After pronouncing everything clear, O'Kelly left and Linc stared solemnly at the trim back of the woman standing in his living room. He couldn't remember the last time he'd had a woman in his house, but he knew what it had been for. His mother would kill him if she knew that he was perilously close to living the chauvinistic adage that women were good for only one thing.

And now he had a woman here, not for sex, but because he'd volunteered to take care of her.

A vaguely recognizable sensation slid through him and it took a few seconds to identify. *Need—purely physical. Undiluted and sharp.* The realization jolted him. His defenses sprang up and he reminded himself of the fear in her eyes and the vicious battering she'd taken, but it didn't lessen the tension coiling through his gut.

On a deep core level, he felt something for Jenna West. Perhaps it was because he knew her. Perhaps it was because he'd seen the cruel handiwork of a vicious man focused on revenge. Perhaps it was that the wariness in her eyes matched the wariness in his own.

Whatever it was, he'd offered her shelter and now here they stood, two quiet strangers edging away from each other. And he suddenly, fiercely, wanted it to stay that way.

She burst on his senses like a sharp explosion. It rattled him. It annoyed the hell out of him. He could still recall the glide of velvet skin beneath his fingers at the hospital, could still smell the faint hint of plain soap and lemony shampoo, could still remember with a clenching gut the way her jewel-colored eyes had pleaded with his.

Help me. Which had to explain why he'd lost his mind and volunteered to take care of her.

She walked into the massive living room, turning in a slow circle as her gaze swept up to the rough-hewn beams of the vaulted ceiling. She glanced over the large oatmeal-colored sectional sofa and love seat, the framed watercolors of animal life on the wall, including one of his German shepherds, Chester and Buckley.

She held her broken arm close to her side, her good one wrapped around her waist. Though she stood about five-seven and exuded a viable strength, she appeared frail and alone in the middle of the big room.

She turned, dark shadows under her eyes. Fatigue drew taut lines around her generous mouth, sharpened the angle of her high cheekbones. "It's beautiful. And so large. I guess I won't be in your way."

"Not at all." He said the polite thing, feeling exhaustion work its way through his body. He'd had less than ten hours of sleep out of the last sixty and he was starting to feel it in the ache of muscle, the burn in his eyes.

The faint whiff of her fabric softener drifted to him and he realized suddenly how empty his house was, how empty he was.

Well, that was the way he wanted it for now. For always, he amended. Though he sometimes would have liked to have someone with whom to share dinner or discuss movies or music, he wasn't interested in furthering a relationship past the physical. He'd dated a few women since Michelle had left and he never called any of them after the first date.

He'd learned the hard way that women couldn't be trusted, even a woman a man thought he knew inside out. He and Michelle had been together through some pretty lean years. He'd worked as a roughneck, supporting her through medical school, then she had supported him through the same grueling four years.

Just as Linc felt they'd gotten on their feet, paid off their medical school bills, she'd up and left with Mike Blaisdale, Linc's good friend and lab partner from medical school who'd become a fabulously wealthy neurosurgeon. And Michelle's lover. And a father—

Jenna faced him, pulling his thoughts from the mire of the past. "I appreciate you letting me stay, but I hope you don't—won't—feel the need to wait on me.'' She lifted her right arm, heavy with the cast. "I'm not a complete invalid. I can still do some things."

Her features were pinched with fatigue, drawing the gash at her temple into stark relief. At the wariness in her sea green eyes, his heart squeezed.

"Don't worry, Jenna. I'll try not to get in your way." He could've given her the soft sell, tiptoed around it, but he was tired. And he felt he owed her the same bluntness she'd given him.

He strode toward the couch, heading for the open doorway and the kitchen opposite him. "Would you like something to eat?"

"You can just show me to the kitchen and I'll fix something."

"I'm going there anyway. I haven't eaten in a while, either."

She regarded him steadily, as if trying to determine whether he told the truth.

He stopped, waiting, and finally she nodded.

"That would be nice." Her voice was still brusque.

He figured she had as much reason to trust men as he had to trust women and that was fine with him.

Just as he turned to go to the kitchen, the doorbell sounded. Startled, his gaze went to Jenna's as he moved toward the front door.

Apprehension clouded her eyes and he acknowledged the same concern. But when he looked out the peephole, he exhaled in relief. "It's Mace. And Devon," he added in surprise.

"Oh," Jenna breathed, visibly relaxing.

Linc opened the door. "Hey, what are two you doing here?"

He stepped back to let the couple inside. His sister-in-law, a dainty brunette with silver-green eyes, smiled warmly at him and walked toward Jenna carrying a casserole dish and a long foil-wrapped package that trailed a scent of fresh-baked bread. Mace followed, closing the door.

Linc moved up beside his brother. "What's going on?"

"Has something happened?" Jenna stepped forward, her wan features once again concerned.

Mace smiled reassuringly. "Everything's fine. My wife wanted to meet you—"

"Actually," Devon interrupted softly, "I thought you might need a hot meal. Left to Linc, you'd probably get a sandwich or something out of a can." Her eyes twinkled with a teasing warmth Linc was coming to appreciate.

Devon and Mace had actually planned to marry last year, before Devon's father had died. After that trauma, Devon had walked away from Mace only to wind up needing his protection from the men who'd murdered her father. Linc believed Devon would only hurt Mace again and he'd been dead set against Mace hooking up with her. But in the weeks since their marriage, Linc had begun to realize he might be wrong about his sister-in-law.

Devon shoved the casserole dish and bread at him, then turned to Jenna. "Hi, I'm Devon Garrett."

"Hello." The wariness in Jenna's eyes disappeared and Linc noted an inviting openness tempered with curiosity in the blue-green depths.

"I'll put this in the kitchen." He inhaled deeply, taking in the rich scent of tomatoes and herbs. "What is it?"

"Baked manicotti. I hope you like pasta," Devon said to Jenna.

The other woman smiled. "Love it! It smells great."

"We won't stay long. I'm sure you need to rest—"

Devon's voice faded as Linc strode into the kitchen. Done in light oak, complemented by green-and-white tile, the room was open and fresh-looking. Oak cabinets gleamed, lining three walls of the room in a U-shape. The refrigerator occupied the space on one end of the cabinets; the sink, dishwasher and trash compactor marched the length of the short wall. There was a large center island for cooking.

He rarely ate here, but when he did, he cooked. At first he'd learned out of necessity, but now he liked it.

He glanced at Mace, who had followed him. His brother now stood in the kitchen doorway watching his wife and wearing the same silly grin he'd worn since his wedding six weeks ago.

"What's really going on, Mace? You checking up on me?"

"Devon is. She didn't believe me when I told her you'd offered to take in Jenna."

"I'm sure you told her you were just as skeptical."

Mace flashed him a sly grin.

Linc shook his head in fond exasperation. He stepped up beside his brother, noting how comfortable Jenna seemed with his sister-in-law. "How is Devon adjusting to being a cop's wife?"

"She's great." Mace smiled tenderly and Linc experienced twin pangs of joy and jealousy.

He'd once thought he and Michelle were that much in love, that committed to each other. Now he knew he would never open himself up to anyone like that again. He tore his gaze from the auburn sweep of Jenna's hair. "Devon seems to have survived that mess with the mobster."

"She has. And once that trial is over, she'll never look back."

"So she's okay?"

"Yes." Mace's gaze, blazing with pride for his wife, met Linc's.

He nodded. This time, Mace and Devon just might make it. Devon had let fear of Mace's job drive her away before, but she seemed much stronger now.

Mace moved back toward the women, who still stood in the entryway. He slid an arm around Devon's waist. "We'd better go, babe."

She nodded, smiling at Jenna. "Please call if you need anything. You too, Linc."

He smiled, moving to the front door. "Thanks for supper, Devon. You were right. I was about to offer Jenna a ham sandwich."

She grinned, her eyes shining at him as she walked outside. "Bye, Jenna."

"Goodbye. And thanks." Jenna smiled warmly and waved at the departing couple.

After Mace promised to come by the next day, Linc closed the door. "We'd better eat before it gets cold."

Jenna nodded and followed him into the kitchen, moving to stand before the floor-to-ceiling window that overlooked the backwoods.

A green-and-white striped valance gave a tidy look without overwhelming the view. A small breakfast table and four chairs were situated in front of the window.

Linc retrieved plates and silverware then dished up the manicotti while she stood quietly at the window, a slender figure who tugged at his heart.

He turned away, cursing silently. The woman was a patient who happened to be an acquaintance, nothing more.

She laughed softly, her voice raspy. "I see Chester and Buckley have raided the woods."

Linc glanced up to see the dogs come racing out of the trees, chasing a rabbit. He smiled and carried two plates full of pasta and bread to the table.

They ate in silence, Jenna staring out the window so quietly that Linc almost forgot she was there until her chair scraped across the floor.

She rose, picking up her plate with her left hand. "Thanks. That was delicious. It was nice to have something besides hospital food."

"My sister-in-law's a pretty good cook."

"Yes. And very nice. I enjoyed meeting her."

He smiled in acknowledgement as he took his plate to the sink. "Just leave your dishes. I'll get them later."

She looked about to argue and he stalled her. "I thought I'd show you to your room. You need to get some sleep."

Defiance firmed her lips, but before she could protest, he amended. "You're probably ready for some."

She hesitated then nodded. "I am tired."

He walked out of the kitchen and back toward the living area. "Right this way."

All the bedrooms were on the far side of the house and Linc crossed the gray flagstone foyer to walk into a long hallway. He flipped on the light and turned to the left, leading the way past two bedrooms and a bath and walking into a room at the end of the hall.

Jenna followed him inside and froze. With open amazement, she stared at the large four-poster bed, swagged with Italian linen and piled high with pillows—round, square, small, large, tasseled. "Wow."

He'd done that for Michelle, too. For nothing.

"Are you sure I should sleep there? It looks too pretty to mess up."

He was floored by a vivid image of her resting peacefully in the middle of that bed, her auburn hair dark against the pale linen of the pillows. "I'd like someone to get some use out of it."

Too late he realized the bitterness in his voice and ignored the sharp glance she threw him. He made no sound on the plush taupe-colored carpet as he walked past the bed and skirted a floral chaise longue and wingback chair to open a door and flip on another light. "You'll have your own bathroom. There should be plenty of towels inside."

"Thanks." Once again her voice was cool, distant.

He realized belatedly that she probably felt uncomfortable in a bedroom with a man. He strode quickly past her and stopped in the doorway. "If you need anything, let me know.

I'm at the opposite end of the hall and I can hear you if you call out.''

''I'm sure I'll be fine.'' Her voice was smooth, but he saw that she fingered her cast nervously. Her gaze darted around the room, stopping everywhere except that big bed.

Compassion welled up in him again and he said goodnight. Upon reaching his own room he closed the door and shucked off his boots, yanking his red pullover out of his jeans and over his head.

This had to be the weirdest time he'd ever spent with a woman, here or anywhere else. He was in his bedroom; she was at the opposite end of the hall.

It didn't matter that he told himself he didn't think of Jenna West in a sexual way. He'd have to be dead not to notice those mile-long legs, that generous mouth, or those eyes.

Just the thought of her sleeping in that bed kicked off a nearly forgotten burst of heat in his belly. It was a good thing they'd both agreed to distance. Neither of them wanted anything else. Neither of them needed anything else, either.

Stripping down to his underwear, he crawled into bed, sinking into the cushy mattress. He closed his eyes, allowing his body to slow down, skimming through all the procedures he'd performed the last few days.

It was an automatic process, the way he unwound after being on duty. He sometimes analyzed his work as the memories flowed over him, relaxing. He'd be asleep in minutes.

Three hours later he was still awake. His body was so tired it ached. His mind was fatigued, yet it kept hurling images and words and procedures at him. Frustrated, he remembered that he hadn't let the dogs in for the night and he rose, grabbing a pair of cotton knit shorts from his bureau.

Opening the door quietly, he saw a silvery light flickering under Jenna's door and heard the soft murmur of the television. So, she couldn't sleep either.

He padded to the kitchen and let the dogs in the door opposite the breakfast nook. Excited to see him, the shepherds whined and sat right on his feet, tails thumping on the floor. He scratched them both generously behind the ears and they panted in excited pleasure.

He fed them, leaning against the center island as they sucked down their food like vacuum hoses and then he snapped his fingers. "Come."

Calmer now, they followed him, sniffing industriously at the floor and the couches they passed on the way to his room. He knew they could smell Jenna and he paused in the hallway. The light was still on, the television still humming. Chester stepped toward her room.

"Stay, boy," Linc commanded softly.

The dog whined, but levered himself onto his haunches, his ears pricking as he looked expectantly at Linc. Buckley did the same.

Linc hesitated. Maybe she was in too much pain to sleep.

He didn't recall that she'd taken any more pain medication at dinner. Some doctor he was, he thought ruefully. Jogging back to the kitchen, he shook out one of the tiny pain pills from her prescription bottle and returned to her room.

Telling the dogs to stay, he walked to her door and knocked softly.

"Yes?" Her voice was flat and unwelcoming.

He cracked open the door, prepared for the sight, but still startled to see her in the middle of his bed. She looked tiny. She hadn't disturbed the pillows except to make herself a path in the middle of them.

"Are you okay?"

"Can't sleep."

"Do you need some pain medication? I didn't think to ask earlier."

She hesitated. "No."

"Are you sure? I think maybe—"

"I said I don't need any."

He eyed her for a moment. "All right."

She looked away, reluctance crossing her features then she glanced back at him. "Look, I'm sorry."

"No need." His gaze went to the TV and he recognized Dick Van Dyke. He chuckled. "That's one of my favorites."

He felt a gust of hot breath against his leg and looked down.

Chester and Buckley peered around him, eyeing Jenna as if she were a Milk-Bone. She saw them and a warm welcoming smile eased across her features.

Even in the garish light, Linc felt the kick of that smile clear down to his toes.

"Hello, boys," she crooned in a smoke-and-honey voice.

Linc had a sudden fierce wish to hear her say his name in that throaty caressing tone. Chester and Buckley wiggled and bumped against Linc's legs, but stayed where they were.

"Can't they come in?"

His heart tilted at the wistfulness in her voice. As if he gave in to women every day, he heard himself saying, "Sure."

Chester and Buckley didn't even wait for Linc's okay. They raced into the room and up to the bed, wagging their tails so hard Linc was surprised they didn't knock over the furniture.

Jenna pushed aside the pillows and scooted to the edge of the bed, reaching down with her left hand to scratch their ears as she murmured to them. Chester whimpered low in his throat and closed his eyes in bliss.

She laughed softly. "It's good to see you, too, Chester."

Linc had a burning urge to walk over there and sit on the edge of the bed with her, but *he* hadn't been invited. Only the dogs. Still, he moved to the bedside table and placed the small pain tablet on the polished wood surface.

"Are you sure you won't take a pill?"

Her smile dimmed. "If I want one, I'll get it."

"Fine." Clearly unwelcome, he turned for the door.

"I guess I'll be apologizing the whole time I'm here." She sounded impatient, though not with him.

He glanced over his shoulder. He knew her anger wasn't directed at him, knew it was tied to the helplessness forced on her by Deke Ramsey.

"It's all right," he said quietly. "You've been through a pretty rough time."

Her gaze met his and he read painful relief in the vibrant depths of her eyes. Her features softened, restoring the serenity to her battered face. "It's no cause to be rude."

His gaze shifted to her lips then away. "You can keep the dogs in here if you want."

She smiled, then winced in pain though the light in her eyes didn't dim. "I'd like that."

He nodded, hesitant to leave though he didn't know why. "Well…good night."

"Good night." She whispered something to Chester and the dog dropped to the floor, settling his head between his front paws. Buckley did the same, flopping down and exhaling loudly.

Obviously dismissed, Linc shook his head and closed the door.

Chapter 3

The next morning, fear and resentment churned inside her, fusing with the pain until she could barely tell the difference. She hadn't slept. The pain medication Linc had offered would've helped with that, but she didn't want to close her eyes.

Every time she did, Ramsey's face leered at her. His vicious words circled inside her head—what he would do to her, how he would do it. Just the thought of Ramsey finding her again made her heart pound hard enough to rock her body.

Her throat tightened, aching painfully and she was reminded anew of his massive hands around her throat, squeezing, pressing until black spots swirled in front of her eyes.

The only thing that kept her from exploding into hysteria was the fact that Linc Garrett was nearby. Damn Deke Ramsey anyway. He had again managed to push her into a corner of dependency. Just when she'd finally gotten her life back on track.

She ignored the little voice in her head that whispered she

still hadn't hurdled the obstacle of establishing a relationship with a man. So what? Every woman didn't need a man.

So what if sometimes her body ached for physical intimacy? So what if sometimes her heart twisted out of sheer loneliness?

She'd tried the intimacy thing and it had been a bust. Deke Ramsey had ruined her for sex, that was for sure. But she had a job she loved, parents and a sister she adored and a best friend who never let her down. She had nothing to complain about.

Even so she couldn't halt the flash through her mind of Linc Garrett's smoky gray eyes and a cocky half smile. Her lips twisted. Dr. Garrett was as gun-shy about relationships as she was.

Still, he had completely reassured her parents about her staying with him. And he'd brushed aside their gratitude as if it made him uncomfortable, even embarrassed. He had also checked on her last night. He had let the dogs keep her company as if he knew how alone she felt in the middle of that unfamiliar bed. Linc was perceptive and had been kind to her, an image that didn't fit with his detached, emotionless doctor persona.

Of course, away from the hospital he didn't much look like a doctor. He wore faded jeans that gloved his lean muscular legs and snakeskin boots that were scuffed enough to belong to a rodeo rider. A couple of days' growth of stubble darkened his jaw, giving his lean face a hawkish, ruthless edge.

Something stirred inside Jenna, a glimmer of feminine appreciation she hadn't felt in years. She didn't welcome it now. Nor did she welcome the memory of how his gray eyes had warmed with kindness when he'd seen her in the middle of that ridiculously sensual bed.

All in all, though, he had remained detached since she'd been brought into the hospital last night. Well, he wouldn't need to worry about her developing a case of hero worship.

She had every intention of keeping her distance. And making certain that he kept his.

If she had to live with him, so be it. But it didn't mean she had to set up house with him.

Frustration plowed through her and she awkwardly shifted the brush to her left hand. She dragged it through her shoulder-length hair, grimacing at her reflection in the sparkling bathroom mirror. Even with the soft daylight showering through the skylight, the cut above her eye looked raw.

Her arm still twinged, and was starting to itch beneath the plaster cast. Her back and thighs and the entire front of her body was splotched with bruises turning from gray-green to dark purple. And the distinct imprint of Ramsey's hands glared against the pale skin of her throat.

Her stomach lurched. Damn Deke Ramsey for getting out of prison! Damn him for coming after her. He hadn't wasted a minute doing it, Jenna knew now. Terror dried her throat. Detective Garrett had told her Ramsey had only been released from the penitentiary in McAlester two weeks before he'd attacked her. And killed Wilbur.

Wilbur. Pain shafted through her and Jenna closed her eyes, pressing her lips together.

Tears trickled down her cheeks. That dear man had lost his life because of her. A heavy sense of responsibility, crested by rage, threatened to overwhelm her. This same relentless rage had stalked her constantly after the rape. As well as this same incapacitating sense of helplessness. She struggled to rein it in.

A heavy sigh eased out of her. She was tired and sore and she didn't know if she could fight Deke Ramsey again.

But she had to. This time the stakes were too high. A chill rippled up her spine. He'd sworn to kill her and she believed him. Otherwise, she certainly wouldn't be here with Dr. Linc Garrett.

She slammed the hairbrush down on the tiled countertop and walked into the bedroom. She shrugged out of her button-front shirt and painstakingly managed to pull on a pair of denim shorts, zip them, and finally slip the lone metal button through the hole. By the time she finished, her muscles ached and Jenna stared in frustration at her clean shirt.

How in the world was she supposed to put that on? She'd slept last night in the one she'd worn from the hospital, but now she wanted to change. Mom, bless her heart, had packed only pullovers.

Jenna figured she could get them over her head, but she wasn't sure how to get her arm into the short sleeve. She wasn't even going to mess with her stupid bra. She stood at the foot of the bed, holding the red plaid polo her mother had sent, staring at it as if she'd never seen a shirt in her life.

Frustration crowded through her, at Deke Ramsey, at her broken arm, at the stupid shirt. She pulled the shirt over her head, trying to decide how to get the cast through the ribbed sleeve.

"Hello—oh." Linc Garrett's deep voice was surprised, then flustered. "Hell."

Jenna looked over her shoulder and her skin prickled at the weight of his gaze on her injured back. "What are you doing?"

"I knocked, but when you didn't answer—hey, I'm sorry. No harm meant."

She heard the door start to close. "Wait." She paused, fighting pride and resentment and a wariness that now seemed inborn. "I think I need some help here."

He was a doctor, right? He'd seen naked bodies before. He'd definitely seen naked women. So why did a shiver stroke her insides?

Because he hadn't seen *her* naked body. But if she was going to get in this shirt, she had to have some help.

"I can't get this on by myself." Her voice was hoarse with embarrassment and she refused to look at him.

He was quiet for so long that she finally burst out, "Well?"

"Just a minute."

She heard his boots thud down the hall, away from her and she glanced over her shoulder. What was he doing?

Her brow furrowed and she brushed away the panic that nudged at her. She was fine. Ramsey was nowhere around.

But when Linc returned, she couldn't halt a sigh of relief. Determined not to show him how uneasy she was, she looked down, feeling a tingle in her nipples that were bare and brushed by air that suddenly seemed cool on her sensitive skin.

"I thought maybe one of my shirts might be easier for you to...get into."

Amazed, she glanced over her shoulder before she even thought about it. He stood in the doorway, holding a button-front shirt that looked about three sizes too big for her.

Her gaze flickered to his. "What a great idea."

He stepped toward her, his gaze sliding across her shoulders and lingering on her bare back. Anger tightened his features then disappeared. His smoky eyes were cool, unreadable.

She stiffened, her gaze moving to the bed in front of her. Being alone with a man, even the man who'd helped her, was not Jenna's idea of smart right now, but she needed him. Thoughts of Ramsey ticked against her nerves like a bomb timer.

"You take off that one first and—"

"All right." She yanked the shirt over her head. With her good hand, she pressed the fabric to her breasts.

Tension laced through her and she tightened her grip on the fabric until it burned her palm. She certainly didn't need Linc Garrett to tell her to cover herself, especially from his intense gaze.

"Okay." His voice was quiet and he walked up behind her slowly, letting her know he was coming.

Nerves jangling, she braced herself to feel his fingers on her skin, but instead she felt only the heat of his body as he stopped directly behind her. At first she was surprised that he didn't simply take charge as he had at the hospital, but then she realized he probably knew to approach her cautiously because of her rape.

She glanced over her shoulder, freezing at the dispassionate look on his face. She thought she saw a muscle flex in his jaw, but she must have been mistaken. Nothing seemed to get to Dr. Linc Garrett, to penetrate that inscrutable facade.

He continued to stand there, not touching her and it occurred to her that he was waiting for a signal from her. Her heart rapped like a broken piston and she clutched the shirt tighter to her breasts.

She closed her eyes. "It's all right. Go ahead."

How she hated depending on someone for something as basic as dressing! Damn Deke Ramsey for putting her at someone else's mercy—again. The details of the attack flashed through her mind and cold sweat slicked her palms.

Linc eased closer and the movement filled her nostrils with his warm-body scent, an intriguing blend of woods and spice and minty toothpaste. His heat caressed her spine, her shoulder blades.

He smelled dark and blatantly male. Jenna's throat closed up. *He's not going to hurt you. He's not.*

Still she held her breath, bracing herself for his touch.

It didn't come. Instead of those warm strong fingers, she felt the smooth glide of fabric across her skin, over her shoulders. She automatically lifted her left arm, sliding it into the sleeve.

He carefully pulled the fabric into place and shifted behind her. She could feel the hard length of him, not touching but caressing just the same. A calm deliberation emanated from him, yet she was about to crawl out of her skin. She swallowed hard, fighting panic and a tantalizing sensation low in her belly.

His warmth teased her and for a split second, she wondered what it would feel like to lean back against that hard, broad chest. To let him wrap those strong arms around her and shelter her.

Shoving away the thought, she lifted her right arm, too quickly and a twinge of pain reminded her why she was here, why *he* was here.

The cast caught on the light fabric and she couldn't get her fist through the armhole. She sighed in frustrated resignation, clutching the red plaid tighter to her breasts as if it were a steel shield and hid her completely from Linc's sight.

In a flat voice, he asked, ''Do you need my help?''

''Yes,'' she snapped, sounding ungracious and petty and not caring at the moment. Anything was better than revealing the stark fear that knotted her belly.

With measured movements, he gently lifted her upper arm with his left hand. His strong fingers were a fraction of an inch away from the curve of her breast.

Jenna didn't breathe, probably couldn't have if she'd tried.

With his right hand, Linc pulled the sleeve over her cast and up to her shoulder. ''There.''

He released her instantly, but her skin tingled from his touch. As she buttoned the shirt, she was amazed to discover that she wasn't repulsed in the least. In fact a slow burn in her belly made her want more, just a tiny bit more.

The thought shot apprehension through her with the punch of speed. And in that moment, frustration, resentment and anger crashed in upon her. Angry tears stung her eyes, but she refused to cry.

She moved away from him, away from the remoteness in his gray eyes, the warmth of his body, the memory of his touch. ''I said you wouldn't have to baby-sit me, but I guess I was wrong.''

''I don't mind.'' His voice was even and controlled, just like his movements.

He was so detached, so self-contained. Jenna wondered if he regretted offering her a place to stay.

She pulled herself up short and turned away. "Thanks for your help. I hope I don't have to bother you again."

"It was no problem. You can borrow my shirts as long as you need to."

His voice held no warmth, no teasing seduction, yet she didn't like the intimacy his statement implied. She could smell the richness of him, the faint tang of his aftershave, and the whole idea of her body being covered by something that had covered *him* sent strange ripples of sensation through her.

She'd survived just fine without that part of life and would continue to.

He turned for the door. "I'll be in the kitchen making breakfast. Come on in when you're ready."

His indifferent invitation made her uncomfortably aware that they were practically strangers. If not for Ramsey's attack on her, she and Linc would still be staying well away from each other. "I don't want you going to any trouble on my account."

"Hey, we have to eat."

Despite his impassive voice, she sensed a restless energy pumping through him. He was probably ready for his house-guest to leave.

"I'm sure I won't have to take advantage of your hospitality much longer," she said stiffly. "The cops will find Ramsey soon."

Linc stopped in the hallway, staring over his shoulder at her. Resentment burned in his gray eyes, the first emotion she'd seen since he'd walked in on her. "You can stay here as long as you like. I thought I made that clear."

"I don't want to put you out any longer than necessary."

Something flickered across his face—impatience? Irritation? "Why is it so hard for you to let people help? Or is it just me you don't want help from?"

She started to deny it out of politeness, but the lie wouldn't come. He did unnerve her, but Jenna wasn't exactly sure why.

She shrugged. "You're right. I'm sorry. I appreciate what you're doing for me."

"I wasn't fishing for compliments."

"I know." She offered a tiny smile, which he did not return. Her smile faded and irritation flickered. "I'll be out in a minute."

"Fine." He turned away and started down the hall.

What was with Dr. Distant? Did anything ever get to him? The man rarely showed emotion. Maybe that was why his wife had left him.

Not fair, Jenna chided herself. She'd asked him to stay out of her way. So why was she peeved that he was doing exactly that?

She didn't understand the spark of heat that passed from him to her whenever they touched. She didn't understand why her muscles, deep inside, clenched when he moved near. Her skin tingled hot, then cold.

Her nerves felt as if they'd been laid bare by a scalpel. And the reason for her unease stood six foot three of brawny male with the sharpest, most probing gray eyes she'd ever seen.

For the first time in eight years, she was acutely, physically aware of a man. Apprehension pealed through her. It would lead nowhere. She knew that. A few years after the rape, she'd tried sex with a wonderful, caring man whom she adored and it had been a total disaster.

For some reason, she responded to Linc Garrett on a physical *and* an emotional level, but she wouldn't, *couldn't,* be seduced by that.

Jenna tucked her hair behind her ear and slid her feet into a pair of deck shoes. A few days at the most. That's all it would take for the police to find Ramsey and put him back in prison. She just had to hold herself together.

Taking a deep breath, she started for the kitchen. Once Ramsey was caught, Jenna would leave Linc's house and go back to her life. Unexpectedly, the thought held no comfort, only a strange emptiness.

She brushed it aside. They had a deal. He was holding up his end by staying out of her way. She would do the same.

Linc wanted to kill the bastard! Wanted to put his hands around Ramsey's neck and squeeze the life out of him, watch Ramsey's eyes turn to agony, just as he'd done to Jenna.

Rage boiled through Linc—sharp, vicious, obliterating his reason. He had never, *never,* felt such fury. Not when Michelle left. Not even when he'd learned about the baby.

Linc strode for the kitchen, breathing hard against the razor-sharp anger that churned inside him. Raw fear had dilated Jenna's eyes, startling Linc until he'd realized *he* wasn't the reason for it. Ramsey was.

And then Linc had glimpsed again the evidence of Ramsey's hatred for the woman who'd put him in prison. Linc hadn't wanted Jenna to see him like that, hadn't wanted to subject her to the savagery that had risen up inside him upon seeing her back, her throat.

Her beautiful skin marred, her flesh bruised and torn and bloodied. Linc clenched his fists, his long strides covering the living room floor. Damn Ramsey for what he'd done to her!

Linc's breath came in short ragged pants. His chest hurt and the rage burned higher. He couldn't believe he wanted to kill someone, not when he'd dedicated his life to saving people. But Ramsey didn't deserve to live. What he'd done to Jenna was malicious, brutal, evil. Linc *hated* the guy, wanted him dead, wanted—

Linc stopped cold in the kitchen doorway. Mace sat at the breakfast table. "What are you doing here?"

His brother calmly lifted one of Linc's oversize black mugs and sipped. "Came by to see how Jenna is doing."

"Well, how do you think she's doing?" Linc snapped, marching over to the stove and yanking open the cabinet beneath. Only now did Linc smell the aroma of fresh coffee. He grabbed two skillets from below the oven and slammed them on top of the stove burner. "She looks like somebody beat the hell out of her!"

"Emotionally, is she—"

"She's starting to heal physically, but she's frustrated that she can't do everything on her own." He recalled the wariness in her beautiful eyes as he'd helped her dress. "She's putting up a good front, but she's afraid. I don't know how safe she feels here." *With me.*

"This is the best place for her at the moment." Mace dismissed his comments brusquely. "You haven't done anything to make her doubt that, have you?"

"Like what?" Linc jerked open the refrigerator door and pulled out a carton of eggs.

In the last day and a half, he'd doctored her and contemplated committing murder for her. Not a very good way to honor her request to stay away.

Mace shrugged. "If you're stomping around like this in front of her—"

"I'm not stomping around." Linc cracked an egg on the cabinet edge and spilled it into a bowl, feeling a slight release at breaking something. "I think she's coming along, but don't push. She's strung pretty tight."

"Who wouldn't be?"

"You got that right," Linc muttered, peeling off strips of bacon and slapping them in another skillet.

He didn't understand how Jenna West got to him so fast and in ways no one else ever had. He had to keep his distance. He didn't want to get *that* involved with her.

Mace set down his coffee cup and rose. "What's really going on here, bro?"

With sharp movements, Linc broke several more eggs and emptied them into the bowl. "What are you talking about?"

"I'm talking about this…anger. I've never seen you like this. Over anybody. Is it because of Jenna?"

"I'd like to shoot Ramsey full of gasoline and watch him die a slow, painful death."

"Listen to me, Linc." Mace moved over to stand beside him at the stove, urgency in his tone. "You've got to get ahold of yourself. You can't play avenger here. We'll handle things."

Linc whipped furiously at the eggs, imagining in his mind that he was striking out at Ramsey.

"Hey, are you listening to me?" Mace knuckle-rapped him lightly on the arm, gaining his attention. "Ramsey is danger-ous. He's a fighter. He comes looking for it."

"You saw what he did to her!" Linc dumped the eggs into the heated skillet, automatically picking up a fork to scramble them.

Mace frowned, concern darkening his eyes to cobalt. "Yes, I did. And I got a look at his prison record today. When he was in the pen he stabbed a guard, Linc. Nobody would even identify the shiv as his. All the prisoners were *that* afraid of him. Don't be thinking you're going to go after this guy. That's my job."

Linc set his jaw. That was exactly what he'd like to do.

Mace grabbed his arm. "Don't take this on. It's not your fight. You can't make a difference. You're already doing what you can by taking her in."

"It's damn little after what I—" He broke off and turned away from his brother. No way would he admit to Mace how he had scared the hell out of Jenna all those years ago in the barn. For which he still hadn't apologized.

"After what?" Mace asked quietly.

He shook his head. "She helped me. I want to help her. That's all."

"You are helping her. Do what you do best and look out for Jenna here. I don't want to have to worry about you going off somewhere on your own. *That* won't help anything."

Linc glared at him, trying to rein in the rage still spiraling through him. "I can take care of myself. I have a gun, too, you know."

"I'm warning you. This won't be good for Jenna. She

needs to be in a place where she can feel safe, where she doesn't have to worry that you might go off half-cocked—''

"I'm not!" Linc scraped the eggs onto a plate and flipped off the burner. "But when I look at those marks on her—she could be dead! He just kept hitting her and hitting her—''

"Hey, man." Mace moved closer, touching Linc's shoulder. Realization settled in his eyes. "You actually care."

"Of course I do!" Linc snapped. "She's my patient. She's my vet. I *know* her."

"It's more than that. I haven't seen you care about anybody like this in years."

"Spare me."

"Hey." Mace held up both hands in a gesture of surrender. "Just making an observation."

"Well, you can shove those."

"Ah, that's more like the doctor I know," Mace drawled, picking up his coffee again. "Is there something going on between the two of you?"

"I just told you she's my patient!"

"I know what she is, bro. But you seem pretty upset over someone who's *only* a patient."

Mace's observation drew Linc up short. His brother was right. He needed to get ahold of himself. He didn't understand why this rage had taken hold of him. Today wasn't the first time he'd seen those marks on Jenna. And even though she'd tried to hide her fear from him, he'd understood by her skittishness and curt words that she was terrified.

And why shouldn't she be? Ramsey was still out there. No, Linc couldn't curb this fierce protectiveness that rose up inside him.

"I mean it, Linc. Don't get any ideas about taking on Ramsey when he finally shows up. He's a killer."

Linc passed a hand over his eyes, the fury still breaking inside him like high tide. "I saw what that bastard did to her, how he tore her up. Dammit, he's out there waiting for her, waiting to finish what he started. And I won't let him!"

Linc realized he was yelling. He also realized Mace had gone very still and his gaze had slid over Linc's shoulder to the doorway. Linc felt it then, a hum of sensation up his back.

He turned, his gaze crashing into Jenna's. Her eyes glowed like heated stones in the chalk-paleness of her face. Those eyes, though wide with disbelief, were still fringed with fear.

Linc's rage eased and regret knotted his gut. After he'd tried so hard to shield her from his anger, she'd heard everything.

Chapter 4

Shock and disbelief slammed into Jenna, weakening her knees. Regret chased across Linc's smooth features. His gray eyes, dusky with self-reproach, locked with hers. The spicy aroma of frying bacon, the sizzle of the meat receded into the background.

Linc Garrett was defending her. She could hardly wrap her mind around it. She knew now why he had been so distant, so remote while helping her dress. Knew now that the marks she bore from Ramsey's beating had been the cause for his inscrutable expression, the flat voice. Linc was furious. *For her.*

Aware that he and his brother watched her carefully, she could only stare at him. Warmth flooded her, prickling her skin, her breasts, and Jenna ruthlessly dismissed it. It was natural to feel grateful for what he'd done, grateful to him for wanting to protect her.

She felt vulnerable after the attack, and especially here in unfamiliar surroundings. But that didn't mean she should be lured by the sense of belonging that suddenly enveloped her, the sense that she was a part of someone other than herself.

Still she couldn't help feeling that she had misjudged him greatly. Unable to pull her gaze from his, she said, "Your brother's right. I appreciate the sentiment, but you shouldn't get involved with Ramsey." She shrugged, forcing a small smile. "Any more than you already have, of course."

Linc's eyes, so cool only moments ago, were now stormy with protest and compassion and simmering rage. He stared at her for a long moment. Then he turned back toward the stove, forking out the bacon that sizzled in the pan.

She felt as if she'd somehow thrown away a gift he'd given her. She hated seeing the deep worry in his eyes, but surely that was nothing more than the caring a doctor felt for a patient. Yes, that's all it was.

Uneasiness nagged as she tried to explain away the savage protectiveness in his voice. Glancing at Mace, she moved into the kitchen and stopped close to the center island, only a few feet away from both men.

"Good morning, Jenna," Mace said. "How are you today?"

"Sore, but I'm coming along. I think my doctor would agree." Though painful, she smiled in Linc's direction, but he frowned and looked down at the pan of crackling bacon.

Tension lashed his broad shoulders and his movements were stiff. He wore tight faded jeans and a worn white T-shirt with fading navy letters that spelled Yankees. The sleeves of the T-shirt were ripped out, exposing hard, tanned biceps.

He was more than her doctor; he was a man. And Jenna was suddenly swept by the urge to touch his arms, see if those muscles were as firm as they looked.

She tore her gaze away, fighting the need to rub at the goose bumps prickling her arms.

Linc carried platters of eggs and bacon to the table, then returned to gather plates and utensils. "Breakfast is ready."

His voice was smooth, calm. There was no hint in his voice of the earlier fury she'd overheard. Jenna moved to the table and eased her stiff body down in a chair next to the window. Sunshine spilled into the kitchen, painting the table and chairs a soft gold.

Mace took the chair to her right, leaving Linc to sit across from her. Still rattled by his defense of her, Jenna was glad to have the distance between them. Even though Mace's leg occasionally brushed hers, Jenna felt no jump in her pulse the way she had when Linc had touched her.

Mindful of her busted lip, she attempted to smile at Mace. "Please thank your wife again for the meal last night. It was delicious."

He nodded. "I will. She enjoyed meeting you."

"I liked her, too."

Mace refilled his coffee cup then handed the newspaper to Jenna. "There's a big write-up about your friend today."

"Wilbur?" She took the paper with shaking hands.

Linc darted a quick glance at Mace, then looked at Jenna. She could feel his gaze on her like a warm touch and for once, she didn't have the urge to bolt.

Unfolding the paper, she quickly found the front page article on Wilbur and began to read. "'Beloved Veterinarian Killed.'" Tears burned her eyes and she blinked them back. Tears wouldn't help Wilbur now.

"Is it good for her to read that?" Linc asked abruptly, pouring milk into a glass for Jenna.

She glanced up, ready to protest that she could read whatever she wanted.

Mace shrugged. "Unfortunately, she already knows more detail than is given in the paper."

Her attention returned to the article, skimming over the details of his philanthropy and the citywide spay-neuter program he'd established. He was dead, because of her. "His funeral is in three days." Her gaze dipped again to the paper. "Wednesday, at two o'clock."

"Yes."

Swamped by sadness and regret, she looked up, studying Mace. Did she imagine the tightness in his voice? "I'd like to go."

"No."

Linc slid into his seat, his gaze flicking from Mace to her.

"Yes! He was my friend." Her body tightened, spurring an ache through her bruised body. "He's dead because he tried to help me."

Mace set his coffee cup on the table. "Ramsey will be looking for you there."

Jenna hesitated, wanting desperately to say goodbye to Wilbur. To apologize. She couldn't bring herself to step foot outside Linc's house, but she *had* to be at Wilbur's service. "Wouldn't that be a good way to get him out in the open?"

Mace shook his head. "Ramsey'll be ready for us. No doubt he's still searching the hospitals for you. When he comes up empty, he'll show up at the cemetery."

"But I want to see Wilbur. It's my fault—" Her voice cracked and she looked out the window, taking a deep breath as she studied the massive oaks and pines behind the house, tuning in to the faint song of a whippoorwill.

Mace spoke quietly, "It's best this way. If you like, I can take you after the ceremony. You can have some private time with him, but you'll be under police protection."

Frustration stirred inside Jenna that Ramsey had taken yet another thing from her. "But—"

"Forgive my plain speaking, Jenna, but if you go to that funeral, you'll be dead, too."

"I assume you'll be there!" she snapped, her grip tightening on the paper.

"Yes, but it would be best if you paid your respects afterward. That way, the funeral crowd will have gone and it'll be easier for us to keep an eye on you. I'm only thinking of your protection."

"So you're not saying she can't go at all?" Linc shot Jenna a reassuring look.

"No," Mace said. "Just that we need to take some precautions. We've got to be smart."

She chafed at the imposed restriction, torn between wanting to be there for the service and knowing that Mace was probably right. She wanted to catch Ramsey, but she didn't want to die while doing it. Resignation shaded her voice. "Yes. All right."

"Good." Mace glanced at Linc. "You come, too. Just in case O'Kelly can't."

Linc's gaze searched Jenna's and she nodded.

"Okay," Linc said to Mace.

Though still reeling from the savagery she'd overheard in Linc's voice, she found the fact that he would accompany her strangely comforting.

Mace took another sip of coffee, then grinned at her. "I saw your parents earlier."

"How are they? Have they talked to Steve?" She refolded the paper and placed it in the empty seat to her left. "Is Puppy all right?"

"They're fine, concerned about you. They didn't mention Steve." Mace grinned and grabbed two pieces of bacon, then surged out of his chair and strode out the door. "But they sent the dog for you."

"Oh!" Jenna rose, having hardly touched her eggs. Relief mingled with the first comfort she'd felt since the attack. "Puppy? Puppy's here?"

"I'll go get him." Mace chuckled as he disappeared from sight on his way to the front door.

"Mace brought your dog?" Linc rose as well, motioning for Jenna to proceed him out of the kitchen and into the living room.

She started after Mace, then wheeled, nearly crashing into Linc. He reached out to steady her, but dropped his hands abruptly before they made contact. Gray eyes, wary and uncertain, bored into hers. His heat stroked her from breast to thigh; something hot and tight grabbed at her insides. Something she hadn't felt in years. *Want.*

Startled at the realization, she retreated a step. She swallowed, then summoned a smile. "You don't mind, do you? About the dog. I should've asked you first, but I had no idea Mom and Dad would send—"

"It's fine," he interrupted, keeping his gaze fastened on hers. "I've got plenty of room for another animal. Chester and Buckley will like playing with a puppy."

"Oh, he's not—"

"Jenna!" Mace called. "Here he is."

"Oh!" She spun away and hurried into the living room. "Hey, boy! Come here, boy."

Puppy raced into the house, shooting past Jenna in a black blur, skidding into a turn at the French doors in the living room and loping back to her. The Great Dane's head reached her waist and she held out her left arm, cradling him close to her. She crooned a hello to him, joy welling up inside her.

"*That's* your *puppy?*" Linc's disbelief echoed through the front room.

Jenna raised her head, smiling broadly. "That's what I was trying to tell you."

Linc walked over to her, his steps measured, letting the dog judge him. The Great Dane's head lifted and jet-black eyes never wavered from Linc. Jenna watched as Linc's gaze took in the sheen of his ebony coat and the white blaze on his massive chest.

"When I first got him, I had an older dog so I just called him 'Puppy.' It kinda stuck."

"I guess so." Linc eyed the animal dubiously.

Sudden concern shot through Jenna. He *would* let Puppy stay, wouldn't he? Linc moved another step closer and the dog growled low in his throat.

"You big goof, it's all right." Jenna kneed the animal playfully in the chest. His tail started wagging and his tongue lolled, making him look as if he wore a dopey smile.

Linc grinned, his gaze going to Jenna's. "He's the size of a Shetland pony. Where do you keep him?"

"In the house, but while he's here, he can stay wherever you want."

"If he's trained, he can stay in here just like my dogs."

"Thank you!" Affection warmed her and she hugged the dog to her again. Puppy's tail thumped loudly on the tile floor and he quivered impatiently, nudging her with his head to get closer.

"Watch out for your arm." Concern deepened Linc's voice and Jenna again felt that strange tightness gripping her down low.

She kept her attention on the dog, whom she could read more easily than Linc Garrett. "Sit, boy. Stay. Good dog."

The animal dropped immediately to his haunches, looking expectantly at Jenna. She scratched his ears with her good hand.

"That's amazing," Linc praised.

"Yeah," Mace spoke from the doorway. "Maybe you can try a little of that training on my brother while you're here."

"Ha," Linc said dryly, his gaze locked on Jenna.

She felt that same sensation she'd gotten in the bedroom, as if her skin tingled with an icy heat. It wasn't unpleasant at all and totally confused her. Seeking to escape the intensity of Linc's gaze, she leaned down to Puppy.

The dog nuzzled her neck and her cheek. She laughed, speaking to him softly as Linc moved behind her.

She could hear his lowered voice as he spoke to Mace. "That is some big dog."

"Yeah. I didn't figure you'd mind and it can't hurt to have another watchdog around."

"I agree." Linc's voice dropped, though it was still audible to Jenna. "And maybe having him here will make her feel more at ease."

"Yeah."

Jenna straightened and turned toward Mace, her eyes glowing. "Thank you so much for bringing him."

"You're welcome."

Her gaze moved to Linc and she was startled by the intensity in his eyes. Overwhelmed with a sudden awkwardness, she looked away. "And thanks for letting him stay."

"No problem." His voice stroked over her and she felt herself wanting to know what he was thinking. Annoyed at the thought, she shoved it away.

Mace shifted in the doorway, bringing something out from behind his back. "Jenna, Captain Price—that's my boss—got a fax of this photo of Ramsey last night. I want you to take a look at it, make sure we're looking for the right guy."

A photo of Ramsey? Fear raked down her spine. She didn't *want* to look at it. She'd given them a name. Why wasn't that enough?

Mace pushed the paper at her and Jenna fought to breathe. *It's only a picture. He can't hurt you.*

"Jenna?" Concern clouded Mace's blue eyes as he shot a look at Linc.

Linc's gaze moved to her, concerned, speculative.

Shaking, she reached out woodenly, her nerves pulsing with revulsion and apprehension. Maybe it was silly to be so panicked, but Jenna could barely escape thoughts of the man as it was. She certainly didn't want another reminder.

But the police needed her help. Ignoring the nausea pushing up to her throat, Jenna's fingers closed over the picture and she drew it to her.

The walls closed in on her; her chest constricted. Time froze as she stared at his handsome raw-boned features and hate-filled dark eyes. Images of the attack tumbled back, mixed with painful jarring reminders of the rape.

Again she felt the violation of her body, the bone-crunching pressure of his weight on her, the slam of her head against the Jeep window as she tried to get away from him. The smell of sweat and beer rancid on her body.

Anxiety overwhelmed her. She wanted to drop the picture and run. A thread of common sense kept her in place. *Just look at it and get it over with.*

His thick brown hair was short and neatly trimmed, as he'd always worn it. Even in penitentiary overalls, his massive shoulders strained at the seams. Bulky arms and a thick neck testified that he was still into weight lifting, as he had been in college.

He looked the same—the deceptive careless smile, the cold, restless eyes, the hard mouth that had spewed such vicious obscenities at her. Pure fear knotted her gut. The only difference Jenna noted from eight years ago was a jagged scar that ran diagonally from his right ear to his collarbone. It had been too dark the other night for her to notice that.

Fighting back the nausea that threatened, she thrust the photo back at Mace. "That's him. Deke Ramsey. It's him."

Mace folded the paper in half and stuffed it into his back pocket. "All right. We're going to release this photo to the press then."

Linc edged closer to her, asking in a low voice, "Are you all right?"

She nodded woodenly, a chill burning from the inside out to ice her fingers and toes. Her panic receded enough so that she could move and backed away from the open door, the stifling heat, reaching again for Puppy, something familiar and comforting. Ramsey's face flashed through her mind interminably. She would never be free again.

Mace squeezed the bridge of his nose. "Your parents called."

"Are they all right?" she asked anxiously.

"Yes. And they picked up your Jeep."

"Good."

His voice, calming and gentle, penetrated her apprehension.

"Jenna, starting tonight I'm going to put a man on your office for a few nights."

"You think Ramsey might go back there?" She kept her hand on the softness of Puppy's head, glad for his company.

Mace shrugged. "Right now, he's probably still checking out hospitals, but when he can't find you, he'll definitely go back there."

"How did he find me in the first place?" Jenna shoved her good hand through her hair, her voice as shaky as her hands.

Mace shook his head. "My guess is he started somewhere familiar. Since he knew you in college, he probably started in Stillwater."

She stilled, horror swelling inside her. She glanced from Linc to Mace. "Maybe he got the alumni newsletter."

Mace's eyes narrowed thoughtfully. "Do you keep up with that stuff?"

"Yes." Agitated, she shifted from one foot to the other. "And I also volunteer every year to take an intern from the vet program."

"That's probably where he found you then," Mace concurred.

She threw up her good hand, her voice bitter. "And there I was, an easy mark."

"Hey, you can't blame yourself for that." Linc's voice was low with conviction.

She glanced at him, compelled by the deep timbre of his voice. "I wasn't blaming myself, not really. I know I did nothing to bring this on except put him in prison where he belongs."

"Good." Linc's gaze held hers. "I'm glad to hear you say it."

She tore her gaze away, flexing her fingers on the dog's head. Puppy's tail flopped happily on the stone tile. "Detective, I have to make arrangements for my animals. I don't mean Puppy. I mean my patients."

Mace nodded. "I can call whoever you want."

"There's a friend of mine—Steve Majors, who's also a vet. He can take over some of my cases. I'll just call and see if he can come out tonight—"

"No. Absolutely not."

Surprise held her speechless for a moment. "Why not? I need someone to look after my animals."

Beside her, Puppy seemed to sense her irritation and he growled low in his throat.

Mace shook his head, his gaze unyielding. "We don't want to get anymore people involved here."

"I can't leave my animals unattended." Despite knowing Mace was only trying to provide security, Jenna couldn't bear to think what might happen if arrangements weren't made for her patients. "I have to do something."

"Come on, Mace." Linc moved so close to Jenna that she could feel his heat wrap around her. "What can it hurt?"

Jenna didn't look at him, but she was surprised yet again. She studied Mace, her mind racing for ways to reassure him. "I haven't seen Steve in almost a month, so if Ramsey has been watching me for the last two weeks, he can't connect Steve to me."

"I don't think it's a good idea. Why don't you write down what you want and I'll get in touch with him?"

"I need to talk to him. I need to see him. He'll be worried about me."

Mace studied her with absolutely no expression on his face. This time, Linc was silent. Frustration churned inside her. "Please, Detective. Steve is my best friend. You can depend on him to be discreet and I really, really need to see him."

Mace frowned, his gaze flickering to Linc. "Linc can help you. He's a doctor. Just tell him what you want."

"For crying out loud, Mace!" Linc exploded beside Jenna. "I treat patients with two legs. All hers have four. Or wings. What do I know about cow udders?"

Pleased at his argument, Jenna nodded. She kept her voice even, trying to control the anxiety swirling in her stomach.

After what had happened, she desperately needed to see Steve. "Linc's right. He can help me do some things, but I'd feel better about my patients if I knew Steve was taking over."

Mace scowled, looking from Jenna to Linc.

"Please." Jenna moved toward Mace, desperation thinning her voice. "Can't I see him and make arrangements? He can help me. He's helped me before."

"Jenna—"

"Come on, Mace!" Linc joined in with her and Jenna couldn't have been more surprised if he'd stripped and run through the house naked. "If the guy's careful, what harm could there be? You can certainly lay down a few guidelines to ensure her security."

"I don't like taking unnecessary risks." Mace's jaw hardened stubbornly.

"Well, you're upsetting my patient and that's risking her health." Linc stepped over beside Jenna, his jaw firmed in the same way as his brother's. "Her blood pressure's probably skyrocketing. Letting this guy come out seems like something you could easily control. Come on. You'll be putting her mind at ease and right now, I think that's what she needs."

Astonished, Jenna nodded and looked at Mace, her fingers working convulsively on Puppy's head. Mace had to let her see Steve.

He had to.

Mace fisted his hands on his hips, glaring from Linc to Jenna indecisively. He threw his hands up in the air. "Oh, all right. Maybe between the three of us, we can pull this off securely."

A radiant smile bloomed in Jenna's eyes and she reached toward Mace, shaking his hand. "Thank you. Thank you so much. Steve will be careful. He will."

"He'd better," Mace grumbled. "All right, give me the

guy's name and number. I'll get in touch with him and see if he can make it tonight.''

Despite the discomfort, Jenna smiled at Linc, noticing that his return smile seemed more a grimace. His features were now tight and closed. Did he regret helping her?

She rattled off Steve's office and home phone numbers as Mace wrote them down. He slid his small notebook into the back pocket of his jeans. ''I'll call you once I hear from him, tell you what's going on.''

''Great!'' Profound pleasure washed through her and Jenna realized with astonishment that it was due to Linc. He'd done so much for her, but nothing meant more than this.

She glanced at him. He watched as his brother walked down the steps and climbed into his Mustang convertible. Mace started the engine and drove off.

Linc lifted a hand in farewell then moved back into the house, closing the door.

''How can I ever thank you?'' Jenna's voice was quiet, her throat tight with gratitude.

He shifted, his broad shoulders moving under the worn T-shirt he wore. ''Don't worry about it.''

''Ah, yes, you're just repaying me for what I did for you.'' She swallowed against the lump in her throat, suddenly wanting, *needing* for Linc to know how much she appreciated what he'd done. So much for staying out of his way. She *and* her dog were here now. In a few hours, Steve would be, too.

Wariness stole into his eyes and he jammed his hands in the front pockets of his jeans. ''Since you brought up repayment, I'd really like to apologize for what I did that night. In the barn. It's way overdue.''

She froze, her mind skipping back to that evening. Even now she could feel the steel of his uninvited grip, the moment of heart-stopping fear when he'd pulled her near. And yet standing here with him, she wasn't afraid. Certainly wasn't repulsed. Still, she didn't want to discuss it either.

She waved him off. "That was a long time ago. Why don't we—"

"Jenna, please let me do this." His voice was hoarse and fervent. "I was drunk that night, but it doesn't excuse what I did—what I *tried* to do to you. I'm very sorry and I hope you'll forgive me."

His gaze drew hers and she couldn't look away. In the gray depths was reflected old pain, deep loss. She saw that now, just as she recognized his remoteness hid a wealth of feeling. "I accept and I hope you'll believe me when I say you didn't harm me."

"Good." Relief shone in his eyes. "I'm glad we got that out of the way. If it makes you feel any better staying here with me, I haven't had a drink since then."

"I'm not worried about that," she said softly. And strangely she wasn't. "Please let me thank you for what you're doing now."

"It's nothing, really." Linc shook his head, taking a step past her.

Without thinking, she put her hand on his forearm, stopping him.

His gaze dropped to her hand, then rose to her face. Electricity hummed between them. Disbelief, hunger and uncertainty clouded his eyes.

Firm muscle and smooth skin warmed her palm. Jenna licked her suddenly dry lips. She rarely touched anyone, outside of family, but a small bit of trust had been forged today with Linc. "Thank you for everything. For letting Puppy stay—"

Upon hearing his name, the dog whimpered and thumped his tail. His dark eyes watched Linc and Jenna.

"For going to Wilbur's grave with me. And for helping me see Steve."

"I understand your concern about your patients." Linc shifted, bringing his hip within an inch of hers. Spice-scented warmth emanated from him and wrapped around her. "And I really don't want you upset."

Her blood heated at the deep huskiness of his voice. Before she even realized it, her gaze went to his lips and she wondered what it would be like if he kissed her, with her consent, with his gentle deliberation.

His muscles flexed beneath her hand and she jolted at the kick of desire in her belly. Her gaze locked with his and she saw hunger flare in his eyes. That raw, frank interest should've scared her; at the very least, she should've stepped away from him.

But Jenna was rooted to the spot by curiosity and a want that unfurled along her nerve endings. Would he kiss her? Should she let him?

His gaze grew more intense, more heated. And he leaned toward her. A thrill shot through her veins, tempered by caution and apprehension, but she waited for him. After so many years, she wanted to know, wanted to taste him just once.

She kept her gaze on his, her breath coming in small ragged pants. His breath caressed her cheek, her lips and she stood completely still, waiting. Hoping. Uncertain.

His muscles flexed under her palm. Tension coiled through his body, spiraled around her. He drew nearer, nearer. Then he closed his eyes and stepped back.

Desire and doubt warred on his features. He opened his eyes, now metal dark with regret.

Why had he stopped? It had been years since she'd felt mutual attraction to any man, but she thought she remembered how it felt. Had she been wrong? Was he unaffected?

He opened his mouth, to form an apology she knew.

She couldn't bear it. Perhaps she should've been embarrassed that she had wanted him to kiss her so badly, but she felt only a sharp disappointment that he hadn't. She didn't understand that, didn't understand why she was so drawn to him. So much for staying out of his way.

Tearing her gaze from his, she felt a blush heat her neck. "Thank you for everything. I appreciate it."

"You're welcome. And Jenna?"

"Yes." Her gaze met his, searching, measuring, expectant.

"I'd like to at least be friends. Do you think we could do that?"

She paused, swept away by the urging in her heart to be capable of more than friendship. But that's all she was good for, thanks to Ramsey. And perhaps Linc inherently sensed that. "Yes, I certainly do. I'd like that, too."

"Good." He smiled, broad and unguarded and it burned her clear to her toes. "I'm glad."

"Me, too." She couldn't draw a full breath and her chest ached. She'd never seen such a beautiful, welcoming smile. A smile that ignited a secret craving inside her, made her want to win it again, to delve deep beneath the scarred layers of the man and see his soul, to be part of him.

Something she would never do, thanks to Ramsey. What man wanted a woman who couldn't respond to him? No man. And certainly not a sensual, attractive man like Linc Garrett.

Friends. If they became even that, it's all they would ever be.

Chapter 5

You idiot, what were you thinking? Linc hadn't thought at all. He'd simply reacted to the sweet heat of her, the sincerity shining from her eyes and the feel of her hand on his arm.

She had touched *him* voluntarily, for the first time. Humbled by that fact, he'd also been spiked by pure need. So, what had he done? Tried to kiss her.

Still, she hadn't tried to pull away from him. There had been no revulsion or horror darkening her beautiful eyes; instead they had glowed with gratitude.

What would've happened if he *had* kissed her? Would she have run from him then? Would that heart-wrenching terror have come into her eyes? Linc was glad he hadn't found out. And part of him was just as sorry.

He responded to her physically. What man wouldn't? But that didn't mean he wanted to get tangled up with her. After what she'd been through, she needed a man who could give himself totally, openly and Linc couldn't do that. He had nothing left to give. Michelle had destroyed every last piece of his soul.

He shouldn't want anything from Jenna West, but he did. He wanted to erase that wariness in her eyes, wanted to coax open those soft lips and kiss her hot and openmouthed and ease some of the desperation coiling in his gut.

He wanted to stroke the velvet of her skin with his hands and tongue, to lave away the bruises—

Stop. This thinking was futile. A dead end. Just because Jenna hadn't bolted when he'd tried to kiss her earlier, didn't mean she was interested in anything physical. And physical was all Linc was interested in.

Disgust rolled through him. How could he be thinking about sex after what had happened to her? She had just been attacked, nearly raped again. What kind of man did that make him? He wanted her. There was no use denying it, but he wasn't proud of it. And he certainly wouldn't act on it, no matter how loudly or insistently his body screamed.

That evening, he still ached from that missed kiss. Regret stabbed at him, but he knew he'd done the right thing by walking away from Jenna. Despite the slow burn of need inching through him, he'd turned and kept going. For the first time, she'd looked at him with something other than wariness in her eyes and he'd started to kiss her.

Linc cursed inwardly. She didn't need that from him. She needed a friend, a protector. Not a lover. But he ached anyway, with regret and unanswered want.

As he watched her and her friend, Steve, standing in his entryway, Linc felt that desire spread through him with the *throb-throb* of a slow pulse.

A savage urgency rose up inside him and he wondered if she would ever look at any other man—*him*—the way she looked at Steve Majors, completely trusting, her eyes shining, her emotions plain on her face.

She looked at the guy as if he were a cross between Mel Gibson and Santa Claus. Linc went with Santa Claus. Dr. Majors had come bearing a grocery sack full of something and in the other hand held two foil-covered pans stacked on top of each other—blackberry cobbler from his mother and peach cobbler from Jenna's.

Mace had called earlier, saying Jenna's friend would be there around eight o'clock. At eight on the dot, the lean, lanky doctor, who looked more like a ranch hand than a veterinarian, arrived.

He and Linc exchanged guarded hellos at the door, then Linc had taken the cobblers into the kitchen and stored them in the fridge.

When he rejoined them in the living room, they stood just inside the front door exactly where he'd left them.

Their voices were low and Linc couldn't catch the words. But the sight of Steve's fingers floating familiarly over Jenna's neck as he examined the marks around her throat had Linc's body tightening as if braced for a blow.

Assaulted by a burning grip on his gut, he moved a few steps closer. "I put the cobblers in the fridge so you can find them when you're hungry."

"Thanks." Jenna hardly spared him a glance, staring up at her friend with affection and absolute trust.

Steve Majors wore long Wranglers with ragged hems that skimmed the tops of his scuffed boots. Upon entering the house, he'd removed his light straw cowboy hat and set it on the polished entryway table. Linc figured Steve would be his exact height without the boots.

Linc stared hard at Jenna and her friend, ignoring the churning in his gut that he didn't understand. The two of them had similar coloring, enough so that they could've been related. Steve's hair was the exact color of Jenna's, but where her eyes were blue-green, his were hazel.

His big hand held her uninjured one as he thoroughly looked her over with gentle concern.

"I told you I'm fine." She touched her throat gingerly, as if to wipe away the bruises there. "Linc made sure of that."

Steve grinned at Linc. "I'm sure that wasn't easy. Thanks, Doc."

Linc started to say he hadn't done it for Steve, but he bit back the words. He didn't like Steve's proprietary air, but Linc certainly had no claim on her.

His gaze swept over her. She seemed stronger today. Was she all right? In the two days since the attack, her bruises had faded from cruel red to a yellowish purple.

Jenna made a face at Steve's jibe, poking at the grocery sack he still held in his arms. "What's in there?"

"Everything you could possibly want."

There was no hint of seduction in Majors's voice, but Linc's jaw clamped tight anyway.

Steve reached into the sack and withdrew a handful of CDs.

"Music for your eclectic little heart—from Alan Jackson and Céline Dion to Def Leppard and the Eagles. All your weird choices."

She held her injured arm close to her side, extending her other hand stiffly to take the discs from him and glance eagerly through them. "Thank you."

From the sack, he pulled a couple of videotapes and his deep voice rumbled out, "And for your viewing pleasure..."

The two of them were so intent on each other that Linc felt like a third wheel. But it was his house, dammit and he wasn't going anywhere. Besides, Jenna might know Steve Majors enough to trust him, but Linc didn't. He leaned back against the corner of the couch, crossing one ankle over the other.

Steve waggled a stack of videotapes at Jenna. "Your favorite Harrison Ford movies, your Civil War movies, including *Gone with the Wind*. I figure you'll have time to watch all of that one now that you're a woman of leisure."

She stuffed the CDs back into the bag and squeezed his arm.

"Thank you. Any books?"

"Yes." He opened the sack, holding it wide for her inspection. "And some vet journals, too. The last two months' worth."

"This should keep me occupied for a while." A sudden sadness shaded her voice and Linc watched her carefully.

So did Steve. "You sure you're okay?"

She nodded quickly. Her pleasure at seeing Steve was obvious, but strain shadowed her eyes, tightened her mouth. Fear seemed to vibrate from her. Linc could feel it, even though she put up a brave front.

She seemed to shake it off, asking Steve in a warm voice that belied any concern, "Can you stay for some cobbler?"

"Sure."

Jenna's gaze swerved to Linc's. "You don't mind, do you?"

"No. Not at all." He was *not* jealous, Linc told himself firmly. Simply determined not to see Jenna disappointed any more today. She might have convinced Mace to let her see Steve, but she'd still had to give up going to Wilbur's funeral.

She and Steve moved toward Linc and he straightened, following them into the kitchen.

Jenna dished out blackberry cobbler—her favorite, Linc learned—then heated it up while Linc scooped out vanilla ice cream. The three of them sat down at the kitchen table to enjoy the dessert.

Steve and Jenna discussed everything from pulling calves to a heart massage Steve had performed that day on an old cow dog. Linc sat quietly, marveling at the difference Majors's presence made in Jenna's demeanor.

She occasionally touched her throat in a nervous, self-conscious motion, but gone were the shadows in her eyes, the tight lines around her mouth. Her mouth was still swollen, but more relaxed.

Though her bruises still looked raw, her lightly tanned skin was flushed with pleasure; her eyes glowed. And she seemed to have more energy.

Majors had done more for her in the last thirty minutes than Linc had managed to do in forty-eight hours. A fierce frustration ripped through him and he shoved it away. He had no claim on Jenna West. Nor did he want one.

Jenna included him in the conversation which, frankly, Linc could barely keep his mind on. He was surrounded by the clean soap scent of her, charmed by the light in those blue-green eyes and frequently cursed himself for not kissing those soft lips, busted or not.

It was obvious that Jenna and Steve had seen each other through some pretty tough times. There was an ease to their friendship which Linc did admit to envying. He only felt such a degree of ease with his brothers, Mace and Sam. And that not all the time. There were some things he could discuss with Mace, some with Sam, but it seemed Jenna and Steve had no secrets. Linc had never had a friend like that, not even Michelle in the early days.

He listened more than he participated in their conversation, trying to read what kind of man Steve Majors was. Jenna obviously trusted him, which put the man in a class held by only one other, Jenna's father.

Linc was suddenly struck with a fervent desire to be included in that elite group, to win Jenna's trust to such a degree that she would share things with him—

Ah, there he went again. Feeling things he'd never felt and wouldn't know how to deal with if put to the test.

He gathered the empty bowls and rose to put them in the sink.

Steve and Jenna pushed away from the table, too, and walked back into the living room.

The tall veterinarian took Jenna's elbow, guiding her toward the front door. "How are the police coming on finding Ramsey?"

"Nothing yet, but they don't think it will take long."

Despite the briskness of her voice, Linc caught a slight tremble in her words, heard the doubt.

She was all business as she told Steve about Wilbur's funeral and how Mace thought it would be best if she paid her respects after the service.

He nodded in agreement, which made Linc breathe a sigh of relief. "Sounds like the smart thing to do. Allie and I will be there. We'll give Bernice your condolences."

"Thanks." Frustration roughened her voice. "I just wish I could go. Wish I didn't have to stay stuck here like a coward—" She broke off, glancing apologetically over at Linc, who was once again standing beside the sofa. "Linc's been wonderful, but it's frustrating."

"Hey." Steve squeezed her upper arm. "It's just for another few days. If it would make you feel better, you can come out to the ranch with me. In fact, that would make *me* feel better. I can keep an eye on you. I'm outside of city limits, too, so—"

"You'd have to clear that through Mace and I doubt he'd approve it." Linc's fists clenched. He didn't know why the idea made him angry, but it did. Jenna was here and she should stay here. "Besides, she still needs medical attention and I can provide that."

Jenna looked at him, then back at Steve regretfully. "He's probably right."

The other man's gaze slid to Linc and his eyes hardened with a challenge. He squeezed Jenna's shoulder lightly. "If you want to go home with me, I'm sure it could be arranged."

She touched Steve's arm, drawing his gaze. "I'm fine here. Linc has been good to me. And as you can see, there's plenty of room for both me and Puppy."

"All right, but if you change your mind, just say the word."

She nodded. "How's Allie? I thought you might have brought her along."

"She's fine."

"Almost have the wedding planned?"

Ah, the best friend had a fiancée. For some reason, Linc's

muscles relaxed a bit and he eased back down on the corner of the couch.

"I guess so." Steve ran a hand through his short hair. "It beats me how something that lasts less than twenty minutes can take so dang long to plan."

Linc silently agreed.

Jenna smiled fondly at Steve, causing that tightness to lock up Linc's body again. "She wants it to be perfect. You're only going to do it once."

"I know."

"Tell her I said hello."

He shifted, suddenly looking awkward. Linc wondered what it was about his fiancée that would spark such a look of discomfort.

Exasperation crossed Jenna's features and she sighed loudly. "You didn't tell her you were coming to see me, did you?"

Steve scratched his chin and stared at something over her head.

"You big dummy." Affection softened her voice. "You're not breaking any confidences by telling her, Steve."

"I just didn't know how much you wanted to be public knowledge," he said in a low voice, shooting a questioning look toward Linc.

"It's all right. Linc knows about it. About *everything*."

By everything, it was obvious that Jenna meant Linc knew about her rape eight years ago.

Surprise clear on his sun-roughened features, Steve looked fully at Linc, his gaze at once protective and probing. Linc held his gaze, giving away nothing.

He resented the implication that Jenna shouldn't have told him and he felt an absurd jolt of male satisfaction that he knew. At the moment, it didn't matter that the information had been given to his brother, the policeman, out of necessity.

Steve could wonder all he wanted about how Linc knew. It wasn't his job to reassure Jenna's friend.

She touched Steve's arm, gaining his attention. "You still haven't told her about the rape?"

"Jenna, I just don't feel I should."

"It's all right. I know she won't tell anyone. And I don't want her having any reason to doubt you. Tell her the truth. Tell her you came to see me and why."

He hesitated, clearly torn.

Linc straightened, now realizing fully that the rape must've been one of the things Steve and Jenna's friendship had weathered. No wonder she trusted the guy so implicitly.

Steve bent and kissed her cheek, smiling tenderly at her. She gave him a half smile, favoring her injured lips and hugged him with her good arm.

Linc strode across the tile and opened the front door. In the distance, thunder rumbled and he noted with surprise that the sky had darkened considerably. To the south, clouds churned thick and fast.

A stout breeze tore across the yard. Looked like they were in for a storm tonight.

Just then, all three dogs bounded up the porch and raced into the house. Seeing Steve, Linc's German shepherds skidded to a halt, growling, their hair bristling. Puppy raced around Jenna's friend, gave Steve's hand a quick swipe with his tongue, then loped inside.

"It's all right," Linc reassured them. "Quiet."

The pair fell silent, studied Steve for a moment then bolted past him to Jenna. She was petting Puppy, who growled happily as she scratched his ears. Chester and Buckley crowded closer, bumping at Jenna's hip, wanting her attention, too.

Chuckling, she complied. Linc's gut kicked at the throaty sound of her pleasure and he fleetingly wondered if he could ever coax anything like that from her.

Steve cast a concerned eye at the sky then stepped up beside Linc and said in a low voice, "Can I talk to you on the porch?"

"Sure." Linc glanced at Jenna, still doting on the dogs.

"Jenna, I'm going to walk Steve out and have a look around."

"All right." Speculation sharpened her eyes as she glanced from him to Steve. "I'm glad you came, Steve. And thanks for everything you brought."

"You bet. I want to hear from you, okay?"

"You know it." She reached down to chide Puppy for chewing on Buckley's tail.

"Love ya!" Steve called as Linc began to pull the door shut.

"Love you, too," Jenna responded in a husky voice.

Linc's gut clenched and he shut the door before he could see if she had tears in her eyes. If she did, he'd probably do something stupid like invite Majors to stay.

"I appreciate what you're doing for her." Steve jammed a hand in his front pocket and studied Linc curiously.

"I want to do it."

The other man nodded. "Yeah, she told me she helped you out a few years back. I guess this is your way of repaying her."

Resentment shot through him. He didn't like the fact that Steve Majors knew about that drunken night in the barn and Linc hadn't known a damn thing about him until today.

Steve settled his hat on his head, his eyes narrowed. "I figure you must be a pretty good guy if you're taking in Jenna *and* Puppy."

"Yeah, some puppy, huh?" Linc smiled, thinking he could probably like Steve Majors if he knew him a little.

The other man's gaze settled thoughtfully on the door, as if he could see Jenna through the heavy wood. "I want you to call me every day and tell me how she's doing."

Startled, Linc frowned. "She just said she'd call you—"

"*You* do it," Steve insisted. "She'll only tell me she's fine, whether she is or not. And I want to know how she's really getting along."

Irritation wound through Linc. He wasn't a damn nurse.

And Steve Majors wasn't Jenna's next of kin, though the man obviously cared about her. "All right."

Relief flitted across Steve's features, then his hazel gaze hardened. "If you hurt her, I'll come after you."

"Hurt her? Why would I hurt her?" Disbelief was quickly followed by rage at Majors's gall. Linc straightened, taking a step toward the other man. "I've spent the last two days *helping* her."

"That's not what I mean and you know it. You hurt her, you answer to me. Got it?"

Linc's back stiffened. Anger swirled through him. "I don't like threats."

Steve's gaze stayed locked on his, unyielding, waiting.

Linc finally conceded saying, "She has nothing to fear from me."

"Make sure it stays that way." Steve nodded briskly and stepped around Linc to open the door again. Moving over the threshold, he walked to Jenna, kissing her on the cheek once more. "Take it easy."

"I will."

"I'll let you know about the Campbells' foal."

"Okay."

Steve rejoined Linc on the porch, gave him one last warning look, then stuck out his hand. "Thanks for helping her, Doc."

"Sure." Linc's gaze narrowed at him. Steve Majors was a little high-handed, but he understood why. Linc shook Steve's hand, silently assuring the man that he would care for Jenna *and* let Steve know how she was doing.

The man nodded and loped down the steps toward his pickup. "Bye, Jenna."

Linc turned in time to see her wave, then wince. Her gaze went from him to Steve, blatantly curious. She moved closer to Linc, though she still stayed in the house. "What were y'all talking about?"

Linc slid a sideways glance at her. "He just wanted to know if you were really all right."

"What did you tell him?"

"That you were perfectly safe here," he answered, his voice taking on a rough edge as he recalled the moments earlier when she'd considered leaving his home to go with Steve. "And you are, Jenna."

Her gaze met his then skittered away. "I know," she said quietly. "I do feel safe. With you."

"You do?" Surprise forced out the words. Relief and profound pleasure welled inside him. "I'm glad."

Her gaze met his fully. A slow smile started in her eyes, lighting them like heated gems. Then the corners of her lips lifted.

Desire, denial, doubt all pumped through him. She smiled at him as if he'd accomplished some incredible feat and he felt his heart crack open another centimeter. Yet a part of him—the scarred, experienced part—retreated from the sense of vulnerability she stirred.

Jenna had drawn the lines where she wanted them and Linc told himself to play by her rules. Despite the fact that he found himself wanting to cross the line with her, wanting to know more, wanting to *be* more.

You're providing safety for her. That's all. You're repaying her for helping you.

His voice turned gruff and he stepped into the house, closing the door with his foot. "I need to call the hospital."

She looked startled, then disappointed. Nodding, all trace of emotion erased from her face, she suddenly looked tired and as if she were in pain. "I think I'll turn in early tonight. Steve's visit kind of wore me out."

Linc nodded, wincing when she bent and scooped up the grocery sack full of goodies Steve had left. He longed to help her, but the distance was back between them, cool and solid. Still he kept his gaze on the stiff lines of her back, her careful gait, the sheen of her auburn hair as she walked quietly down the hall and disappeared from view.

This was the right way to handle things, he told himself. Never mind the loneliness and regret pressing heavily on his chest.

Outside, thunder roared and rain lashed the windows. The wall opposite her bed creaked. Jenna's nerves stretched taut.

She'd come to bed three hours earlier and the storm had exploded in full force about an hour ago, nudging at her fears about Ramsey, stoking her unease. *He was going to take everything.*

In an effort to manage the apprehension, the anxiety hammering at her, she forced thoughts of him out of her mind.

Her bruised body ached keenly though she could tell some improvement. Her lips were still swollen and stiff, the marks around her throat and face still rawly conspicuous. And tonight, like each night since the most recent attack, she couldn't sleep. Only tonight, Ramsey wasn't the sole cause. Nor was the howling storm.

Trying *not* to think about Ramsey triggered other thoughts she tried to dodge. Thoughts of Linc. A smoky frustration scraped along her nerves, knotted in her gut. Hot edgy desire slid through her, beckoning, coaxing her to explore it.

Linen sheets caressed her bare legs, prickling them to sensitive awareness. She was acutely aware of her silk panties and a growing heaviness in her breasts.

With a muttered curse, she yanked the sheets up to her chin, then pushed them down to her hips again. *Why was she still thinking about that kiss? It had happened—or not happened—hours ago.*

She didn't have to close her eyes to imagine Linc's hands on her body, his lips on hers. Though she had welcomed these thoughts to distract her from Ramsey, she found the images of her and Linc equally disturbing.

Forcing them away, she concentrated fiercely on mentally

cataloguing her clinic's supply cabinet—surgical scrub, spray disinfectant, gloves, syringes.

Outside the wind sighed like an old woman, wasted and feeble; in the next instant it screamed like a wounded animal. The noise played in the background of her mind, ebbing, falling, coiling through her nerves.

Thoughts of Linc slipped through her mind like insidious fingers of fog, winding past her defenses, easing around her objections until she throbbed low and deep between her legs. A frantic heat sizzled under her skin.

Okay, so she was feeling things—physical things—that she hadn't felt in years. Her hormones, silent for so long, were putting up a fuss. That's all it was. Why now and why Linc Garrett, she didn't know.

But she wouldn't be seduced by it. She'd tried a sexual relationship after the rape. She'd failed. And she'd moved on.

Still she couldn't forget the heat in his eyes, the impatient hunger. A shiver chased up her spine and she squeezed her legs together.

Tentatively she allowed the memory of that morning, when he'd almost kissed her. She could feel his breath misting her lips, her cheek. His body heat mingled with hers. And his eyes grew dark as he drew nearer, closer, his lips reaching for hers. She lifted her face, wanting his kiss, needing it—

Groaning, she pushed herself into a sitting position and propped her elbows on her knees, her cast rough against her skin. Good grief! Since she'd gone to bed, she had been tortured continuously by these thoughts.

She wished he had kissed her.

There. She'd admitted it. Here in the dark, *alone,* it didn't seem so bad, but she knew it was dangerous. Knew that wanting his kiss might lead to other, more complicated wants and she couldn't follow through on anything more intimate than a kiss.

Shoving her hair out of her face with her good hand, she surged out of bed and tugged down her light cotton nightshirt.

The blue and white plaid material fell to her knees and she padded silently to the bedroom door. Rain pounded against her windows. Away from the house, a door, maybe to the barn, clattered in the distance.

Fatigue washed over her, followed by a sense of complete helplessness. Since the attack, she lived on fear, jumping at every noise, afraid to go outside. Just the same way she'd been after the rape. She had made every decision based on fear, but she had finally freed herself of that. Until now. Now it was starting all over again.

The only thing that kept her from unraveling completely was putting on a front for Linc. She didn't want him to think she was a total basket case. And these chaotic thoughts of first him, then Ramsey were eroding her self-control, eating away at the little strength she had left.

Her mind was tired, her body weak. Just for a while, she wanted to escape thoughts of Ramsey *and* Linc. She wanted a break from the stalking fear and from the unexpected sensations Linc stirred in her.

What she needed was a movie. Harrison Ford. He could take her mind off anything. She opened the door and peered into the hallway. Faint light glowed from the living room. At the opposite end of the hall, Linc's room was dark. *He* was probably sleeping peacefully, she grumbled under her breath.

Checking to make sure the buttons that ran the length of her gown were fastened, she walked down the hall and out to the foyer, crossing to the living area. The rain seemed louder here, more violent, hurling sharply against the French doors.

Now she saw that the light came from the kitchen and she slowed, wondering if Linc was up after all. A quick check of the kitchen proved it was empty and she decided to leave the light on, comforted by the warm glow that spilled into the darkened living area.

She padded into the living area, her gaze sweeping over the spacious room. Despite the tall ceilings, it was cozy. The love seat and couch were arranged in an L position, with the love seat angled toward the television and the couch facing the fireplace. Linc had placed her sack of CDs and movies on the hearth.

She walked between the love seat and a broad square oak coffee table, reaching the hearth and digging through the sack. Thunder cracked and she tensed, glancing toward the back doors. Lightning flashed through the night like clashing swords, its silvery light illuminating the backyard and the massive oak trees that bent in the wind.

Jenna's gaze automatically swept the yard. It was empty. No face stared back at her beyond the windows. She deliberately forced her mind from wondering about Ramsey, refusing to be intimidated by the violent storm.

"Ah." She pulled her copy of *Raiders of the Lost Ark* from its cardboard case, walking over to plug it into the VCR.

Spying the remote control on top of the television, she palmed it and walked back toward the love seat. A framed photograph on the mantel caught her eye and she paused, recognizing Linc with his brother, Mace, and another dark-haired man she didn't know.

The three were dressed in hunting gear and each of them knelt behind a buck. A broad smile creased Linc's normally serious features and his eyes glowed with laughter. Jenna found herself smiling at the change in him, at the obvious camaraderie the three shared.

"What are you doing?"

The gruff masculine voice triggered the anxiety that had been mounting in Jenna all night. She whirled, stifling a scream as horror flashed through her.

"That's me with my brothers."

She sighed in relief. Linc spoke from the doorway of the kitchen. She clutched the remote to her breasts, her heart thudding wildly against her ribs.

"Hell," he muttered, looking disgusted. "I didn't even think I might scare you. Sorry."

"No, I'm fine. I just didn't hear you come in."

Water shimmered on his strong features. His hair was slick from the rain and he wore no shirt. Dragging her gaze from the sleek broad sinew of his chest, she noticed he held a towel. As he raised an arm to rub his hair, muscles flexed at his motion.

Her gaze shot toward the hallway. "I thought you were in bed. Asleep," she added unnecessarily, suddenly aware that her nightshirt came only to the tops of her knees. And beneath it she wore only panties. Her thumb fiddled with the button between her breasts.

Dark water spots dotted his jeans and he'd removed his boots. White socks gleamed in the light from the kitchen. "Yeah, I couldn't sleep either." His voice was grainy with fatigue. "I decided to look around outside."

"Did you hear something?" Concern sharpened her voice. Even though she told herself no one was out there, she half expected him to say there'd been trouble.

His gaze drifted over her and he answered absently, "Just the storm."

"Oh." She felt suddenly caged in, acutely aware of his broad bare shoulders and the fact that they were alone. Trying to ignore the flutter of sensation in her stomach, she gestured toward the photo on the mantel. "I recognize your brother, Mace."

"The other one is my brother, Sam. He's the youngest." Linc's voice was polite, but distant. "He's a cop, too."

Jenna nodded, knowing now that Linc's aloofness could mean anything. She tried to read his features, though the kitchen light behind him hampered her efforts.

She touched another photo, one of a tux-clad Mace and his wife in a beautiful bridal gown. "How long have Mace and Devon been married?"

"About a month and a half."

"I like them both a lot."

"Yeah." A faint smile flashed across his features then his

gaze bored into her. He abruptly reached out and flipped off the kitchen light, plunging them into darkness for a second.

Lightning flashed through the room, haloing him in silver. As the light faded and Jenna's eyes adjusted, she could see him moving toward the foyer. "Well, I guess I'll see you in the morning."

Pale light filtered through the French doors behind her and she could see his face clearly now. She gestured toward the TV. "I hope I won't disturb you. I was going to watch a movie."

"Go ahead." He paused, faint bars of light falling across his chest, glittering on his chest hair. Shifting, he jammed his hands into his back pockets. "What are you watching?"

She told him, feeling compelled to invite him to join her. She wasn't sure he should stay, but she suddenly didn't want him to go. His presence wrapped around her like a quilt, comforting, soothing.

"Well, enjoy your movie."

As Linc turned to leave, she offered tentatively, "You're welcome to join me."

Ramsey was still out there, watching, waiting, planning. Nothing had changed in the last few hours, except that she was now torn between eluding all thoughts of Linc and having him close by.

He glanced back, his gaze flat and measuring. "Are you sure?"

A shiver worked through her at his low voice, igniting that heat she was coming to expect when around him. But it also resurrected her old doubt, the wariness. She edged over to the love seat and sat down on the end closest to the hallway...and escape.

Acutely aware of being naked beneath her flimsy nightgown, she smoothed the fabric over her thighs. "Yes. Of course."

After a long moment, he nodded. "I'll just put on some dry clothes and be right back."

"Okay."

She watched him go, unable to tear her gaze from the rain-sleeked sheen of his muscular shoulders, the cut and flex of sinew in his arms.

That startling, potent awareness moved through her. Want pierced her, enough to make her teeth ache and leave her winded. He disappeared into the hallway and Jenna flopped back on the love seat, her skin hot and clammy at the same time.

She shouldn't have asked him to stay.

Chapter 6

He would *not* kiss her. Jenna had shown trust in him by asking him to stay; he wasn't going to jump on her the first chance he got.

Linc had changed into a dry T-shirt and shorts, then returned to the living room. He sat on one end of the love seat, she sat on the other. They didn't touch. Yet, he could smell the soft woman scent of her, inhaled it as if it were part of him, anticipated it as if he needed it to breathe.

The storm slashed violently through the night. Lightning flared in and out of the room. He resolutely kept his gaze on the television.

Though she had drawn her nightshirt down as far as it could go, he could still see too much sleek thigh for his peace of mind. She had strength in those legs, legs that would fit exactly right around his hips and—

Linc cut off the thought and thumbed at the sweat on his upper lip.

Outside, the barn door slammed open and shut; the wind howled around the house. Jenna shifted, drawing Linc's gaze.

"It's all right," he said softly. "The dogs will let us know if something happens."

She nodded, barely glancing at him.

Anxiety pinched her pale features and dark circles ringed her eyes. In the flickering light, the bruises around her throat were dark smears. She looked exhausted and he realized she probably hadn't slept much since she'd been here. "Are you in pain?"

"That seems to be getting better." She offered him a slight smile, keeping her attention on the television screen.

"Do you need more medication? I can give you more."

"No. I don't like to take it."

Sudden suspicion snaked through him. "Have you taken *any* of it?"

When she didn't answer, his voice was sharp with surprise. "None? No wonder you look like death warmed over."

"Thanks," she said with dry humor. "That's what every woman wants to hear."

He bit back a smile. "You need to rest, Jenna. It's the best way to heal. And I know your ribs and arm must still be painful."

Her jaw firmed and for a moment he thought she would ignore him. Finally she looked at him. "I know you're right, but those pills would knock me out."

"That's the idea," he said wryly.

"I don't want—I can't—I don't want to close my eyes," she whispered, her eyes huge in her colorless face.

"You need to rest—oh." Linc's medical reasoning died on his lips. She was *afraid* to sleep, afraid to be caught unaware in case Ramsey did show up.

Linc's voice gentled and though he longed to take her hand, he didn't. Instead, his fist clenched on his thigh. "I can understand your concern, but I'm here. I won't let anything happen to you. I promise. The pills will help you rest. You'll feel better, get your strength back faster."

She stared at him, uncertainty warring with protest in her

eyes. She shook her head. "Thanks, but I honestly think I'm over the worst pain now. I don't want to be drugged out if something happens."

Linc wanted to protest, order that she get some rest, but he couldn't bring himself to do it. Staying here with him, waiting for Ramsey to make a move already had to have her feeling vulnerable. Powerless. By refusing to take the pills, she was exerting some control and Linc knew if their situations were reversed, he would be the same way.

A deafening crack of lightning split the rumble of the storm. Jenna jumped. Senses piqued, Linc's gaze moved quickly to the back doors.

The trees bent and twisted against the wind; rain slashed at the windows, but he could discern no threat.

Glancing over at Jenna, he saw that she had huddled into a tight ball, her features strained.

"Hey, the dogs are snoring over here so they can't be too worried. Okay?"

She looked at Puppy then the shepherds, all sprawled lazily on the floor, and her shoulders relaxed. "Okay."

She seemed more calm after that, even going so far as to curl up into a more comfortable position on the love seat. An easy silence settled between them as they watched the movie.

Linc tried to keep his mind on the adventures of Indiana Jones, but he was too distracted by the clean-air-and-sunshine scent of Jenna's heat, the tantalizing closeness of her foot to his leg.

He recalled how she'd looked standing by the fireplace when he'd come in earlier. Light from the kitchen had filtered through the thinness of her nightshirt and Linc had seen enough to make out the full curve of her breasts, the concave dip of her belly, the slender strength in her thighs.

At the memory, his mouth went dry and he shifted, trying to ease the growing tightness in his shorts. Tension coiled through him, carving a hole in his gut. Finally he glanced at her, only to see that her eyes were closed, her features relaxed in sleep.

Asleep, the lines of strain were gone; her skin was smooth. She looked fragile, pulling at that foreign part inside him that wanted to defend, make promises he couldn't keep. Desire and protectiveness roared through him and he marveled that he could still feel both things for a woman.

She moaned, stirring restlessly, her forehead puckering. Automatically, he reached out and laid his hand on her leg, just above her ankle.

She quieted and a small smile twisted his lips. He was surprised she'd actually drifted off. He knew she wouldn't have if she didn't trust him.

The thought spread a wave of warmth through his chest. He should probably move his hand, but he couldn't make himself do it. He enjoyed the feel of her. Gently, like the touch of a butterfly wing, he stroked her skin with his thumb.

Beneath his palm, her muscles were firm and sleek, her skin supple. Warmth seeped from her body into his. The nightshirt came to her knees and didn't reveal anything above there, but Linc knew she wore only panties beneath. Heat surged through him though he tried to ignore it.

Outside the rain battered the house. Webbed in a seductive lethargy, Linc wanted to run his hand up Jenna's leg, palm her thighs, delve gently between her legs for the heat he knew he would find there. His body tightened and his arousal throbbed keenly.

Just then Puppy's head shot up and the shepherds leapt to their feet. All three dogs rushed to the back doors, toenails clicking sharply against the tile. Hair ruffled on their necks as they posted themselves a foot apart.

Concern rose inside Linc and he glanced at Jenna, glad to see that she still slept. Careful not to disturb her, he removed his hand from her leg and pushed himself up from the love seat.

Walking to the back doors, he murmured quietly to the dogs, "Good boys. Good dogs."

The animals settled on their haunches, all growling low in their throats.

Linc peered through the rain-blurred windows, searching the hazy night. Twigs cartwheeled across the yard. The massive oaks bent and swayed, leaves ripped from their limbs to spin across the yard in a violent dance.

He moved silently to the windows adjacent to the fireplace and stared out at the barn. The door flopped back and forth, clacking loudly. But he saw nothing out of the ordinary, no menacing shadows, no dark shape edging up to the house or around the back porch.

He glanced again at the dogs, all three of whom now looked completely unconcerned. Puppy's tail flopped happily on the floor. The shepherds were stretched out, this time beside the Great Dane.

Linc checked the doors and the security alarm just for good measure. When he turned back, Jenna was sitting rigidly upright, watching him with wide frightened eyes.

Compassion tugged at him, along with that fierce desire to protect her. He wanted to pull her against him, but he moved back to his place on the love seat, keeping a good foot of distance between them. "Everything's all right. I didn't see anyone."

Her features were eerily flat. She stared straight ahead, beyond the doors. Huddled into herself, hands clasped tight between her knees, she looked defenseless and distant. "He's out there, just waiting for me."

With some surprise, Linc realized this was the first time Jenna had brought up Ramsey on her own. He wanted to ease her fear, bring some color back into her pale features.

He reached over her, picking up the remote to mute the movie. "Mace will find him, Jenna. Until he does, you're safe. Ramsey doesn't know where you are. He'll never find you here."

"We don't know that."

How could he argue with that? Irritation flickered at his helplessness, though he imagined it was small compared to what she must feel. "Mace *will* find him. Soon."

"Will he?" She turned her head and looked at him, her eyes bleak, ancient. "Will he find Ramsey before the sadistic scumbag finds me again?"

Linc had never heard such hopelessness and he fought a growing rage, fueled by the same impotence he'd felt upon looking at Jenna's battered body. He knew Mace was right and that he shouldn't try to go after the bastard, but Linc once again considered how he could do just that.

"I hate this," she said with quiet vehemence. "I want to stalk *him.* I want him to know what it feels like to lose control, to lose his confidence, his sense of…self. I want him to know what *this* feels like."

"Jenna—"

"I know," she acknowledged bitterly. "I know I can't do it. It's not smart. And I wouldn't even know how to go about it. But I want it all the same."

The helplessness, the forced retreat—Linc suddenly comprehended what these things must do to her. He wanted to tell her that it would all be over soon, but he didn't know that.

He only knew that the emptiness in her face propelled him to reach out and take her hand. She didn't jump, didn't pull away. Her gaze riveted on their joined hands and Linc realized he hadn't asked if he could touch her. He'd just done it, thinking only of how he could comfort her, not of how she might perceive the gesture. He started to pull away.

"No." Her gaze lifted to his.

In her eyes, Linc saw the same desire he felt, the same desire he'd tried to deny and ignore, the same desire that curled through him right now. Stunned by the curious invitation in her eyes, urged on by sensations that drowned his logic, he moved toward her.

This was different than before.

If she'd looked at him with fear or revulsion, he would've stopped right then. But she didn't. Curiosity and want burned in her eyes. Just as those things burned through him.

She lifted her head, her nostrils flaring delicately. Linc slowed, but didn't stop. Her eyes were wide, wary, yet tentatively expectant. He wanted to give her time enough to run, if that's what she wanted, but damn, he wanted to taste her, just once.

She remained perfectly still, waiting for him. Her gaze searched his face, then dropped to his lips, lingering so long that his heart threatened to pump right out of his chest.

Anticipation hooked into him and his arousal surged. He thought he should offer some reassurance that he wouldn't hurt her, but he knew if she allowed this, his words wouldn't be the reason why.

Then...his lips brushed hers. She kept her eyes open, locked on his and the blue-green depths were dark with uncertainty.

His throat tight, he whispered against her lips. "Tell me no, Jenna. If you don't want this, tell me."

"I...will."

He froze, barely registering her words. She hadn't refused, hadn't bolted. Her breath caressed his lips, drawing him on a razor edge of need. Then his lips covered hers.

Careful of the cut on her lips, he touched her lightly. No demands, just savoring the warm honey of her mouth.

Jenna sat motionless, not breathing, not running from him, but offering no encouragement.

Doubt stabbed at him. She didn't want this. He shouldn't have—damn!

Her hands slid into his hair and her mouth opened tentatively, cautiously under his. He felt a shudder move through her. His breath jammed in his chest and for an instant, his mind blanked.

After a long moment, her hands lowered to his shoulders,

resting lightly, holding him there. Want flared through him and he fought the urge to haul her onto his lap.

He increased the pressure of the kiss, not enough to hurt her, but he wanted inside, wanted to taste the dark heat of her. He cautioned himself to go slow, remember who she was, what she needed from him.

Desire lashed at him, straining at his control. Slowly, gently he slid his arms around her and pulled her closer, letting her ease into the feel of him against her. Her heart beat a wild tattoo against his chest. Her breasts felt full and soft against him; her nipples puckered.

A groan erupted inside him and he tamped it down, not wanting to scare her. He coaxed her gently with his tongue, touching the seam of her lips, teasing her until she opened tentatively.

She gasped. The sound was part pleasure, part surprise and his nerves twitched like water on flame.

Easy, he told himself. Don't hurt her. Trembling with the effort to go slowly, his tongue slipped into her mouth, caressing the hot sleekness.

Her arms tightened around his neck, then her tongue shyly brushed his. Unable to hold back this time, he groaned. He wanted to pull her onto his lap, press her hips into his, but he forced his arms to remain loose around her. No pressure. No demand.

She stiffened. At first her resistance didn't penetrate the sensations raging through his body. He angled his head, seeking a better fit, wanting to soak her into his skin.

She pushed at him, whimpering in the back of her throat, insistent, then determined, desperate.

The soft sound speared through his lust and he withdrew immediately. "I'm sorry, Jenna. I'm sorry."

Lifting shaking fingers to her lips, she gulped in a deep breath. "I've never—we shouldn't have done that."

Damn. Linc's heart sank and agony razored through him.

"I'm really sorry. I don't know what I was thinking. Hell, I *wasn't* thinking!"

"Don't, Linc. Don't blame yourself. It wasn't just you."

"I didn't stop when you asked."

She rose from the couch, the nightshirt riding up her firm thigh. Lightning flashed through the room, showing features that were now pinched with agony.

Jenna hugged her good arm around her waist, pulling the material taut across her breasts, outlining in vivid detail the hard points of her nipples. Linc swallowed, forcing down the want that slashed through him.

"We can't do it again. It can't go anywhere."

"It was just a kiss, Jenna." He rose, too, concerned at the paleness of her face, the strange flatness threading her words.

She stared blankly at the floor. "For now. For now it was just a kiss."

"I wouldn't push you further than you wanted to go," he said softly.

"I know you wouldn't want to."

"I *wouldn't*." Stung by a sudden thought, he asked, "I didn't hurt you, did I?"

"No."

Even in the flickering light, he could see the waxy sheen of her skin. He ran a hand across his face, feeling miserable, wanting to apologize, but not wanting to make it worse for her. Regret and arousal tangled inside him. "I swear, I never meant— Look, Jenna, I know I went too far, too fast, but— did I scare you?"

She hesitated, her eyes glittering brightly. "No."

"Did you like it? Just a little?" He grinned, hoping she would admit to feeling what he had.

Uncertainty flashed across her features. "Yes, but—"

"I liked it a lot. And I'd like to do it again."

"No!" Panic sharpened her words and her head snapped up. Fear glittered in her eyes. "No, we can't."

"You're right. This is too fast. I pushed you—"

"Linc, stop." Her voice shook. "It's not you. It's me. I can't do this."

"Can't or won't?" He wanted to bite his tongue, but the frustration clawing through his body drove out the words.

She stared at him for a long excruciating minute. The storm screamed around them, taunting him. Pain flashed through her eyes, then they darkened with resignation. "Can't."

"I thought you did it pretty well." *Shut up, Garrett. Just shut up.* Still he watched her, wanting, *needing* to know if she'd felt even a fraction of the desire he had. Needing to know why she wouldn't admit to it.

She met his eyes, though he could see it cost her. "It will never go anywhere, Linc."

Her words were so final, so certain that they sparked another spurt of irritation. "Because that's the way you want it? All right, I can accept—"

"Because I'm frigid."

And she walked out.

She left him standing in the living room, looking dazed and disbelieving.

Touching trembling fingers to her lips, she allowed herself to relive the gentleness of Linc's mouth, the minty, dark taste of him. His kiss had been so sweet, so searching yet possessive that tears had stung her eyes.

And then she'd ruined it.

I'm frigid. She couldn't believe she had just blurted it out. But she had to tell him the truth. Part of her had been compelled by the desire not to encourage him; the other part had been spurred on by the powerful, reckless desire that had rushed through her body on a tongue of fire.

"Jenna?" Linc's voice came softly, achingly through the door. "Are you all right?"

She swallowed on a hard lump. "Go away."

"That was quite a bombshell you dropped back there. I think we should talk about it."

"No." She backed up a step, even though he couldn't reach her, couldn't touch her, couldn't even see her. "I'm sorry I blurted it out that way, but it's...true. You need to know that."

"We shouldn't talk about something like this through the door." Confusion deepened his voice. "Let me in. I promise not to crowd you."

That sultry baritone was soft, cajoling and Jenna found herself wanting to go to him, open the door and apologize. But she'd only told the truth.

And right now, trembling with reaction from his kiss, pummeled on every side by the taunting presence of Ramsey, she couldn't handle this discussion.

"I don't want to talk about it. Go away." She meant to sound firm, but her voice was whisper thin, bald with a plea. *Just go away.*

"Jenna, I know you're frightened. I know these feelings are...overwhelming." He gave a short laugh. "Believe me, I know. But that was not the kiss of a frigid woman. I promise you—"

"Linc, please." Frustrated, appalled at what she'd said, she couldn't face him. That kiss was just another thing, like Ramsey, that she was running from.

She had responded to Linc's kiss without fear, without second thought. She had never, ever responded to a man like that. And she couldn't bear to see the hunger in his gray eyes turn to pity. As must surely be happening right now.

"Jenna?" He knocked again. No yelling, no banging on the door, no commands. Just a quiet plea that nearly undid her.

"Go away."

"Jenna—"

"I'm not going to discuss it, Linc. I can't." She held her breath, waiting for him to try the door more forcefully, demand that she let him in. "Please."

After a long pause, she heard the scrape of his boots on the floor, then silence.

He was gone. The relief she expected never came. Instead she was swamped by guilt and regret and an insane desire to go after him. But she stayed where she was.

She had nothing to give. This was best. It was the only way.

Frigid. The word screamed through Linc's mind. How the hell could a woman turn a man inside out with a kiss like that and really believe she was frigid?

But Jenna did believe it. He'd seen the hopelessness, the bleakness in her eyes. She wasn't frigid, but how could *he* convince her? He groaned in disgust. What made him think she would even want him to try?

Three days later, the agony of some elusive loss still throbbed through her. Jenna knew she would have to face Linc and soon.

She knew she couldn't put off the discussion he obviously wanted to have. And that he deserved.

But right now, on the way to Wilbur's grave site, was not the appropriate time.

Still, as she sat beside Linc in the back of Mace's unmarked detective cruiser, Jenna dreaded it. The other night, Linc hadn't pressed her, hadn't returned to her room, hadn't acted as if anything had passed between them. But since she'd joined him late this morning, he'd been quietly solicitous.

She caught his gaze on her several times—intense, probing, speculative. But the pity she'd expected to see wasn't there. While that thawed a frozen place deep inside her, Jenna knew it wasn't enough. She knew they would have to discuss what she'd said, but not now. Not here.

As the car rolled through the gates of the Memorial Park Cemetery and followed the winding path to the far south side bordered by woods, Jenna looked down at her borrowed yellow shirt and wilted khaki shorts. She wished she had something nicer to wear. Not because anyone would see her, but out of respect for Wilbur.

The car rolled to a stop. After Mace declared the area safe and empty, Jenna stepped out of the car into the soggy heat. She took a couple of steps, then stopped, staring at the freshly turned grave blanketed with fresh flowers. A sob lodged in her chest.

Wilbur had hired her on the spot after she'd graduated from veterinary school. He'd given her a start, not caring how green she was, never asking questions about why his new associate was so jumpy around men.

She'd eventually confided in him about the rape and he'd never treated her as anything less than a daughter. He'd always given her his love, his loyalty.

Her fingers gently grazed the bruises on her throat as she remembered Wilbur's last words to her.

I'm comin', Jenna-girl. I'm comin'! Get away from her! Get away!

He had helped her as he always did and it had cost his life.

She pressed her knuckles to her lips, glad for the sharp stab of pain it caused, hoping it would stanch the agony welling up inside her.

"Jenna?"

Misery knifed through her. She turned toward Linc, shaking her head. "How can I ever make this up to his wife?"

"She doesn't blame you."

"Wilbur's dead because of me. I can't believe Ramsey would do that because of me."

"Jenna, torturing yourself won't bring him back." Linc's quiet concern unraveled the last of her tenuous control.

She gave a choked sob and tears spilled out.

Compassion darkened his eyes and, careful of her cast, he drew her to him. Strong arms closed around her and Jenna felt the first warm stroke of peace over her soul.

It was ridiculous, she thought even as her tears wet the

front of Linc's denim shirt. She'd pushed him away and yet here he was, offering comfort and support. The solid steadiness of his body.

"I'm sorry," he whispered against her hair. "I'm so sorry."

Pain turned his words ragged and she knew he hurt for her, for the loss of her friend. The realization made her feel a connection to Linc that before she had only ever felt for Steve.

She wanted to be strong, capable, but right now she felt worn down, vulnerable. Yet as she stood with Linc, felt his breath stirring her hair, felt the warmth of his body mingle with hers, a new strength infused her. Grateful for the comfort and the friendship, Jenna steeled her nerves and pulled away from him.

Wiping her eyes with her good hand, she suddenly found she couldn't look at him. "I've made a mess of your shirt."

"It's all right." The deep conviction in his voice compelled her to look at him. He nodded. "It's all right."

He was talking about more than the shirt; he was encouraging her, telling her he was there for her. Fresh tears burned her eyes, but she blinked them away. "Thanks."

She managed a weak smile, her cut lips stinging only slightly. Encouraged by the warmth in Linc's eyes, she turned toward Wilbur's grave.

"I'll stay here, unless you want me to come with you."

Grateful for Linc's thoughtfulness, Jenna nodded and walked alone the several steps to the edge of her friend's resting place.

The anger that always seemed to hide behind the fear surfaced. Would the police ever catch Ramsey? If they did, would he go to prison, only to be released again one day to torment her further?

The man deserved to die for what he'd done to Wilbur. And to lose his freedom the same way she had.

Fighting back her tears, she curled her hands into fists and silently vowed to Wilbur that Ramsey would pay for what he'd done. Somehow he would pay.

It was as if God had created a perfect day to bring Wilbur home. The August temperature was pleasantly warm instead of scorching. Sunshine flowed over the well-tended grounds, sparkled in the shooting water of a small, nearby fountain. Majestic oaks and maples spread welcoming arms, draping the manicured green grass in shadows.

Wilbur had chosen a peaceful spot for his burial just as he had chosen for his home. Nestled on the edge of the cemetery, bordered by trees, the place was restful and serene. No closed-off spot in the middle of the grounds for Wilbur. He had preferred the openness of the woods.

Goodbye, my dear friend. Thank you so much for everything you gave to my life, for the very life you lost.

Tears blurred her vision and she lifted her face to the sun, closing her eyes and soaking in the peace of the place, listening to the gentle twittering of birds in an effort to soothe her ragged nerves.

But she only felt more vulnerable, more targeted. Her body ached, a constant reminder of Ramsey. Behind her, she could hear the rise and fall of Linc's voice as he spoke to his brother. She knew where they stood, knew they watched her. Focusing on the sound of Mace's and Linc's voices, she tried to take comfort that she wasn't alone. Yet a sudden tension prickled between her shoulder blades.

She shifted, trying to dispel the sudden sense that someone watched her. Foreboding, relentless and insistent, pushed at her. Something was wrong.

She opened her eyes, her gaze riveted on Wilbur's grave as she willed away the feeling. It was normal to feel so uneasy after the attack. And especially on her first day outside since then.

But the feeling of dread persisted, hovering, growing thicker in the peaceful quiet. Heavy, dark, menacing. The sensation strengthened as if someone telegraphed a threat to her.

Her skin tingled. Cold sweat slicked her palms. Though she tried not to, Jenna scanned the edge of the woods yards away.

A distinct sense of danger—blatant, immediate—slammed into her. Her gaze moved along the border of trees, tried to probe the shadows beyond. A flash of light glinted from the woods.

She froze and her head came up slowly.

Eyes glittered in the shade of trees and a face stared back at her. Even as her mind tried to force away the image, she registered it. It wasn't a trick of her eyes. Or a product of the fear that hounded her.

A large, black shape, now plainly that of a man, stood in the trees. Dark eyes bored into her. The man moved slightly forward, only enough to bring his face into the light. His arm lowered and Jenna dimly registered that he held a camera.

Ramsey!

Her body tightened painfully. Every beat of her heart slammed like a punishing blow against her ribs. For an instant, she stood paralyzed, raked by horror. Denial. Disbelief.

In that moment, he smiled at her. Broad and smug and evil, that smile unlocked every nightmare she'd ever had about him.

He'd come for her, just as Mace had predicted.

Panic exploded, blanking her thoughts, her reason for an instant. A scream rose in her throat and her mouth opened, but no sound came out. Then the horror broke free.

She screamed. Spinning toward Linc, she screamed again. "It's him! He's in the trees!"

Chapter 7

Jenna bolted toward Linc, her ribs and bruised thighs protesting. Fear pumped through her, diligent, relentless.

Mace, gun drawn, sprinted past her. Linc followed, leaping a headstone on his way toward the woods.

Get him. Oh, please, get him. Jenna swallowed hard, her heart racing, torn between following and crawling into the back seat of Mace's sedan. "Be careful!" she whispered after them, her throat closing up.

Mace dodged several graves, then yelled over his shoulder. "Linc, go back! Stay with her!"

Linc skirted a small sitting bench.

"Go back!" Mace waved his brother toward Jenna.

Only then did Linc stop. He skidded to a halt, looking from Jenna to Mace. Startled realization crossed his features and he wheeled around, sprinting back toward her.

He stopped in front of her, his sandy hair disheveled, sweat glistening on his forehead. "Are you okay?"

She nodded, her gaze locked on the woods as Mace disappeared from sight. Sheer terror clawed through her. *Deke Ramsey was here. He'd seen her.*

The words sliced through her restraint, leaving her quivering next to the car. *Ramsey, Ramsey, Ramsey.*

She couldn't pull her mind from the words. They circled viciously in her head and she wrapped her good arm around her waist, huddling into herself in an effort to escape the terror, the uncertainty tightening around her neck like a noose.

Where was Mace? She wanted to see him.

Linc peered closely into her face, panting. "I'm sorry I took off like that. It was just—I didn't even think about it."

She nodded again, hearing what he said, but barely registering the words. Her ears pounded from the sound of footsteps crashing through undergrowth, the startled chatter of birds and animals as humans interrupted their sanctuary.

She could hear Mace shout at Ramsey, order him to stop.

Her gaze moved to Linc's and they shared a moment of dread.

"He'll get the bastard, Jenna."

She nodded, not believing anymore, tears stinging her eyes as panic knocked at her. She couldn't fall apart. She wouldn't. The crackling of undergrowth grew dimmer; the shouting stopped. Her nerves stretched taut, anticipating a gunshot. Waiting. Waiting.

A shot rang out. Then another.

Jenna jumped, fear clawing through her. Linc swore viciously. Both their gazes riveted on the woods. Birds screamed and tore through the trees in squawking protest. Then...nothing.

The birds settled. One second stretched into a moment, then longer, abrading her nerves, eroding her control.

"Where is he? Where's Mace?" She turned to Linc, praying his brother was all right. "Why haven't we heard anything?"

He shook his head, concern darkening his gaze to metal gray.

"Maybe you should go—"

"No, I won't leave you." Despite his authoritative tone, he looked torn.

She moved closer to him, reassured by the warmth of his body, by his solid presence. Dread hammered through her; her muscles snapped tight against the threat circling around them.

Where was Mace? What was happening? Fear and hate and anger collided inside her. Damn Ramsey for disturbing today, of all days! He had ruptured the peaceful silence at Wilbur's grave. Ramsey's appearance spilled onto the sacred day like an encroaching black tide, dimming the sunlight, turning the air from clean to putrid and heavy with the scent of fear.

Again, he had violated something pure, destroyed, invaded. Jenna felt dirty and angry. Weighted by a growing sadness, a shudder rippled through her. Time scraped by and still no sign of Mace. No sound of gunfire or struggle from the woods. *What was happening?*

A touch on her arm pulled her attention from the woods. Linc spoke, looking at her with alarm in his gray eyes.

His touch was gentle yet firm on her elbow. He leaned down, his gaze examining as he looked into her eyes. "Jenna, talk to me. Jenna?"

"I can hear you," she said woodenly.

His gaze searched hers, deep and measuring. Realization filtered through the numbness of her mind. Ramsey could've killed her, could've killed Linc. *Might already have killed Mace.*

She trembled, so fiercely that her muscles clenched painfully in an effort to control it.

"You're shaking like a leaf," Linc muttered, anger vibrating from him. Glancing at the woods, he moved slightly to shield her body with his.

Her control slipped; she wanted to throw herself at Linc, wrap herself around him. Gritting her teeth, she held on, praying for strength, some sign of Mace.

"Jenna, look at me." Linc's sharp voice penetrated her panic. "Stay with me."

She tried. Tried to focus on the caring eyes of the man in front of her, the broad expanse of his denim shirt, the steadiness of his voice.

He had turned to face her and now looked her over from head to toe, peered again into her face, then opened his arms, stepping toward her. "I won't hurt you."

That old wariness surged through her. But this time it was combated by a fierce longing to gather strength from someone. *From him.*

He watched her. Worry about Mace fringed his eyes, but he waited patiently for her, offering whatever she wanted.

She wouldn't fall apart, but oh, how she needed his strength. She took in his features, worried pale beneath his tan. Her gaze locked on his, she stepped forward, one step, then another. He waited, making it plain she could take only what she needed, what she wanted.

Jenna felt as if she were reaching, stretching, fighting the old fear, the old scars of her soul. Then she stepped into his arms. They closed around her, strong and big and safe. Relief and comfort sluiced through her.

"It's all right," he whispered against her hair. "You're safe. I won't let him hurt you."

For a long moment, she stood stiffly in his embrace, her body rigid, poised for a fight. A little voice in her head urged her to surrender, to give in to the urge to sag against him, but Jenna was afraid that if she did, she would break down and sob.

Linc stroked her back and held her close, saying nothing for a while, offering unconditional support with his body.

When he spoke, he said softly against her hair, "It's okay, Jenna. You're okay. I'm only going to hold you. I won't hurt you."

She wanted to tell him she knew that, knew he would never

harm her, that he only wanted to comfort her, but the words wouldn't come.

The strength of his body seeped into her, sawed through the last thread of her restraint. Her shoulders sagged and she leaned into him. Closing her eyes, she burrowed her face into his neck.

Dark musky male assaulted her senses, wrapped around her like a teasing curl of smoke and her good arm went around his waist. Her palm flattened against the strong sinew of his back and she held on, waiting for Mace, for some word of Ramsey.

For the first time in long seconds, she took a breath. She was safe. Linc was safe. For now.

She needed to feel his warmth, the weight of his body against hers. She pressed close to him, closer. Still she trembled.

He held her tightly, solidly and after a moment, the fear receded. She surrendered to the comfort. Her body relaxed into his; she shifted her head in the crook of his neck, inhaling his scent, his strength. A sense of safety flowed over her.

Linc's heart thudded sharp and evenly against her breasts. Lean powerful thighs braced hers. His warm breath stirred the hair at her temple. She wanted to collapse, to sink into him, to forget.

A sound stirred in the trees. Footsteps rustled through the grass, moving toward them. Jenna and Linc glanced around.

Mace trotted up, breathing hard. "The SOB got away. He took a shot at me."

She lifted her head, her gaze scouring over him for signs of blood, any sign of injury.

"You're okay." Linc's exhaled statement mirrored the relief Jenna felt.

Mace's gaze moved between her and his brother, taking in the way Linc held her. "Yeah, I'm fine."

With the back of his hand, he wiped the sweat from his

forehead then jogged around them to his car. Sliding into the passenger door, he grabbed his radio, calling the station.

Static crackled over the still air. Jenna heard a disembodied dispatcher's voice, heard Mace give Ramsey's description, then request a radiogram on him from this location, heading east toward I-35.

Linc pulled slightly away from Jenna, though her arms tightened around him. "You okay?"

She nodded, her teeth chattering too much to speak yet.

"You sure?"

She took a deep breath and met his gaze. "Yes," she said finally. Tears burned her eyes, threatened to spill over again, but she forced them back. Ramsey was still out there. This nightmare wasn't over. Jenna didn't know if it ever would be.

Linc's arms remained warm and comforting around her, but Jenna realized how easily he or Mace could've been hurt. How she would've been dead if she'd been here alone. Still trying to quell her trembling, she dropped her arms and stepped back from Linc.

Concern clouded his gray eyes as his gaze tracked over her with professional thoroughness. "We need to get you home."

"I'm ready."

Another thorough inspection. "You sure you're okay?"

"Yes."

He tilted her chin up, staring straight into her eyes.

"I'm here. So is Mace. Ramsey won't come back."

Not today anyway. She nodded, fighting back the terror that threatened to explode inside her. She could still feel Linc's heat, his strength, still needed it, but at the thought of his leaving, she was covered by a chill, a dark heavy sense of being cold, lost, alone.

"Linc, you could've been hurt. Mace, too."

"He can't get us all."

But he could, Jenna realized on a sharp stab of terror.

Deke Ramsey *could* kill them all. "You're in danger because of me. He killed Wilbur. He just shot at Mace. He won't hesitate to kill you.''

She'd said the same thing at the hospital, but after what had just happened, the reality of that statement now sliced through her with fresh horror.

"I'm fine." Linc's features hardened. Determination glinted in his gray eyes. "I'm not hurt and I'm not going anywhere."

"Maybe I should."

"What?" His brows snapped together and his body went rigid.

"I'll have Mace move me somewhere else."

"He won't let you move to Steve's." Anger rumbled beneath Linc's low controlled words. "It would be too hard for him to keep tabs on you out there."

"No, not with Steve. I mean somewhere else. Somewhere…alone. I couldn't bear for either of you to get hurt or die because of me. Like Wilbur did."

Fear clawed through her at the thought and she tried to step out of Linc's embrace.

Linc held on, not hurting her, but tightening his arms around her anyway. With one finger, he tilted her chin up, forcing her gaze to meet his. "Listen to me. Crazy as it is, this is Mace's job and he won't walk away from it. I'm not going anywhere and neither are you. I won't let you. Whatever happens to you, happens to me."

"That's what I'm trying to tell you," she moaned in frustration, fear clawing through her.

"No," he said quietly. "That's what I'm trying to tell *you.*"

She saw the loyalty in his eyes, the pure stubbornness and understood that he intended to stand by her. Despite the risk, despite what had happened between them a few nights ago, he didn't want her to leave.

His loyalty and protectiveness soothed her battered emotions. Jenna wanted to be convinced. She felt safe with him and grateful not to be alone.

Gratitude squeezed her throat tight and she fought back tears. Looking up at him, she managed a small smile with her swollen lips. "You don't have to do this."

He searched her eyes for a long second. "I do, Jenna. I do. I will."

Reflexively she reached up and caught his hand on her shoulder. He smiled, though it didn't reach his eyes. Then his hand folded around hers, warm and solid and strong.

Jenna tightened her grip, needing the connection, the steady feel of his support and presence. He held her hand as they settled into the back of Mace's car.

She didn't want to let go. She'd forgotten what strength a simple bond like this could bring, forgotten that solid intimate connection with another person, a man.

"You okay, Jenna?" Mace asked from the front seat.

"Yes."

Linc squeezed her hand.

"How about you, Linc?"

"I'm fine." Linc glanced at Jenna, offering a reassuring smile.

Mace hit the steering wheel with his palm. "I can't believe that bastard got away!"

Recalling the blazing hatred in Ramsey's face, Jenna gripped Linc's hand tighter.

"We *will* get him, Jenna," Mace said vehemently. "I swear."

She nodded, hoping that happened before it was too late for all of them. "He had a camera. *What* was he doing with a camera?" Her voice rose, grew sharp. "Watching me? Taking pictures of Wilbur's grave—"

She broke off, drawing in a deep breath, trying to calm nerves that were scraped raw by what had just happened. "What a psycho."

"He is, Jenna. And he'll pay."

Linc squeezed her hand again and she knew then that whatever happened, her life would be inextricably connected to his forever. For good or bad. For death. He knew it, too. And he was willing to stand by her. But for how long?

A mixture of frustration, anger and arousal hummed through Linc. Jenna stayed close to him in the car, gripping his hand as if he were her main line to oxygen.

Mace dropped them off, saying he would call them, then he sped off in a cloud of dust. Linc recognized his brother's frustration over Ramsey's escape because Linc felt it himself.

Virulent rage swept through him as he recalled that bastard watching Jenna at the cemetery. Linc's hand tightened on Jenna's and she wiggled her fingers. He loosened his grip, struggling to rein in his temper. The last thing Jenna needed was to see him lose control. She needed someone cool, steady.

She released his hand only when they walked inside his house. Once there, he saw her visibly relax. He saw no outward signs that she was in pain, that she had strained anything during those tense moments at the cemetery. Still, Linc watched her unwaveringly.

She prowled restlessly around the living area, keeping the dogs close to her, stopping in front of each window to stare outside at the glittering midday sunshine.

He resisted the urge to go to her and whisper reassurances she must surely be tired of hearing. "Jenna, do you want to talk about it?"

"What's to talk about? Deke Ramsey's out there, like I said. And he won't stop until he kills me."

Her voice was hard, foreign. Compassion twinged sharply in Linc's chest. He wanted to hold her, kiss away the shadows in her mind, erase the ugliness of Ramsey.

"Do you want to lie down?"

"No." Her voice was resigned, distant.

Compelled to do something, offer *something,* he stepped

toward her, then stopped. Though he battled the thought, it came anyway. Linc wanted to lay her on *his* bed and peel the clothes from her body, gently, slowly kiss and caress every inch of her until Ramsey was obliterated from her mind.

Until she admitted that she wanted him the way he wanted her. His body tightened, urging him toward her, but he knew she didn't want that from him, at least not yet.

Seeing Ramsey had rattled Linc's nerves good and he could only imagine what it had done to Jenna. He had offered her shelter knowing full well the danger, the risk he was taking, but until today he hadn't realized how twisted, how sickly determined Ramsey was to get at her.

The last thing she needed was to dwell on what had happened at the cemetery. "Are you hungry? I can fix something to eat."

"No, thanks." She stared outside, holding her cast close to her side as if warding off a blow.

She looked so frail, so alone that Linc's heart clenched. He stepped toward her. "We can take out the horses if you'd like."

She turned toward him, forcing a smile. "I don't think I'm ready to go out just yet."

Well, that hadn't been too swift. Linc's gaze traveled around the living room, searching for something to distract her. His gaze fell on the TV. "We can watch another movie. I'll pop some popcorn or make some cookies—"

"*You* are the sweetest man." She turned from the window, her pale features finally warming with color.

Sweet? Linc eyed her dubiously.

"You are," she insisted. "You're trying to keep my mind off Ramsey and I appreciate it, but he's real, Linc. I can't make him go away."

"It doesn't mean you can't forget for a little while."

"Until he's caught, I can't forget at all." She hesitated, fear flashing across her face. Then she squared her shoulders and walked to him. "I know you don't want to hear this, but I really think I should talk to Mace about moving me."

"I thought we'd settled this." Linc planted his hands on his hips, fighting to keep his emotions on an even keel. She was only trying to do something, *anything*, in order not to feel so helpless.

"You saw him! He means to kill me and he'll do the same to you."

"No!"

"Linc, you know what he's capable of—"

"The only thing that's changed here, Jenna, is what happened between you and me the other night."

She blanched. "Don't try to make this about that kiss."

"Why not? That's what it's about."

She sighed, exasperation flushing her features. "Do you ever hear anything you don't want to?"

"You feel safe with me." He threw out the words as a challenge. "Isn't that what you said?"

"Yes."

"Then why leave?" He moved over to stand in front of her, wanting to tuck a stray strand of hair behind her ear, gather her in his arms and stroke her back until she allowed herself to be reassured, to be comforted. She wouldn't answer, wouldn't look at him.

"Admit it," he said. "It's because of what happened that night. I kissed you. You kissed me back." His gaze bored into her. "You're just afraid, Jenna. It's new for you. It's new for me, too. That's okay. I can go slow—"

"No," she said through clenched teeth, finally looking at him. Her fists curled at her sides so tightly that he figured she wanted to take a swing at him. "Listen to me, Linc. *I'm frigid.* That's real, just as real as Ramsey coming after me. It's not something I imagine. You mustn't believe that it is."

I'm frigid. He hadn't forgotten her words, not for a moment, but he had shoved them to the back of his mind, intent instead on making certain she was all right. Now he could no longer ignore them. He hadn't meant for this to come up, but he knew this was at least part of the reason she wanted to leave.

Jenna looked decidedly uncomfortable, but also as if she might explode. He knew the feeling. She hadn't denied wanting him.

She'd never said she didn't like kissing him. She'd only said she couldn't give anything more than that because she wasn't capable.

"If what you say is true—"

"It is."

"If it's true, how could you respond to me the way you did?"

She swallowed hard, her gaze falling to his chest. With obvious effort, she again looked him in the face. "I'm attracted to you—"

He grinned.

"I can't believe it." Frustration roughened her voice. "I certainly never expected it."

"Thanks," he said dryly.

Looking discomfited, she shifted from foot to foot. "I've never—I haven't felt like this in years and it scares me."

"It's a little scary for me, too."

She didn't look reassured by his confession. "This…thing between us can't go anywhere, Linc. And it's not fair for you to believe it will."

"*You* be fair, Jenna," Linc said evenly. "I didn't ask for anything from you that you weren't willing, and able, to give."

She blushed. "That's true, you didn't. Not yet. But I know where that kiss was leading, Linc. Look, I know how this sounds. I should probably stop right now. It's been so long for me since I've done anything like this—I'm way out of my league. Maybe things between us would never go further than they did the other night, but you've got to believe what I said."

"You're the one who needs to be convinced," he said fiercely, shoving his hands in his pockets in an effort to keep from reaching for her. "You're a flesh-and-blood woman, Jenna. You were affected when I held you. I felt it." His gaze dropped to her lips, then slid to her breasts. "I saw it, too. Lady, there's nothing frigid about you."

Heat suffused her face, but she didn't look away. "You're not making it easy for me to believe what I know to be true."

"Good," he said gently, though he fought an unfamiliar desperation spiraling inside him. He wanted her to believe *him,* not the curse that Ramsey had laid at her door.

She shook her head. "Yes, I kissed you back. Yes, I enjoyed it, but—" Darker color suffused her face and her gaze wavered from his. "Kissing is all I can do. I can't— I'm not able—oh, good grief!"

She eased down on the love seat, her gaze pinned to the floor.

Torn between needing to hear her out and wanting to forget the whole thing, Linc sank down onto the arm of the small couch. "Why do you think you can't make love with me, Jenna?"

She groaned and covered her face with her good hand. "I can't believe we're having this conversation."

Linc reached and snagged her wrist, then gently pulled her hand down. "Why?"

Her gaze shot to his, eyes glittering with defiance. "Because I've tried before, okay? If it didn't work with Steve, it won't work with you."

"Steve?" Linc's jaw dropped. *"Steve?"*

She nodded, fiddling with her cast.

"You've been with Steve?"

"Thank goodness, our friendship was stronger than that…that fiasco."

"Steve Majors?"

She eyed him drolly. "Try to stay with me here."

"I am. I think." Something hard and hot shoved up beneath his ribs. "When was this?"

She pressed her lips together, still looking uncomfortable. "About six years ago."

"You shouldn't assume things will still be the same for you. Maybe you weren't ready. Obviously, you weren't," he said under his breath.

"I've survived just fine without sex." Her glare softened. "But I couldn't have survived without friendship—"

"I mean, that was a long time ago and—"

"Linc, stop. Don't do this. Please."

The desperation in her voice finally penetrated his denial. He looked at her, seeing the pain, the unease, the total conviction in her eyes. It didn't matter what he believed. It mattered what *she* believed.

She rose, her shoulder brushing his, her gaze locked on him. "You can't 'fix' me, Dr. Garrett. You can't make it better. It's not something you can treat or bandage. It can't be surgically removed." She took a deep breath, her voice aching. "This is just the way things are. I thought leaving might make it easier on both of us."

He struggled against the sting of her words. He *did* want to make her better, but this was about something more. "I don't want you to leave."

"If I stay, what happened the other night can never happen again." Her voice was soft, but firm.

Helplessness swamped him and he clenched his teeth in frustration.

Compassion darkened her eyes even as they urged him to believe her. "I know you think I'm saying this because I'm afraid and maybe that's true, but I also know, I *know* that things will never be any different for me."

Every part of him that had been trained to restore and heal cried out inside him to do that with her, to try just one more way, one more argument or procedure. But he knew he couldn't change her mind, knew she would have to do that herself. Finally, he nodded grudgingly.

"I'll do whatever you say, Jenna, but I know some things, too."

Sad resignation settled in her eyes, but she studied him soberly, waiting.

"I want you. And you want me." The words sounded harsh in the silence, almost forbidding.

Discouragement pulled at her features. "Didn't you hear me? It doesn't matter what either of us wants."

"I won't push you. I won't do anything you don't want." He shifted, inhaling her clean, lemony scent, savoring the teasing closeness of her breasts. "If you want me to stay fifty feet away from you, all right, but it won't change the fact that I think you're the sexiest, most stubborn female—"

"I have a black eye and busted lip," she exclaimed. "How can you find that sexy—"

"You're beautiful and I want you in my bed." Conviction lowered his voice to a husky rasp. "If you change your mind—"

"I suppose I should be coy here and say you'll be the first to know." Uncertainty flared in her beautiful eyes and for a moment, just an instant, hope rose inside him. Then she shook her head. "I won't change my mind. I can't."

"I still don't want you to leave." He shoved aside his disappointment, focusing instead on the fact that she had agreed to stay. For now. "Whatever happens to me, happens to you. I meant that."

"All right." Her gaze, softly pained, searched his face.

He wanted to lash out, demand she give this thing between them a chance, but he couldn't.

With a grateful smile, she stepped away and walked toward the hallway, then disappeared.

Linc shoved a hand through his hair. He didn't want her damn gratitude. He wanted *her*.

Frustrated, he sank back down on the love seat. He couldn't

give her what she needed. She would want too much from him. He knew both those things and right now, they seemed insignificant. Sometime, somehow the situation between him and Jenna had changed.

Yes, he wanted to sleep with her. Yes, the strongest, most primal part of his ego wanted to be the man to give her sexual pleasure. But there was also something more, something he couldn't define. Something he wasn't sure he could admit even if he knew what it was.

His wounded soul, his defenses screamed at him to do what she asked, to back off. Linc knew he wouldn't. Or maybe he couldn't. He only knew he would be there for whatever she wanted from him. When, if ever, she wanted it.

Now, he'd seen her and he had to find her.

Frustration ripped through him and Deke fought the urge to throw the chair through the wall. Where the hell was Jenna West hiding? Seeing her earlier had given him no clue.

At the cemetery, the camera lens had revealed in satisfying detail the bruises marking her face, the cast on her arm. A slow smile spread as he recalled their little meeting in her office parking lot, his hands around her slender throat, the fear in her blue-green eyes.

The old man had interrupted Deke's attack, but it didn't matter. He had other plays to run, plays that allowed *him* to call the time-outs, the penalties. And Jenna West would be the one penalized.

Seeing her at the cemetery today had given him a hard-on. Not only because he wanted to tear into that sweet body again, but because he'd been positive she'd show up there.

But he hadn't known about the two men. One of 'em, the broad one with dark, wavy hair, was a cop. Deke drummed his fingers on the computer console. He had known that, even before seeing the man's badge and the shoulder holster.

Deke had spent too much time in prison not to be able to smell a cop from any distance. Still, he'd checked out the license plate on the Internet and learned the four-door sedan was indeed an unmarked police cruiser.

But the other man... Who was the other man? The one who'd held Jenna West, the one who'd never left her side? Obviously, he meant something to Jenna. He was a little taller, leaner than the cop, and looked confident and arrogantly assured.

That man was not a cop. Deke had seen no gun on his lean frame, no badge. What was he? *Who* was he?

Cold, brutal fury slashed at him, the way it did every time he thought about Jenna West and what she'd done to him. She'd ruined his life, stuffed him in prison where, as far as the NFL was concerned, he was dead. She'd destroyed his life and he would destroy her.

Slowly, systematically, he would rip away every security she'd ever known, cut off her support, test her sanity. And he would have her again before it was all over. At least one more time.

Fingering the camera in his lap, Deke smiled. After developing these photos and adding his own special touch, he would send them to Jenna.

The digital clock beside the computer flipped past another minute. Elaine would be home soon and Deke didn't want to be here. She was easy enough to manipulate, but her questions about his job hunting were starting to wear thin.

The night he'd been sprung from the pen at McAlester, he'd met her in a bar. She had picked him up and they'd enjoyed hot, fast sex in the front seat of her Volvo. Deke had told her he'd been injured in an on-the-job accident and only just been released after a long hospital stay. He'd then *allowed* her to convince him to come home with her.

Elaine wasn't like any accountant Deke had ever known. She was good in bed and it seemed her brain for numbers didn't extend to other parts of her life. Her questions about his efforts at job hunting could be quelled with a certain look. She didn't take the daily newspaper, so he'd picked one up. His picture had been plastered all over the front page, but Elaine hadn't seen it. He'd never told her his real name so she paid little attention when the radio or television newscasters talked about Deke Ramsey. And he would've known by now if she'd recognized him for the photo they flashed on television.

Every night when the news came on, he made sure to keep her occupied. It wasn't hard, since her entire world revolved around sex or deciding what bar to visit. She'd noticed nothing yet. If and when that changed, he was ready to move. Or kill, if he had to.

He needed Elaine's place to stay until he could find Jenna West. Rage roared through him again.

Until he found Jenna, he didn't want her to forget he was out here, waiting for her. And he knew just where to leave another message.

Chapter 8

Relief washed through her. At last, she'd explained fully to Linc about her problem. He didn't believe her, she admitted wryly, tamping down her frustration. But she'd told him.

He'd said he wouldn't push her, wouldn't try to convince her that she wasn't frigid. And she knew he meant it. Still, she had seen the denial, the determination to prove her wrong glinting in his eyes. If he tried, it would only lead to heartache for both of them.

For the past three days, he'd been polite and reserved, not mentioning the issue again. Just after noon, a knock sounded on the door, interrupting her thoughts.

It could only be Linc and Jenna swallowed hard, hoping he didn't want to talk about her or what had happened between them. She opened the door. "Hi."

"Hi." A light blue oxford molded his broad shoulders. He'd rolled the cuffs back, revealing his strong wrists and forearms lightly dusted with hair. Well-fitted khaki pants, creased with knife-edge precision, emphasized his lean, muscular legs. His gray eyes searched hers as he held out a stack of envelopes. "I swung by your office this morning and picked up the mail. These looked legit."

"Thanks." She took them, careful not to touch him, avoiding the spark that always seemed to flare between them.

"You're welcome."

"I didn't know you'd gone anywhere." She didn't like the sense of disquiet that inched through her upon learning Linc had been absent.

He shrugged. "I figured you were still asleep. It didn't take long."

Jenna nodded, glancing quickly through the stack, recognizing several bills, a notice from her dentist, and a large manila envelope from Oklahoma State University. Curious about what her alma mater might be sending, she lay the other envelopes on the dresser and opened it.

A piece of filmy peach fabric floated out and she frowned.

"What's that?" Linc gave a bemused chuckle.

Peering into the envelope, Jenna saw a small bundle of the peach-colored fabric. She dumped the contents onto the dresser. Fluffy, sheer material and a photo.

Now she recognized the fabric. Dread iced her veins and she made a helpless sound in the back of her throat.

"Jenna?"

With an unsteady hand, she reached out and flipped over the photo. Her gaze riveted on a full-color shot of her and Linc standing at Wilbur's grave. Something was written across the picture.

Nausea roiled through her. Horrified, yet unable to look away, she raised the photo.

Linc touched her arm, sending a jolt through her. "Jenna, what is it? What's wrong?"

His voice sounded tinny, distant. "That's one of my negligees."

"What!" He reached around her, fingering the filmy material.

Jenna focused on the photo, realization slamming into her.

Scrawled across her and Linc's bodies were the words *No Defense.*

She trembled, so violently that she bit her tongue.

Linc's fist closed around the peach-colored scraps of fabric and alarm sharpened his voice. "Your negligee? What else is there? What do you have?"

She dragged her gaze from the photo, tears stinging her eyes as she looked at Linc. With a shaking hand, she held out the picture. "He's been in my house."

Tension lashed her shoulders and she rolled them, wishing for relief. Stark images of Ramsey and his evil grin strobed through her mind. She kept reliving the weight of his gaze at the cemetery, touching her like a clammy hand, turning her skin to gooseflesh. Kept seeing her lingerie, the photo of her and Linc.

Mace had taken it all as evidence, but she couldn't erase the images. Or the sense of numb futility that dogged her. She eased up to the bed and wrapped her good hand around one of the smooth cherry wood posts.

A tightness gripped her throat. How much longer would she have to stay here? What would Ramsey do next?

Jenna didn't want to think about him. But neither did she want to think about Linc. Her confession about being frigid weighed as heavily on her as Ramsey's games. She knew Linc had only avoided the subject because of the menacing package she'd received.

The thoughts, the uncertainty tortured her, circling through her mind until she thought she would scream. Staying in her room only plucked at her fear, heightened the sense of help-lessness she'd felt since the cemetery and since receiving the photo with her shredded lingerie.

Deliberately blanking her mind, she shook her head and moved away from the bed. She walked to the window and stared out at the setting sun, the shadows stretching across the hills behind the house.

She had tried to call Steve, but he was out. Her sister's line had been busy. Laurel had probably taken the phone off the hook because the youngest set of twins was asleep. Jenna's nerves jangled, pricked raw by the fear that needled at her constantly.

The walls closed in on her. Anxiety stretched tight across her chest and the air thinned. She didn't want to think about Ramsey. Or Linc. She had to get out of this room, out of this house or she would go crazy.

Outside. If she could just get outside. She wouldn't go far, wouldn't wander from the house, but she needed some fresh air, some open space, a place where she wouldn't be watched, a place where Ramsey hadn't been.

Restless now, and agitated, she left her room and walked into the living area. Silence pressed in on her. A soft stillness pervaded the house.

"Linc?" she called, hoping he wouldn't answer. He didn't. Walking to the kitchen, she found it empty.

There was no sign of the dogs or the master. A relieved breath eased out of her. She was grateful for what he'd done, but she needed some privacy. For a few minutes, she wanted to think about nothing more strenuous than the dogs' whereabouts.

She wanted to walk around the backyard, check on the horses. Sick of her enforced imprisonment, she moved to the French doors and looked out through the windows of the enclosed porch. Caution tempered her impulse to rush outside.

The sun set in a glorious burst of red, orange and gold. Vibrant light spilled through the windows. Jenna touched the door glass, as if she could catch the warmth, the hope in that sunset. She'd lived to see another one. Ramsey hadn't gotten her. *Yet.*

Bathed in the glorious flush of late afternoon, it was easy to believe that everything was all right, that she hadn't seen Ramsey that day at the cemetery. But she had.

A chill crawled over her. Tired of cringing every time his

face popped into her mind, she shook off thoughts of him, firmly determined to let her thoughts drift blankly about nothing.

She flung open the French doors and stepped out onto the enclosed porch. Fresh, hot air greeted her and she drew a deep, full breath, the first one that day.

Anxiety rolled from her shoulders and a knot she hadn't been aware of unraveled at the base of her neck. In the distance, she heard the dogs barking. An urge swept through her to disappear into the woods and never look back. She stared longingly at the screen of thick-leafed oaks and maples and pines, wanting to go, but knowing she wouldn't.

She wanted the comfort of animals. With them, she didn't have to talk or put on a front. She could just *be*. Maybe the horses had wandered up to the fence behind the barn.

She started across the expanse of backyard, enjoying the stretch of her muscles. Her shadow lengthened in front of her. Innately wary, she glanced around, checking around the trees, the side of the house, but she saw nothing.

Relieved, she angled behind the barn. The day's warmth hovered in the air and she perspired lightly with exertion. It felt wonderful, freeing. She drew in another deep breath, appreciating the scents of rain-soaked earth and grass and the subtle lilt of wildflowers.

Jenna lifted her face to the sun, which glittered over the land in a ripple of amber and scarlet. Warmth rained down on her and she smiled, her busted lips barely twinging. The horses weren't at the fence and she turned back, skirting the corner of the barn. She strode to the front, working out the soreness in her legs and buttocks and ribs.

She held her injured arm close to her, while swinging the other. Exhilaration moved through her. She checked the urge to glance over her shoulder, refusing to feel vulnerable or exposed. She was safe here, at least for now and the knowledge warmed her.

She reached the front of the barn and drew to a halt. One

of the double doors was closed, leaving the interior hazily lit. The odors of hay and manure and dust tickled her nostrils. From the woods, she could hear the distant, excited bark of the dogs, signaling that they'd found a rabbit or a raccoon.

Sunlight wavered into the barn, gleaming on pieces of straw and oats on the dirt floor, bleaching the grayed wood of the inside walls and stall doors.

Peace rippled through her. Out here, she was alone with God and the force of nature. Out here, she could forget Ramsey. Forget the hunger in Linc's eyes, the disbelief, the denial. Out here, she didn't have to pretend, didn't have to think. She could relax, escape Linc and those unsettling sensations he triggered in her body.

A light tuneless whistle sounded, then Jenna recognized the unmistakable baritone of Linc's voice. It carried from the back of the barn.

She squinted past shadows to where the sunlight slanted through the back wall, angling across his broad shoulders covered in blue denim, trimming one lean jean-clad thigh.

She recalled what had happened the last time they'd been in this barn together, but today she felt no wariness of Linc, no revulsion, no uncertainty. She told herself to leave, but instead she stole closer, her senses narrowed to only him.

He groomed one of the paints. The mare, Dixie. Jenna realized he must've gone for a ride without her. Good, no need for them both to stay chained to the house like prisoners.

Murmuring low words to Dixie, Linc rubbed the mare's nose. Birds twittered in the loft and Jenna could hear the steady *whisk* of the grooming brush.

Bars of sunlight fell across his hair, gilding the ash brown color with gold. His strong, capable hands worked from the horse's flank and up her side toward her head.

He shifted into a pocket of shadow, putting the sun at his back. Golden light blurred around him. Powerful, broad shoulders narrowed to a trim waist, lean flanks. She had leaned on those shoulders only days ago. Her throat closed up. He was a beautiful man.

His deep voice rose and fell like a sweet seductive melody, touching off a deep throb inside her, coaxing her closer. A slow burn unfurled in her belly and Jenna walked slowly toward him, unable to tear her gaze away.

"Did you think I'd forgotten you, girl?" he murmured huskily to the mare. "I'll take you out for another ride tomorrow."

A shiver, purely sensual, chased down her spine and Jenna savored the feeling, tucked it away to recall when their time together was over.

Linc moved to the horse's head, and she could see that his denim shirt was unbuttoned down the front. Sunlight played over his chest, skimming over the dusky hair that veed between his pectorals then thinned to his navel.

He lifted his arm to swipe the brush down the horse's neck. Muscles flexed up his forearm, buckled the taut ridge of his belly.

Licking her suddenly dry lips, she allowed her gaze to roam slowly down his body. His worn jeans were buttoned. They fit snugly, outlining his masculinity, his muscular thighs and sleeking down the length of his legs.

His hands moved over the horse, stroking slowly, steadily, and into Jenna's mind popped an image of his hands moving like that over her. Caressing, his slender fingers covering her breasts.

She swallowed hard, feeling suspended on a thin wire. In a flash, her breasts grew sensitive and heavy. Warmth tickled the core of her, causing her to squeeze her thighs together reflexively.

In that instant, she acknowledged the chemistry between them, admitted that she wanted him. Wanted to make love with him. Wanted to be normal for him. Wanted to try.

But in the next breath, sanity returned. She hadn't lied

about being frigid. She hadn't lied about trying before. Things would be no different with Linc.

She remembered his earlier words to her, the refusal in his voice to believe what she told him. Sadness wound through her. He had to believe it. She couldn't bear to hurt him, couldn't bear to bruise his ego the way Steve's had been.

Unsettled now by the raspy quality of his voice, she shifted. She no longer wanted to hear him, couldn't allow the sensations fluttering at her core.

Linc moved to the mare's side, his voice low and hypnotic.

"Maybe I can convince Jenna to come out with us. She'd like it."

Tearing her gaze from his bare chest, she walked toward him. She told herself she was steady, yet her voice came out hoarse.

"I *would* like it. I think I might want to go riding tomorrow."

"Great!" He looked up, mild surprise on his face at her entrance. He rested one forearm on the horse's neck.

Hunger flared in his eyes; his gaze lingered on her lips.

Bracing herself against the sensual web spinning between them, she said briskly, "But right now, I'm going to call Mace, see if he can take me to the office. Since it looks like I'm going to be here for a while longer, I also need some more things from the house."

His gaze stroked over her. "I can take you."

"There's no need. Mace can—"

"I don't want you to go without me." He straightened, steel threading his voice.

Jenna halted about a foot from him, her gaze holding his. In all honesty, she didn't want to go without him. Which was exactly why she should. "You've had to baby-sit me all day. I'm sure you'd like a break."

"You mean *you'd* like one," he said flatly, giving the horse one last stroke with the brush. "I'm coming."

His tone was too possessive, too authoritative, and it made her bristle. "Suit yourself."

He gave a curt nod. "Just let me put Dixie out and I'll be ready."

"Fine." Jenna turned on her heel and walked out, alternately annoyed and glad. Of course she couldn't go alone, but she found herself depending on him entirely too much.

It was too easy to turn to him, to take comfort and strength from him. She couldn't allow herself to become used to it. When this was all over, they would go their separate ways. Why couldn't he see that? Why wouldn't he respect the distance she tried to place between them?

Jenna admitted that her frustration stemmed from her own inadequacies. She wanted more than protection from Linc Garrett, but she couldn't ask for more, couldn't reach out and take the promise of the attraction that shimmered between them. Because she couldn't give him what he needed in return.

Despite trying to forget him, forget the hunger in his eyes, being with Linc was preferable to dwelling on Ramsey. Still, pressure closed like a giant fist around her. Ramsey wanted her life.

Linc could take her soul. She wasn't ready to give up either one.

She sat on the passenger side of Linc's truck, hugging the door. He had done nothing except what she wanted, yet she found herself tortured by a nagging frustration. She didn't know what to make of it.

Irritation wound through her. She wasn't annoyed at Linc, exactly. She slid a sideways glance at him. He drove with one wrist resting over the top of the steering wheel, his body comfortably sprawled in the seat, making his jeans stretch taut across his thighs.

She tore her gaze away and looked out the window, but it didn't diminish her awareness of him. The bench seat of this truck was entirely too small for two people, she decided. Even from here, she could feel his heat reaching out to her, smell the clean sweat from his body, the faint odor of horseflesh. Erotic, arousing, it tapped against those buried sensations she had more and more trouble ignoring lately.

She felt his gaze on her and steadfastly studied the passing fields and fence posts as they drove east on Danforth from MacArthur. Resolutely she focused on the white faces of newborn calves and the sight of the occasional horse. Despite keeping her gaze averted from Linc, Jenna could feel his on her as if it were a brand.

A flush rose beneath her skin and her breasts grew heavy. Her lips tingled.

With a fresh burst of annoyance, Jenna realized it wasn't Linc who perturbed her. It was her. Or rather her body's reaction to him. Watching him in the barn a moment ago had sent a shower of flame through her, of such heightened awareness that her nipples had peaked.

Just being this close to him wore at her resistance. She couldn't let herself be seduced by the stirrings of her body or the fierce hunger in Linc's eyes.

She crossed her left arm over her right, gripping the cast to remind herself why she was with Linc in the first place. Thoughts of Linc, *of her and Linc,* were starting to stalk her every bit as much as Ramsey. They were deceptive, coaxing her to believe things could be different with Linc, that *she* could be different with him.

She knew better.

She told herself she felt only gratitude for him, but when she thought about the kiss they'd shared, she was not grateful. She was…aroused.

Tentatively, her gaze slid to him again. He watched the road now, instead of her. Jenna's gaze traced the smooth planes of his face, the stubborn jaw, those sculpted lips. Her body softened in a flood of weakness. Since that kiss, her body had hummed with a renewed vibrancy, vitality. It exhilarated her. And unbalanced her.

She didn't want to respond to him this way, yet she could no longer deny it. She *wanted* him to kiss her, wanted him to make everything disappear and make her believe that she could be whole.

He glanced at her and she looked quickly away, fixing her eyes on the telephone poles that sped past the window.

"Are you okay? About what happened this morning, I mean."

She didn't want to talk about Ramsey or the package she'd received. But she couldn't bring herself to discount Linc's concern. She nodded. "I'm glad for the chance to do something normal. Go over the charts Steve left. Get some extra clothes from the house."

She felt his gaze on her, steady, probing, but he didn't pursue his questions about Ramsey. He braked at a four-way stop sign.

"Your bruises look better today."

Her gaze swerved to his. Concern burned in his eyes, but also something else, something sharper. Desire, she realized.

He reached toward her slowly, deliberately. She didn't flinch when his fingers floated gently over her throat. Instead she wanted to arch her neck, give herself over to his touch. She wanted his fingers to trail over her throat, her breasts.

She bit her lip and looked out the car window, squashing the tantalizing thoughts, thinking she shouldn't have come with him. She should've waited for Mace. "It's your turn."

Linc accelerated through the stop sign and the truck picked up speed as they continued east.

His large hand settled lightly on her left thigh. "How's the arm doing today?"

"Fine," she replied choking out the words. She couldn't get a full breath. A spiral of heat worked from her leg to her belly. He was simply checking on her medical progress, she told herself. Still her heartbeat raced at a ridiculous rate.

The road stretched before them, empty still before they reached the city limits of Edmond. Sunlight glittered off the truck's mirrors, bouncing along the blacktop.

Again she felt Linc's gaze on her and she bit back a demand that he watch the road.

His knuckle grazed her chin and turned her face toward him. His gaze roamed her features, his eyes dark and mysterious with a banked light. She told herself it was professional concern in his eyes, not heat.

His gaze dropped to her lips and he rasped, "Your mouth looks good."

She swallowed, her heart kicking against her ribs. She knew he meant that the swelling had gone down and the cuts had started to heal, but that didn't douse the want that flared to life inside her. She resisted the urge to close her eyes, to slide over on the seat next to him.

She tried to ignore the growing heat in his eyes, the unmistakable desire. Yet she couldn't misread that sensual gleam in his eye, the way his voice dropped to a husky rasp that primed her nerve endings.

Shifting against the awareness he stirred, she said sharply, "If you're going to examine me, maybe you should stop the truck first."

He grinned. "If you're asking for a full exam, I'd be more than happy to do it."

"No," she said quickly, stunned by a sudden, fierce craving to feel his bare skin next to hers, feel his lips on her breasts.

He chuckled as if he'd read her mind. Part of her wanted to play along, but she couldn't tease him that way. She couldn't allow him to think things would be different between them when they wouldn't. No matter what amount of attraction between them, she could never be enough woman for him.

He'd said he accepted that she was frigid, that he wouldn't

try to convince her that she could be different with him. So what was he doing?

Frustrated, she blurted, "Are you trying to seduce me?"

"Would you let me?"

Her breath lodged in her chest. Did he want the answer for future reference? Or was he asking permission—for now? She shook her head. "You said—"

"I know what I said." He slammed his palm against the steering wheel. "There's a real big part of me that wishes I'd never promised to leave you alone."

She closed her eyes, regret, reluctance chasing through her. "But you did promise. It would never work."

"I don't agree."

"Linc—"

"I don't agree, but I said I wouldn't push. And I won't."

She glanced at him, seeing his features tighten as he stared straight ahead at the road. "Thank you."

"Dammit." He looked out his own window.

They rode in silence the rest of the way. Jenna swallowed more than one apology, but she knew this was right. If things escalated between them, it would be a disaster, just as it had been with Steve.

They turned at the stop sign on Coltrane and drove north about a mile then Linc pulled into her clinic's gravel parking lot. Up near the side of the building, Jenna noticed a patrol car.

A balding man who looked vaguely familiar stepped out of the black-and-white unit. Jenna remembered him now as the policeman who had spoken to her in the hospital, Officer Sikes.

Her modest brick building stood alone, surrounded by trees and honeysuckle bushes. The potted red geraniums on the porch had wilted from lack of water, but still sturdily survived.

From the outside, the dark brick structure resembled a

small house. Jenna liked that; she'd had it built to be welcoming and comfortable.

Reaching across to open the door with her left hand, she hopped out. She deliberately kept her gaze from the spot just behind her, under the floodlight. She didn't have to look to remember in full, grisly detail what had happened the last time she was here. What Ramsey had done to Wilbur. And her.

"Ah, Dr. West. I wasn't sure who you were." The barrel-chested policeman strode forward, his gait smooth and strong.

Jenna smiled at him and indicated Linc with her free hand. "This is Dr. Garrett, Mace Garrett's brother. He's been helping me."

The older man reached out to shake Linc's hand. "Nice to meet you. I'm Officer Sikes."

"Yes, I remember." Linc smiled, his gaze moving around Jenna's property.

Officer Sikes walked with them to the front door. "Just got here a couple of hours ago myself, about six. I've been on the last two nights. So far, there's been no signs of disturbance."

"Good." It should've reassured Jenna, but she knew Ramsey was just biding his time. Still, she refused to think about him anymore today.

Slipping her key from her jeans pocket, she unlocked the front door and walked inside.

"I'll be right outside if you need anything," the policeman called behind her.

"Thanks." She walked to the opposite wall and flipped on the light switch. Fluorescent lights flickered then illuminated the room.

She turned in a half circle, her gaze skipping over Linc as she scanned the windowless front room of her office. Her desk was to the left of the door. The waiting area was roomy enough to accommodate six chairs along the far wall, her filing cabinets and across from her desk, medicine cabinets.

The trash cans were empty. The tile floor gleamed spotlessly, indicating the cleaning woman still followed her regular routine.

Steve had left things in perfect order. Several files were stacked neatly on the desk and Jenna's calendar had been flipped to today's date.

The filing cabinets were closed. Her undergraduate and veterinary diplomas were framed in blue velvet, giving a splash of color to the sterile environment. More color glowed from the bulletin board behind her desk, where pictures of animals crowded the cork surface.

Everything was just as she'd left it. Still a heavy foreboding pressed down on her.

She shook it off. After what had happened at the cemetery and with the photo, her nerves were understandably rattled. But Ramsey wouldn't be fool enough to show up with a policeman and Linc both here.

Moving to her desk, she sank down in the chair and opened the first chart. Steve had delivered the foal for the Campbells just this morning. He would probably call her about that later tonight.

His notes were neat and easy to read. He detailed his procedure in the same way she did and she smiled. After about ten minutes, she had looked through the charts and made a few notes about one of her horses with cancer. She wanted him to check the mare tomorrow, make sure the tumor hadn't grown any larger.

Linc sat quietly in a chair across from Jenna. "Can I do anything to help? Need anything moved or want me to get something for you?"

"I think I have everything I need." She rose from behind her desk and moved to the door adjacent to Linc, which led to the exam room, lab and kennel area. "I want to check the temperature back here, make sure my instruments are where Steve can find them if he needs to."

"All right." Linc rose, his gaze following her as she

reached the door beside him. "Would you like me to put up those files for you?"

"You don't have to—"

"I'll just do it," he said tightly.

Evidently, he was still annoyed by their conversation in the truck. Jenna stepped into the back room, flipping on the light switch. "Thanks."

"Do I file by the animal's name or the owner?"

"Owner." Both metal examining tables gleamed. On the waist-high cabinet behind the tables sat the heavy autoclave used for sterilizing instruments. Her stethoscope, otoscope, and ophthalmoscope lay beside it. Packets of gloves and syringes were stacked neatly in one corner of the counter. Pills, medicine and antiseptic were hidden behind the cabinet doors.

In the back part of the room, recessed lighting was dim, leaving a darker, more soothing atmosphere for the sick animals she sometimes kept here. At the moment, there were just a few dogs that Steve was watching over.

Her stainless steel refrigerator, which held antibiotics and other medicines, gleamed dully in the light. Its motor emitted a light hum.

Everything appeared in order, yet Jenna couldn't dismiss the tension stretching across her shoulders. She listened closely, hearing only the scrape of file cabinet drawers as Linc put away her files.

They were the only two in here. Steve had been here earlier, but that didn't explain the sense that something dark, something vicious lingered in the air. No doubt it was due to the last incident. But she was safe. Ramsey wasn't here now.

She turned around, her gaze passing the anatomy chart she'd framed and hung over the first exam table. Next to the chart hung a framed, enlarged photo of her and Steve on the day they'd graduated from vet school. But something was stuck over the picture. A paper of some sort.

She stepped toward the wall, reaching up to see what it was. She froze, a scream welling inside her.

Cold sweat slicked her body. She trembled, her muscles clenching as if for a blow and a low moan ripped out of her.

"Jenna, I think that's the last of them. Anything else you want me to do?"

Linc's voice sounded strained and small, as though he were deep in a cave. Fear wrapped tight fingers around her throat and she couldn't speak, couldn't draw a breath. She could only stare. In some part of her brain, she was aware that he had walked into the room.

"Jenna?" Alarm roughened his voice. "What is it?"

Shock rippled through her body. Her vision blurred. Then she was aware that Linc stood in front of her and her gaze finally focused on him.

"He's been here," she said woodenly.

Linc turned and cursed violently as he saw what she had.

There, plastered over the picture, was a certificate of death. Filled out with her name.

Chapter 9

Fury ripped through him and Linc shook with the force of it.

He and Jenna sat in the waiting area of her office. Mace and Officer Sikes were in the exam room. Linc had gotten Jenna out of the other room and though he'd wanted to tear that paper from the wall, he'd known enough, even in his rage, not to touch it.

As soon as he'd settled her in a chair, he'd called Mace, then yelled out the door for Officer Sikes.

Less than fifteen minutes later, his brother had arrived and gone into the back room with the patrol cop.

Jenna sat quietly unmoving beside Linc, staring straight ahead. Her hands lay limply in her lap. Her features were sucked dry of color, her eyes wide and startlingly bright in her face. There were no tears, no hysterics. Linc could find no trace of emotion at all.

It was as if she'd closed down. He kept a close watch on her, watching to see if her teeth chattered or if she began to tremble, but she didn't. Nor did she exhibit any other signs of shock.

He wanted to comfort her and didn't know how. He wondered if he should put his arm around her or leave her alone. Pure rage swelled inside him and he stuffed down a roar.

Linc had seen gang violence. He'd seen brutal stab and gunshot wounds, heard of demented murderers, psychologically twisted sickos. But he'd never been face-to-face with live evil like Ramsey.

Mace and Officer Sikes walked into the room. Mace, his tired face drawn in grim lines, closed the door to the exam room softly behind him.

Officer Sikes halted in front of the door, murmuring to Mace, "I'll call Captain Price and let her know what's going on."

"Would you let my partner know, too?"

"Sure." Officer Sikes let himself out, closing the steel door behind him.

Rubbing a hand over his face, Mace turned, still gripping the plastic bag containing the death certificate. His gaze settled on Jenna.

At the sight of Ramsey's handiwork, Linc surged out of the chair. "How did that bastard get in here?"

Mace's gaze, hard with a warning, sliced to him, but Jenna didn't move. Didn't speak or even acknowledge that she'd heard Linc's venomous outburst.

"How?"

His brother shook his head, shoving a hand through his wavy hair. "Hell if I know. Obviously—"

"What's the good of putting a man outside if he can't protect her?" Rage boiled inside him, searching for a release. Linc battled the urge to ram his fist into the wall, through a window, something.

Mace leveled a flat stare on him. "As I was saying, obviously Ramsey got here before Sikes did. I'm sorry, Linc. We just don't have the manpower to put someone out here twenty-four hours a day. The thing to concentrate on is she's safe. No one was here during Ramsey's little visit. No one was hurt.''

"This time! You saw him this morning at the cemetery. You know what he wants to do to her!''

"Keep your voice down,'' Mace growled, glancing at Jenna. "You're not helping her.''

"Nothing can help her,'' Linc said bitterly, running a hand through his tousled hair.

Since he'd called his brother, he'd been divided over whether to tear up the countryside looking for Ramsey or to stay here and offer solace to Jenna. From where he stood, he wasn't doing a damn thing about either one.

He took some comfort in the fact that he had his rifle behind the seat of the truck, but a fat lot of good that had done. Ramsey had come in here, violated Jenna's space and left a blaring message. *I'll get you when I'm ready.*

He turned to his brother, noting the stubble on Mace's jaw, the exhaustion lining his features. No doubt he'd been working around the clock. Linc reined in his anger. "Of course it's not your fault, or Sikes's, that Ramsey was here. I just feel so damn helpless.''

"Well, you *can* help. You've got to be strong for her, be there for her.'' He frowned and tugged Linc a few feet away from Jenna.

"Is she in shock?''

Linc's gaze moved to her and his heart clenched at the sight of her sitting in that chair, solitary and stoic. "No. But I'm afraid she's giving up.''

Mace looked at him sharply. "On what?''

"That you'll ever get the guy. That she'll ever be free of him.''

Mace rubbed at his red-rimmed eyes. "We got a lead from someone who's seen him in a convenience store. And now we might have someone who's seen him in a bar.''

"What good is that!" Linc exploded. "*Here* is where he's been. The cemetery—"

"We can start tracing his steps, maybe find where he's holed up." The impatience in his brother's voice softened. "We will get him, but it's going to take some time."

"I hope it's soon." Linc watched Jenna, unable to look away. What was she thinking? What was she feeling? Why wouldn't she say something? "If not, I don't know what will happen to her. I think she's hanging on by a thread."

"Can't you help her?"

"Not if she won't let me." Sadness crowded through him. He ached at the sight of her perched stiffly in that chair, fighting off invisible demons. Alone.

Mace turned to him, concern darkening his eyes. "Don't let Ramsey take control of your life, Linc. That's what he wants."

"He's already got Jenna's," Linc noted bleakly.

"Isn't that what matters?"

Mace paused, then lowered his voice. "Did you check her out? She hasn't said a word since I got here."

"She hasn't said a word since we found that damn piece of paper and she told me Ramsey had been here." Linc exhaled loudly. "I don't know how to reach her. I don't know what to do for her."

"I need to get a statement. Can you help me do that?"

Resigned, but knowing it was necessary, Linc nodded. He walked over to Jenna and knelt in front of her. Careful not to touch her, he said her name softly.

Her gaze, vacant and dull, dropped to him. "What?"

A wealth of leashed pain ached in the word; restrained fear shaded her voice. Linc didn't want to be the one who broke the dam on her control, but he didn't think it was good for her to shut down this way.

He shook from head to toe. She sat calmly in the chair. Rage poured through him, throbbing in a wake of helplessness. Her features were pale, yet serene. He wished she would get angry. Wished something would crack that marble facade. But he wasn't sure he wanted to, or should, be the one to instigate it.

"Mace needs a statement. Do you think you're up to it?"

"Of course, Detective." Her voice, smooth as cream, rippled from her throat. In flat, hollow words, she said, "I arrived just after eight o'clock with your brother. After going over some charts, I went into the exam room to double-check medical supplies, but before I could, I saw the paper covering my picture. Then, Linc...you—" She faltered, her gaze going to Linc's. "How did Mace know to come here?"

"I called him," he said quietly, his heart clenching at her stoic restraint. He wished she would cry or scream or throw something, just to release the fear he knew she had to feel.

"Linc called you and here we are." There was nothing in the husky tone to hint at the hysteria Linc could sense bubbling inside her.

Feeling totally impotent and incompetent, frustration razored through him. He turned and looked at Mace, shaking his head.

Mace scribbled the last of his notes, then asked Jenna if she would be willing to come downtown and sign the statement.

"Of course."

Linc rose, clenching his fists in an effort to keep from gathering Jenna to him. Certainly after what Ramsey had just done, Linc didn't want to frighten her. Hell, she'd let him help at the cemetery. What had changed?

He knew what it was. He'd said he wouldn't try to challenge her idea that she was frigid, but in the truck, he hadn't been able to keep his hands off her. Was that why she wanted no support from him?

Jenna rose from the chair and Linc saw her chin tremble. Instead of looking at him, she turned to Mace. "Would you like me to come to the station now? I'd just as soon get it over with."

"That would be great." Mace frowned in concern over Jenna's shoulder and Linc shrugged, shaking his head.

Mace wanted to know if she was all right and Linc had no idea. "I'll take you to the station, then if you want to go by your house—"

"Maybe tomorrow. Not tonight." Her voice was tight and thin with unvoiced emotion.

Linc knew it, he felt it, but he could do nothing about it. "Sure. Whatever you want."

"Good." Mace walked to the door. "I'll meet you there."

Jenna moved around Linc to follow Mace, but Linc gently touched her arm. "Jenna?"

She stopped, but wouldn't look at him.

Linc shot a glance at Mace, silently requesting to be left alone. Mace acknowledged him with a small nod and walked outside, closing the door noiselessly.

"Are you all right?"

"I'm fine."

Did he detect a slight wobble in her voice? He peered closely at her. "I'm worried about you. You haven't said anything, except to answer Mace's questions."

"What would you like me to say?" she asked blandly.

He frowned, moving in front of her so he could see her face, look into her eyes. "You don't *have* to say anything, but aren't you angry? Don't you want to kill him?"

"What would that accomplish?"

Her voice was eerily calm, and if he had blinked, he would've missed the sheen of moisture in her eyes. But he saw it. She wasn't unaffected. She was trying with everything in her to hold it together, not break down.

"You don't have to handle this alone, Jenna. I'm here. I can help you."

"You can't do anything, Linc."

"Jenna, you're frightened." He refused to feel slighted at her words. "You've a right to be. You've also got to be mad as hell—"

"It doesn't matter."

Her voice was steady, stubbornly so, but her body shook. He noticed the trembling in her hands, her shoulders. Then he saw the light sheen of perspiration on her face. "I'm here, Jenna. Let me help you."

"I'm fine. I *am*."

"That's why you're shaking as if you have pneumonia." He couldn't hide the anger in his voice. He wondered if he should forget all common sense and pull her into his arms. "Why won't you let me help you? There's nothing wrong with needing help, with asking for it."

She shook her head, looking away from him. She swallowed hard and he saw a tear seep out of her eye.

His heart clenched with pain. "You let me help you this morning. We can get through this together, Jenna."

"I don't want...I can't—" She broke off, choking back a sob.

Linc moved reflexively, intent on wrapping her in his arms, only forcing them down to his sides at the last minute.

"I can't think straight." She covered her face with her hands. Frustration roughened her voice. "I can't see things clearly."

"Let me see them for you, Jenna. I'm here. I'm not going anywhere. Let me help you."

"Don't get close to me!" She dropped her hands and whirled away from him. "Why can't you understand I have nothing to give? I can't be what you want!"

Her impassioned declaration caught him totally off guard. Desperate to hold her despite what he'd just said, to have her look at him, he said quietly, "I only want you to be safe."

"You want...*me*. You can't have me!" Fear spilled out, sharp and biting. "No one can!"

"Jenna, listen to me."

"You can't have me, Linc. You can't."

Alarm screamed through him, robbing his breath and leaving him speechless for a moment. "I'm not trying to take over your life like Ramsey is."

Had he completely ruined her trust in him by teasing her in the truck? He stepped around her, leaning down to look into her face.

"I don't want to own you or possess you or hurt you and you know it." Pain threaded his words, making his voice raw. "All I want is what you want to give and right now that's trust. We've built that, haven't we?"

He waited for her to nod, or to deny it, but she said nothing. She did nothing.

"I won't hurt you, Jenna."

"You're the only man I trust, besides Dad and Steve. He's trying to take that away from me. He'll kill you, just like he killed Wilbur."

"No—"

"Wilbur tried to protect me, too," she cried. Her eyes were wild, her face ashen. "What makes you think Ramsey won't come after you?"

"We're ready for him, Jenna. We're waiting for him."

"We weren't ready for this," she said baldly, gesturing toward the exam room.

Panic fringed her eyes, making them glow brilliantly against her wan features. She swiped at the tears on her cheeks. "It's all a game to him. A sick, twisted game. He's making me paranoid. I'm starting to doubt whether you'll live through this." She gave a short laugh. "I'm starting to doubt I will. He wants me to doubt everyone, everything—"

"Do you doubt *me?*" Linc stepped closer, wanting her to look into his eyes, to know that he was the one person she could rely on. "Do you?"

Her gaze locked with his. "No, but—"

"Then he doesn't control everything. Not yet."

Restless energy pulsed from her. "But he's trying to take my life, Linc. It's slipping right through my fingers." Her voice trailed to a frantic whisper. "I know how he works and yet, he can still do it to me."

A fierce urgency shot through him. Linc wanted to wrap his arms around her, hold her so tight she would fuse right into his soul. "Don't doubt me, Jenna. Don't doubt yourself. Don't let him win."

She stared into his eyes, a tear trickling down her cheek. "I know you wouldn't hurt me, but—"

"But what?"

"But I should stand on my own. When this is over, I'll be alone."

"Right now, you're not." He wanted to remind her that she *wasn't* alone, would never be alone, if he had anything to say about it. Instead, he urged her with his eyes, his voice to let him help her.

She hesitated, then acceptance crossed her features. "No, right now, I have you."

She still wouldn't let him touch her, but she no longer shied away from him. They walked out to his truck, her gaze darting nervously around, her injured arm pressed close to her side. Linc's eyes burned.

Officer Sikes walked up, his dark eyes concerned. "Dr. West, I'm sorry. Maybe if I'd gotten here earlier—"

"It wasn't your fault." Fierce conviction etched her voice and she reached out to touch his hand. "I appreciate that you're here now. I know you're working past the clock."

Faint color suffused his blunt features, but he nodded, glancing at Linc.

Linc nodded. "Yes, thank you."

The other man smiled and walked back to his car.

Linc opened the truck door for Jenna and when she slid inside, he stepped up to fasten her seat belt. He leaned over her, his chest against her thigh, but she didn't cringe, which sent a wave of relief through him. Clicking the buckle into place, he glanced up to find her staring at him, her eyes big with uncertainty.

"Just hang on a little bit longer, Jenna. That bastard will make a mistake and when he does—"

"Let's just go to the station, okay?" Fatigue strained her voice, shadowed her eyes. "Then home."

"You got it." Linc wanted to caress her cheek, press a soft kiss on her lips, but that was probably the last thing she needed. Or wanted. He closed the door and hurried around to the driver's side.

Though unsettled by the events of the day, he knew one thing. When this was all over, he didn't want Jenna to leave. He wasn't sure exactly what he wanted, but he knew he wanted to explore something with her. The problem was convincing her.

The image of that death certificate flashed through her mind. Over and over, tedious, paralyzing, terrifying. Numbed by a brutal chill, Jenna felt as if she looked down on herself from a great height. Knowing she was supposed to do something, feel something, and able to do neither.

She slid out of the truck and preceded Linc into the house, only now becoming aware of her surroundings. All during her statement at the police station, she had operated like an automaton, deliberately blanking her mind. Now, juxtaposed images, conflicting messages whirled through her mind.

Ramsey's silent, but explicit threat, made clear by the death certificate. *I'll get you. You'll never escape me.*

Linc's unwavering support. *You're not alone. We'll beat him together.*

She desperately wanted to believe Linc, to grasp on to his words and draw strength from them, but his promise seemed a fragile hope in the face of Ramsey's vicious determination.

She couldn't think, couldn't sleep, couldn't even breathe without Ramsey slithering into her thoughts, triggering the fear, the uncertainty, the paranoia, all as brackish and lethal as a dose of poison.

He had forced her into seclusion. *The cops* repeatedly ordered her to stay hidden. *Even Linc,* though he meant no harm, monitored her constantly. She wanted to go outside without a bodyguard, walk from one end of the house to the other without feeling as if she were this month's specimen under a microscope.

Through her numbness seeped the realization that Ramsey had already succeeded in at least one thing. She had no power over her own life.

That comprehension sent a charge of energy through her. Silence enveloped the house, broken only by the low murmur of Linc's voice from the kitchen and the *click* of the dog's toenails on the tile floor.

The quietness should've pricked her nerves, but she found it soothing. As she did the fact that Linc was here. Slowly she became aware of the soft lights from the lamps he had flicked on behind her. Hearing footsteps, she turned as he walked in from the other room.

His gaze, intense and careful, settled on her. "I let the dogs out."

Meaning the animals would patrol the grounds and alert them if someone arrived. She nodded, wanting to do something, say something, but uncertain as to what. Something niggled at her. Something she'd said…

At the clinic, the stress of seeing the death certificate, the almost constant uneasiness of the last weeks had crashed in on her. Her control had shattered and paranoid fear had driven out those awful words.

You want…me! You can't have me. No one can!

"Linc, I want to apologize."

"For what?" He looked startled as he walked toward her.

"For what I said at the clinic. I don't know what possessed me to accuse you that way, to say those things—"

"Jenna, stop."

"I know you don't want to control my life the way he does. I don't know why I said it."

"How about because you were scared to death?" He

reached her, soft lamplight reflected in his beautiful gray eyes. "Or maybe operating on psychological shock?"

"It's no excuse." She recalled the pain in his eyes, the hurt that had pinched his features. "I'm truly sorry. I never meant to hurt you. You've been only wonderful to me and—"

"It's forgotten, Jenna. I understand what you're going through and—"

"Would you please let me do this, Linc? Stop finding excuses for me. I hurt you. I was wrong. I owe you an apology."

"After what you've been through—"

"It doesn't give me the right to hurt you. And I did," she said quietly. "I hate that."

His hand rose to her shoulder. "Hey, I'm fine. You're the one I'm worried about."

"Well, don't!" She hadn't meant for the words to be so harsh, but that brutal icy fear burned through her. Ramsey was closing in. She could feel it, sense it, and panic fluttered at her. "I'm sick of everything being about me. Aren't you?"

He shook his head, confusion plain in his eyes.

"Be honest." She laughed shortly. "Everything revolves around how I'm doing, how I'm holding up. It makes me sick. It's got to bother *you*."

"I just want you to be all right. What can I do to make that happen for you?"

"If you were smart, you'd run the other way," she muttered, only half joking.

"Not an option." His jaw firmed. "Stop trying to get rid of me and enjoy the fact that you have me at your beck and call."

"That's not what I want." Frustration rippled through her.

"Then what?" he asked quietly.

"I don't know." A second later, she tilted her head. She was sick of being the focus. She felt like the invalid matriarch who waited to die while everyone hovered over her, scrutinizing, studying relentlessly. "Yes, I do. Tell me about yourself."

That fast, his concern changed to wariness and he moved away from her, walking over to the fireplace. "What's to tell? You know everything about me that's worth knowing."

"There are parts of you I know nothing about."

He stood at the mantel, hands shoved in his pockets, his back to her. "Like what?"

"Like your family, for instance." Her gaze moved above his shoulder and rested on the framed photograph atop the oak mantel. She walked over and took it down. "What about your brothers?"

Linc studied her as if weighing the consequences of her request. Then he gently lifted the frame from her hand, affection shining in his eyes. "Well, you know Mace. And I already told you Sam is a cop, too. He's the…charmer of the family, I suppose."

"He works Vice, did you say?"

"Used to. Just transferred to Homicide after—" He broke off, indecision and pain shadowing his features.

Curious, Jenna prodded. "After what?"

"He and his partner were in a shoot-out." Linc's gaze measured her and she knew he wondered if she could handle what he was about to say.

She nodded, urging him on.

"His partner was killed and Sam blames himself for it. He shouldn't, but he does. Sometimes we don't see him for weeks."

"I'm sorry."

"We all handle pain in our own way, I guess." He shrugged, replacing the frame. "I wouldn't win any prizes for the way I've dealt with some things, especially concerning you."

"You're talking about that night in the barn. Please forget that. You didn't hurt me—"

"I scared the hell out of you," he exclaimed.

She hesitated, wanting to deny it, get the focus off herself. "Okay, you did, but—"

Regret carved his features and she added quickly, "But I was fine. You were the one who didn't seem able to escape the pain."

"Yeah, that was over Michelle," he muttered derisively. "Hard to imagine now."

"Why?" She barely breathed, hoping to finally learn more about the pain that had nearly him to kiss her that night. "You *were* married to her."

"Yes, but—" He pivoted away, shoving a hand through his hair. He paced to the windows overlooking the backyard, the sound of his boots muffled by the carpet. "You don't want to hear about that."

"I do." *You have no idea how much.* "I don't know what happened between you two and I'd like to. But only if you want to tell me."

Hazed in deep pockets of shadow, he looked over his shoulder at her. She could see the gleam of his eyes, the vague outline of his jaw. Turning to stare out the window, he told her in a resonant, distant tone how they'd worked their way together through medical school. How, after they'd begun practicing, Michelle had become involved with one of their friends, another doctor and run away with him.

Jenna had guessed this much from helping him that night in the barn, yet she sensed he held something back.

Moving away from the window, he strode back to the love seat and sat down on the end closest to where she stood. He leaned forward, his voice contemplative, his wrists resting on his widespread knees. "She ripped out my heart. My soul, too. I haven't cared about anybody since then.

Jenna eased down to the floor at his knee. Her bruises barely hurt now and she crossed her legs to sit Indian style. "Is that why you chose to do emergency room medicine rather than have your own clinic?"

His gaze sliced to her. "What do you mean?"

"This way you don't have to develop relationships with anyone or get close to them or have them become dependent on you."

His lips twisted. "You sound like a shrink."

"Still, you took *me* in," she reflected softly. "I've become dependent on you. Too much so. You knew that would happen, yet you did it anyway. Why?"

"You know why." His voice hardened and he stared straight ahead.

"Yes, because you wanted to repay me, but there's still something inside you that cares very much about people in need, Linc."

"Trust me," he said with a snort. "There's not."

"Of course there is—"

"You're one to point fingers about separating from people," he said impatiently. "You prefer to work with animals. I don't think your view of humans is much better than mine."

At his frank reminder of the rape, pain snatched her breath, but she knew he hadn't brought it up to be cruel. "Right now, I can't disagree with you."

The grim reference to Ramsey hung between them. No matter how she tried, she couldn't outrun reality. "What if he starts doing things to you? That will be my fault."

"He's not going to," Linc said firmly.

She almost believed him, but she knew better. "You think he only wants me, but he wants to ruin my life and you're part of that."

"I *want* to be."

"No!" Agitated, she pushed to her feet. Her voice rose sharp and thin. "Linc, please don't start again."

"I'm already a part, Jenna." He stood, too, moving in front of her. "If Ramsey knows it, believes it, why can't you?"

"You just want sex," she cried out, frustrated.

He laughed, a full deep sound she'd never heard and it riveted her to the floor. She stared at him, totally mesmerized by the sight of joy on his face.

"I do want sex," he admitted ruefully, still grinning. "But you make me want so much more than that, Jenna. You *are* so much more than that."

She was aroused and humbled by his words, but it was dangerous to believe them. "I couldn't bear to think I had caused Ramsey to come after you."

"Let's get something straight, Jenna." His smile faded. "You don't *cause* him to do anything. You know that. You're just apprehensive, understandably so, but what Ramsey does is not your call."

"No, but he calls every shot of *my* life," she said bitterly. "He's taken control and it's sliding right by me."

"I know it feels that way because you're cooped up here with me and the way things are right now, you have to let other people handle things for you. That's hard."

She cocked her head. "How do you understand so much?"

"I remember how it felt when Michelle decided to leave me, turn my life upside down. I had no say over that." He added harshly, "Or anything else she decided to do."

Jenna nodded. "That's exactly how I feel."

He shifted closer to her, his hard thigh brushing hers and setting off that butterfly spark of heat in her belly.

"I know you want to do something, but Mace is right. We should let him handle this." His breath misted her cheek. "We can stay put, right here until they find him."

"*If* they find him." She swallowed, having trouble concentrating.

"They will." Belief, promise, determination gleamed in his eyes, making her want to believe.

She checked the urge to caress his face, to run her fingers along the strength of his jaw. "I couldn't bear to disappoint you the way Michelle did."

He stiffened. "Never, *ever* compare yourself to her."

"I didn't mean—"

"You could never hurt anyone the way she is capable."

"It's very possible you will get hurt because of me, Linc," Jenna reminded him sadly.

"It's not the same thing."

"I'm not saying I could hurt you in the same way she did. Of course, you don't feel for me what you felt for her—"

"You're right!" He shifted, his chest brushing her breasts, his eyes bright with conviction, his fists clenched. "You could never hurt anyone that way! You're too caring, too compassionate, too courageous to do any of the things Michelle did."

What had his ex-wife done to produce such bitterness? "Was there no chance of reconciliation between you two?"

"No! No." Linc rubbed his face, then dropped his hands, stepping back. "Especially after she took my—"

He broke off, agony ravaging his features. He looked so tortured, so utterly vulnerable that Jenna's heart clenched tightly and she automatically reached for his hand.

"After she took your what?" She held her breath, dazed by the anguish she'd seen, the revelation that there were even more layers to this man than she'd suspected in her innocent query to know more about him.

He stared blankly at the floor, then shook himself as if he could dislodge the pain, shake it off like a mist of rain.

A hard, tight knot formed under her ribs. Her hand tightened on his. "Linc?"

"She killed my baby, Jenna." He lifted his head, his tortured eyes boring into hers.

Jenna's heart stopped; air jammed painfully in her lungs. She couldn't possibly have heard him correctly. "She... what?"

"She killed my baby, without even telling me."

Chapter 10

He ran his hands over his face again, looking haggard and grim. "I've never told anyone that before. Besides Sam and Mace, I mean."

Stunned, she could only stare for a moment, searching for words. A raw ache tore through her body. She wanted to hold him, comfort him, but that seemed such a small, insignificant gesture in the wake of what he'd revealed. "How? Why?"

For a moment, he looked uncertain, regretful that he'd even mentioned it. He jammed his hands in his pockets and stared fixedly at a point on the floor. "It was after the separation. I didn't even know she was pregnant and then one day, at the hospital, I heard some nurses talking about it. At first, I just assumed it was Mike's baby, so I confronted her, wanted to know how long she'd been carrying the...child—" His voice broke. "And that's when she told me. She didn't want to start her new life with Mike carrying any baggage from me."

"Oh, Linc." Horrified, Jenna pressed her knuckles to her mouth to keep from crying out at the sheer agony of hearing it. She couldn't imagine feeling it firsthand. "That day in the barn?"

"Yes, I'd just found out. When Michelle left, it hurt my ego more than anything else. But learning about the baby…"

How could a person be so cruel? Jenna could hardly take it in.

"It was years ago. I guess I should move on."

"Don't!" she cried, reaching for his hand. "Don't diminish it. You were devastated. You had a right."

"Did I?" He looked genuinely uncertain. "I felt betrayed, still do, but it wasn't as if the child was ripped from my body."

"That doesn't make your grief any less real. Oh, how can you doubt that? It's real, Linc, just as real as that baby was."

"Yes." He nodded slowly, searching her face as if seeking validation. "But I still always wondered, was it my fault about the baby? Is that why she—"

"No! You didn't force her to take an innocent life," Jenna protested vehemently. Those deep scars echoed in his voice and she ached at the pain he'd endured. "She made the choice to hurt you that way. In a way, what Michelle did to you is exactly what Ramsey did to me."

"It's not the same at all!" Aghast, Linc stared at her, his eyes stormy with disquiet. "Ramsey took your body, your innocence, your trust."

"And Michelle took part of *you,* your trust."

Linc shook his head. "I wasn't comparing, Jenna. I don't—"

"Linc." She laid her hand on his arm. "This is why you seem to understand me so well. You *really* understand."

Now she knew why she shared such an unfathomable connection to him, how he always seemed to know exactly how far to push her, when to retreat.

Relief flickered through his eyes. "It feels good to tell someone." His gaze caressed her features. "*You.* It feels good to tell *you.* After everything you've been through, there's this part of you that hasn't been touched, that refuses to be bitter or cynical. You see the best in people, want to help.''

"You're talking about me again," she reminded dryly, uncomfortable with the praise.

"It's true." He hesitated, then looking into her eyes, his hand gently grazed the swell of her right breast.

Her heartbeat jumped and anticipation shot straight through her. Still, she stiffened.

He dropped his hand immediately, though his gaze never left hers. "There's a solid core of steel in you, Jenna West, right there. It can't be destroyed by anything that Ramsey may do."

At the faith, the conviction in his voice, tears stung her eyes. "No one's ever said anything like that to me before."

"I don't know why. It's true."

She shook her head and he caught her chin gently between his thumb and forefinger. "It is."

His gaze traced her features, tender affection in his eyes.

"No matter what happens, you always keep going. You're more concerned about me than yourself—"

She opened her mouth to protest.

"You have every right to lash out at the people around you, yet you don't."

"I did earlier," she reminded with a grimace.

"Hush," he said with a soft fierceness. "You're concerned about how other people are doing when your whole world has been shaken up. Like Steve's wedding or your sister's twins or your patients. Or me. Most people would want everyone's attention on them."

She squirmed, her gaze falling to the hollow in his neck and riveting on the steady tap of his pulse under the skin. "You're embarrassing me."

"I don't mean to, but you *are* amazing, Jenna." He lowered his hand, shoved it into his pocket as he shrugged self-consciously. "I just wanted you to know."

A stilted silence grew between them. Eager to ease the

moment, she grinned. "I think I should keep you around for confidence building."

But he didn't smile, didn't attempt to make light of what he'd said.

Helplessly, her gaze rose to his. Drawn in by the heat, the sweet caring in his eyes, Jenna said softly, "I think you're pretty amazing, too."

"Amazing enough to kiss?" he asked huskily.

Though slightly surprised, she *wanted* him and at that moment, she refused to allow herself the thought that she couldn't have him. "Yes."

Pleasure lit his gray eyes. He smiled and bent his head, his lips brushing hers gently.

She opened to him, aching to feel the rough velvet of his tongue against hers.

He shifted, his chest pressing against her breasts, one hand sliding gently into her hair. Changing the angle of his head, he deepened the kiss, setting off a firestorm in her blood. Desire, stark and desperate like she'd never felt, ripped through her. She wanted to follow the lure of this tempting fire, explore the heavy throb that began between her legs.

Her good arm looped around his neck, straining to draw him closer, feel his heat merge with hers. His broad chest cushioned hers. Safe, gentle strength surrounded her and inside a wild, unfamiliar recklessness broke free.

He drew away briefly, enabling her to take a breath and she followed him, seeking his touch like a bud searching for nourishment from the rain. His lips found hers again, then his tongue slipped inside her mouth, hot and sleek and wet. Lust coiled tightly in her belly, beaded her nipples into sensitive points. On some distant plane, she realized she had never responded to a man like this. Never. And she wasn't afraid.

Her senses focused on now, here, Linc. His musky heat webbed around her. His hand glided gently over her cheek, then slid under her hair to cradle her nape. She leaned into him, reaching for more of the energy that flamed through her.

She wanted him, wanted to feel his bare skin next to hers, wanted to forget.

His palm brushed her breast. She froze, her breath wedging painfully in her chest. Desire jumbled with prudence; wariness roared up inside her.

He waited, his lips on hers, coaxing the resistance out of her body. She wanted to know what his touch would feel like, but the old caution held her back. Still, he didn't move, but simply waited on her. For her. She relaxed, silently surrendering to him.

His left arm slanted carefully across her back, drawing her to him so that her injured arm was protected. He kissed her again, teasing her lips with small nibbles, igniting a low throb between her legs. Then his hand squeezed her breast, gently, reverently and her nipple beaded against his palm.

She couldn't breathe. She could only exist on a plane of heightened sensation that went beyond desire, beyond reality. Her soul fused to his. Knowing that it was because of shared pain didn't dim the exhilaration skimming through her.

A vivid spectrum of color opened up before her and she gave herself over to the taste of him, the weight of his hand on her breast, the quickening thrum of his heartbeat against her.

Her tongue touched his shyly at first, then with more daring. His arm across her back tightened and he pulled her into him, the ridge of his desire hard and insistent against her hip. She felt no revulsion, only curiosity and an aching anticipation.

Then his hand skimmed over her jean-clad hip and slid between her legs. The touch ignited every fear she'd carried since the rape.

Reflexively she jerked away from him, breathing hard, fighting the horror that rose up in her. This was Linc. He wouldn't hurt her, wouldn't do anything she didn't want.

She knew it, yet she couldn't stop trembling. Blood that

had burned only seconds ago now congealed in cold apprehension. "I...can't. I can't. I can't."

"Jenna, it's okay." Linc's quiet voice shook. "It's okay."

He didn't reach for her, just tried to calm her with his eyes. Those beautiful eyes that had looked at her with such desire, such gentleness. Now they were reassuring, concerned. Still she glimpsed something sharp behind the concern. Pain. Pain she'd inflicted.

Regret swelled in her throat. "I'm so sorry," she cried. "I knew I couldn't do this. I knew I would hurt you."

"Stop. You didn't. Yes, I want you, but I'm willing to wait—"

"Oh, no!" Tears stung her eyes and panic flooded her. "Please don't, Linc. Please don't wait for me."

"I don't know that I have a choice anymore, Jenna." His hoarse words seemed to surprise him as much as they did her.

She stared into his eyes, hurt rippling through her as she wished she was different, *whole,* wished she was ready to give herself. But she wasn't. She couldn't.

She was a coward, but she couldn't bring herself to say the words, to again warn him off and spoil what they'd just shared. Feeling battered and bruised and weak from today's events, Jenna stared into his eyes, knowing she could never be exactly what he wanted. And he knew, too. The knowledge hung between them, sharp in the brittle light of his eyes.

"I think—" She drew in a deep breath, struggling to control the huskiness in her voice, the trembling in her legs. "I'll go to bed now."

Desire flared in his eyes, and, before he could mask it, dark rejection. Jenna bit her lip, cursing her stupid choice of words.

On rubbery legs, she stepped around him and walked toward the hallway. Agony clawed through her. She couldn't bring herself to again tell him this would go nowhere, that he couldn't change the way she was.

She had tried not to lean on him, but he was there, solid,

strong, dependable, easing past all her defenses, making her doubt everything she knew about herself, her buried sexuality.

No matter how she fought getting closer to him, it was happening. She had the sudden feeling that they were…inevitable. And, like Ramsey, she had no control over that, either. At the realization, she expected to feel panic, but she didn't.

She and Linc shared a bond she'd never expected, forged by cruelty and violation. She already felt more intimately connected to him than she ever had to any other man. And still she couldn't give herself to him.

At the thought, a sense of helplessness and loss welled up inside her.

He was knotted up tighter than bad catgut. Even the next afternoon, Linc could still feel the seductive heat of Jenna's mouth, the weight of her breast in his hand, the absolute trust she'd given him. They'd come together out of shared pain, a tragic understanding, yet that kiss had shredded his control. Desire axed his middle and he drew in a deep steadying breath.

He sat in the living room on the love seat, one ankle across his knee, the paper spread over his lap. He was still on the same sports page he'd been on for the last half hour. Once again, his attention wandered to Jenna, who sat outside on the enclosed porch.

He couldn't believe he'd told her about Michelle and the baby. He'd never shared that pain with anyone outside his family. He wore it close like a badge, protected it, buried it and a part of him wanted it to stay buried.

He'd expected to sleep poorly last night, haunted by the images of the past, but he'd slept soundly. An unexpected release had come after telling Jenna. And with her total acceptance. Relief that had eluded him for four hellish years now seemed his due.

Sunlight flowed into the room and the dogs stretched lazily

in the sun, sprawled in a line between him and the French doors, which she'd left open. She had pulled away from him last night, but there had been no revulsion in her eyes, no horror. Instead, they had been startled and dark with uncertainty and fading desire. Linc focused on that.

She was starting to come around. Once again he recalled the satin stroke of her tongue against his, her soft curves melting over him.

He hardened in a surge of lust and shifted on the small sofa. She'd enjoyed that kiss and his touch, until he'd gone too far.

They had eaten lunch in relative silence. All day she'd been quiet and distant and Linc had silently acknowledged her boundaries.

Fine. He'd tried to steer clear of her, even though it was driving him stark raving mad. From where he sat, he could hear the grate of the glider every time she moved, the crackle of paper as she turned the pages of the book she read. If he looked up, he could see the back of her head, her hair bathed in sunlight, warm with distinct shades of chestnut and red, a flicker of gold.

She wore another of his shirts today and the green fabric slid off her shoulder, baring velvety skin bronzed by the sun.

He ached to go out there, put his hands under that shirt and cup her breasts, kiss them and taste them until she moaned with need for him. He wanted to slowly peel those shorts from her body and sink into the sweet, tight heat of her.

If he got any closer to her, he might try to kiss her. She didn't need that today, not after the way she'd left things last night.

She seemed to be holding it together quite well. Though pale, she was getting stronger every day. She didn't jump as frequently at sudden noises, but he noticed the tight set of her shoulders and wondered if that was due to Ramsey or what had happened between the two of them last night.

As large as the living room was, he felt chained to the

space, unable to move, to breathe. The walls pressed in on him. In a surge of impatience and sexual frustration, Linc rose, dropped the newspaper to the floor and went into the kitchen to call Mace.

A few minutes later, he walked to the open French doors and stood looking down at the top of Jenna's head. Sunlight flowed over her, making the cast stark white against the glow of her skin. His gaze moved over her strong, capable hands and his body tightened.

Her hand stilled on the book, which lay facedown in her lap, and she slowly looked up at him. So, she hadn't been reading after all. He wondered if she was as aware of him as he was of her. He ached to touch her hair, to gather her to him and finish what they'd started last night, but that wasn't what she needed.

Despite the churning turmoil of his hormones, he wasn't sure he needed it right now either. "I just talked to Mace and—"

She sucked in a breath, fear and expectation dilating her eyes. "Has he—"

"Sorry." Linc cursed himself. Of course she would assume he had news of Ramsey. "No news. I just wanted to tell you that I'm going to the hospital for a couple of hours and Mace thinks that will be fine, if you're okay with it."

She tried to hide the disappointment on her face, but Linc saw the bleakness cloud her eyes.

"I'm sorry," he said again, feeling inept and clumsy. "I didn't mean to make you think I had news."

She shook her head and rose from the chair, closing her book and gripping it in her good hand. "I'm sure I'll be fine. I have the dogs."

"And the phone if you need it."

She nodded.

"You have my number at the hospital?"

"It's in the kitchen, by the phone?"

"Yes." He studied her, trying to probe past the serenity of

her features, wondering if her emotions were as jumbled as his. "I won't be long."

"It's all right. I'm sure you have things to do. I don't expect you to stay with me all the time."

"I can go later or—"

"No, go!" She smiled slightly. "I'll be fine. You shouldn't have to stay cooped up like I do. It's been nice out here on the porch. It will be good for you to get out."

He nodded, studying her face. She didn't seem eager to see him go, but neither did she seem to mind the idea. He turned to leave. "When I get back, we'll go to your house. Unless you want me to go by there and get some things for you."

"No, I'd like to go."

"All right." He stepped back into the house, then paused, his hand on the door frame. "Jenna, if you need it, I have a gun in my bureau drawer. Top right."

Protest flared in her eyes. "I'm sure I'll be fine."

"Just in case," Linc said quietly, wishing he hadn't needed to mention it. Wishing this whole thing was over.

Torture ravaged her eyes and he very nearly hauled her to him. But she firmed her lips and nodded. "Just in case."

He pulled out of the driveway feeling at once a strange release and a heavy pressure on his chest. How could he be both relieved and reluctant to leave her? He didn't know, but he was.

Just in case. Jenna hated those words. Hated the apprehension, the anxiety they triggered. Hated the fear that lurked inside her ready to explode at the slightest noise, the slightest disturbance.

She sank back down in the glider, hearing Linc's truck engine fade into the distance. Knowing he had a gun within her reach was slightly reassuring. Remembering her response to him was not.

He wanted her, wanted to wait for her to change her mind, to let him convince her she wasn't frigid. She'd thought of nothing else last night or today. Her body thrummed with unanswered want. Desire now coursed through her like blood, so much a part of her that she wondered if it would ever fade away.

It was the first passion she'd felt in years and a deep, secret core of her hoped it always lingered. Yet, it was a living, active torture, bubbling through her, reminding her that she couldn't—*or wouldn't*—reach out and take the promise of passion that Linc offered. She was too bound by fear.

Resentment and apprehension crowded through her, but those feelings weren't directed toward Linc. She'd wanted that kiss, still did and he'd stopped when she'd asked.

Linc was responsible only for the gnawing ache in her belly, the denied hunger that shadowed her every thought, but he wasn't to blame for the anxiety. That was due to Ramsey. He was getting to her, just like he wanted.

Linc was her sole support, the one person from whom she hadn't been cut off. If she surrendered to the craving of her body and slept with him, it would be a total disaster. And he would withdraw from her. Maybe out of embarrassment, maybe out of shame or even anger. It didn't matter.

What mattered was that he would be emotionally distant. If she lost Linc's support, she would unravel. And Ramsey would win.

Linc hated seeing that hope flare in Jenna's eyes when she'd thought he was going to tell her that Mace had some news about Ramsey. But she'd quickly masked her disappointment.

His body burned to possess her, to sink into her, but he'd promised to wait.

They both needed some distance. At least he did. Needed some place away from her to sort out his jumbled emotions of arousal and hope. Of arousal and concern. Arousal and caution.

So he'd left for the hospital. Walking through the double

doors, Linc expected to feel the familiar rush of adrenaline, the urgency that had always coiled within him.

Instead, he felt...disoriented, as if he'd stepped into a world that was foreign, unfamiliar. As people streamed around him, his gaze scanned over the churning mass of waiting patients, orderlies, nurses and doctors scurrying through the emergency room.

What he knew as organized motion, choreographed to the split second, now looked like chaos and madness. He'd been gone too long, he decided, waving at Bridget Farrell as he walked past the nurses' station and headed for the doctors' lounge. He'd catch up on some charts, dictate some reports. That should take his mind off Jenna.

But half an hour later, he sat at a sturdy wooden desk, hunched over a chart reliving that kiss last night, still hearing her hopeless words. Instead of focusing on the medical report in front of him detailing a follow-up visit on an emergency tracheotomy he'd performed, he wondered what she was doing. Wondered if he should call her and check in.

He tossed the pen onto the slick wood and leaned back in the chair, shoving a hand through his hair. Why couldn't he stop thinking of her? Yes, he wanted her, more desperately than he could ever remember wanting any other woman, but his interest in her went deeper than physical, despite all his attempts to keep her at a distance. Despite all *her* attempts to keep *him* at arm's length.

He wanted to protect her, encourage her, convince her to accept herself as the woman he saw—sexy, courageous, *responsive*. The heat, the eagerness with which she'd returned his kiss last night encouraged him to believe he would be able to change her views, but it would take time. Time he was now willing to spend.

Even though Linc knew Jenna was nothing like Michelle, he still didn't know if he was capable of giving her what she needed. But he wanted to try. For the first time since his wife had destroyed his world, Linc wanted to take a chance.

And it scared him to death.

Shoving away the thoughts, he picked up the phone on the corner of the desk and pulled a piece of paper out of his jeans pocket. He didn't want to call Steve Majors, but he'd promised, so he dialed the number.

The vet picked it up on the third ring. "Yeah, Dr. Majors."

"Steve, it's Linc Garrett."

The other man's voice immediately deepened with concern. "How is she?"

"She's fine, but—"

"What is it?"

"She saw Ramsey a few days ago."

"What!"

Quickly Linc explained about the cemetery, then the clinic.

Rage vibrated in her friend's voice. "Why are you just now calling?"

"This is really the first chance I've had. We got home from the clinic rather late." He wasn't even annoyed at Majors's demanding questions. He knew exactly how helpless and furious Jenna's friend felt about Ramsey's machinations. "We stopped by the police station so she could give a statement."

"How is she? Really."

"She's fine now. I was a little worried about her last night." Strangely Linc found it comforting to talk to someone who cared about her as much as he did.

"Where is she now?"

"She's at the house."

"I'm going out there."

"It's not necessary." Linc's protest stemmed, strangely enough, from the sense that Jenna needed some time to herself, friend or no friend.

Finally he managed to convince Majors that Jenna was indeed fine and, only after Linc promised to have her call, did the veterinarian calm down.

After hanging up, Linc tried again to concentrate on his charts, but restless energy pumped through him. Instead of seeing the procedure detailed in front of him, he saw Jenna's eyes, dusky with passion. As he scribbled his name on the bottom of a chart, he recalled the feel of her sweet, hot mouth.

He felt as if something inside him had been knocked loose and was only now sliding back into place. Was it only due to telling her about the baby?

Maybe he should keep his distance, wait for her to make a move, but it seemed every time he was with her, his good intentions dissolved like ashes in the rain.

All the things he'd said were true. He wanted her, wanted to be the man who changed her view of herself, but was he the *right* man? He was only now unchaining himself from the innate distrust spawned by his ex-wife, the wariness that had taken root in him after he'd learned about the baby.

Michelle's betrayal had radiated like a black, toxic cloud through his soul, strangling everything in him that cared about or gave to another person. The resulting wound had hardened into a shell that curbed any softer feelings, any sign of vulnerability, but Jenna had somehow managed to penetrate that wall of scars and betrayed trust and resentment.

Before he'd brought her home with him, his soul had been empty and hollow and charred. Now warmth flickered there, a glow he couldn't explain and that he'd thought never to feel again. A vitality, a stirring belief that he could make a difference in her life, that they could change each other's lives.

She even made him want to consider private practice. Somehow opening up to her made him feel capable, once again, of giving to a patient, of really connecting, not just treating them.

Linc hadn't felt so empowered since medical school and though it was in a slightly different vein, the sense was just as affecting, just as profound.

He wanted a chance with her for a future. He couldn't allow her to just walk out of his life when this was over.

He'd hoped that she felt the same, but he was starting to

believe her when she told him things would never be any different between them.

No amount of persuasion or seduction on Linc's part could make her feel what she didn't feel, believe what she thought was impossible. And with every part of him, he hated that fact.

Nervous and edgy, she sat in the chair on the porch for what could've been hours. She was alone, truly alone for the first time since the attack. At first, it felt treacherous, as if she'd stepped onto shifting rock. Then the silence wrapped around her. The tension and anxiety that had gripped her like a vise slowly eased.

She wanted to go outside like a normal person, but ingrained caution held her back.

Restlessness and defiance charged through her. She opened the door and stepped outside, her bare feet sinking into thick green grass. The dogs raced past her, stretching their lean muscles as they loped toward the border of trees.

Glorious freedom beckoned to her. Birds warbled in the trees, spiraled overhead in a glass blue sky. She could hear the uneven cheep of crickets. The dogs crisscrossed through the expansive backyard, stopping here and there to sniff the grass or lift their heads to the wind.

She tilted her face to the warmth of the sun. She wanted to shed every inhibition, run through the grass, get lost in the woods, but she wouldn't be so rash. She walked into the yard and stopped on a small downward slope several feet away from a wrought iron bench that sat beneath a leafy redbud tree.

Seized by a fierce impulse, she lay down on the ground, shading her eyes with her good arm and resting her cast on her stomach. Grass prickled her shoulder blades through the fabric of Linc's shirt. The scent of fresh grass rose around her, mixed with the lemon of her shampoo and the dark spice that was Linc. She could still taste the heat of his mouth last night, the dark wine of his hunger that unleashed the same in her.

She closed her eyes, holding the memory close, wanting to savor it without trepidation, without the niggle of fear that always attached itself. The sun's warmth soaked into her. Clean, fresh air brushed her face.

The dogs bounded up, their paws rustling through the grass. They rooted noisily around in the grass next to her, then the three of them chose a spot and stretched out beside her.

Puppy laid his head carefully on her belly and she opened her eyes to find his dark ones on her, steady and calm, as if to say, *See, I'm here. I never left.*

She lay there for several long minutes, relishing the warmth, the open space, the scents of bruised grass and fallow earth, the odor of dirt and dog. Slowly, her nerves settled. Things shifted back into perspective. She could do this. She could hang in there until the police caught Ramsey.

And what about Linc? a little voice whispered. Jenna tried to dodge the thought. She'd already told Linc how things were. She couldn't force him to believe it. And when this was over, he would have his life back. She would have hers.

After being with him, her old life seemed dull and tedious. But it wasn't, she told herself. It wasn't.

Her body now craved more of the passion he'd shown her, ached to try physical intimacy with him. But her head—and her heart—knew things couldn't be any different for her.

It wasn't just the rape. She could probably get past that physical trauma. But even before the rape, she hadn't been that comfortable with intimacy. Her first attempt at sex had been awkward and painful. She'd attributed it to her inexperience and that of her college boyfriend. But even with Steve, who'd been gentle and wonderful and giving, she'd failed. She couldn't bear to fail with Linc.

She squeezed her eyes tight against a burn of tears. She couldn't risk intimacy with him. She couldn't. Because she wasn't brave enough to risk failing. Or losing the piece of himself he'd given her.

She was grateful to him for giving them this time apart. She'd needed some space to right her world, to decipher what was real and what wasn't.

Ramsey was real. Being with Linc was just a temporary dream, a visit to her imagination where anything was possible.

She rose and walked back to the house. The dogs stretched, then padded along behind her. She moved through the enclosed porch and stepped into the living room, blinking to adjust to the dimmer light.

A flash of movement from the kitchen caught her eye and she froze, staring hard at the doorway. She heard a noise.

Linc? She opened her mouth to call out and suddenly the dogs, entering the house, went wild. They bolted across the living area and into the kitchen, barking shrilly, frantically, without pause. The sound swelled through the house, piercing, deafening and Jenna winced as it bounced around the room.

Just as the dogs reached the doorway, a man appeared there. *Ramsey!*

Even though she couldn't see the man's features, it was her first thought.

Her blood froze even as the dogs leapt into the air. The man cried out, put up an arm to defend himself and the dogs tackled him like an opposing lineman. He fell to the floor in a head-cracking thud.

Chapter 11

Immobilized, Jenna stared, her stunned mind moving sluggishly. The gun. The gun. What had Linc said about the gun?

The dogs barked ceaselessly, viciously. The man's shouts tangled with the shrill noise until she couldn't tell human from animal.

Finally, the muscles in her legs unlocked and she raced for Linc's bedroom, holding her cast against her ribs. She yanked open the top right bureau drawer with her left hand and reached for the gun.

Her trembling hand closed over the sleek metal grip and she pulled out the short-barreled weapon. She checked the safety, saw it was on even as she wheeled back out of the room. The dogs' barking grew more frenetic. Now, she couldn't hear the man at all.

As she neared the kitchen, she saw him still on the floor.

It wasn't Ramsey. At the sight of the lean, lankier body build, relief shuddered through her, though she didn't know the man. Long legs were wrapped in faded denim, one outstretched, the other bent at the knee with his foot braced against the floor. He spoke softly, soothingly to the dogs.

She moved around him and into the kitchen, leveling the gun at him as she reached for the phone. Her hand shook and the gun wobbled as she aimed at his chest.

"Dr. West?"

At the sound of her name, fresh panic sliced through her.

How did he know her name? Had Ramsey sent him? Fighting off the hysteria that reached for her, she stared through the sight at him, registering dully his dark, thick hair and a few days' growth of beard.

"Dr. West. Please."

She then became aware that Puppy was the only one still growling. The shepherds lay on either side of the man, licking his face ecstatically and wagging their tails. Puppy had planted both huge front paws on the man's torso, snarling viciously every time the guy so much as breathed.

Operating on pure adrenaline, Jenna struggled to register the scene in front of her. She knew the man wasn't Ramsey, but who was he?

Still holding the phone, she inched forward for a better look, keeping the gun trained on him.

He stared up at her, blue eyes wary and grim, looking unexpectedly familiar.

"Ohmygosh." Her breath whooshed out and she slammed down the phone. "Back, Puppy!"

Immediately the massive animal stepped away and sat back on his haunches, still baring his teeth.

Swamped by anger and a knee-wobbling relief, Jenna's eyes narrowed. "You're Linc's other brother, aren't you?"

"Almost the *late* Garrett brother, it appears," the man drawled. With a wary eye on Puppy, he slowly pushed himself to a sitting position, resting one wrist over his bent knee. "And you're Dr. West."

She nodded. It wasn't Ramsey. Only Sam Garrett. The glint

of a police badge clipped to his waist did little to ease the tension lashing her shoulders. Or to diminish her earlier panic and surprise. "You should've called out or something," she snapped. "I was ready to shoot you."

"I did call out," he said evenly, his eyes darkening to indigo. "Got no answer. I had begun to think you'd left with Linc."

She hadn't heard because she'd been in the backyard. If he had been Ramsey, she would be at his mercy now. Her hand shook and nausea rolled through her. "Oh."

He nodded warily toward the gun. "Why don't you put that down now?"

"Oh. Yes." Aware that she still held the gun on him, she quickly placed it on the kitchen counter. Her heart still pounded wildly and cold sweat slicked her palms. "You startled me. I don't like that."

"I'm sorry." Keeping his hands in front of him, he rose slowly, letting her see his every move. "I guess I should've phoned."

"Yes, you should have."

He straightened to his full height, just a shade taller than Linc and peered closely at her. Where Linc's eyes were that beautiful smoke gray, Sam's were blue. As deep blue as cobalt and narrowed on her like steel as he took her measure.

Then a beautiful smile spread across his unshaven features, showcasing strength and a sultry sensuality that was apparent even to her. His eyes crinkled at the corners as he extended a large hand toward her. "Let's do this properly, Dr. West. I'm Sam Garrett. You should leave my brother and run away with me."

Jenna blinked.

"*That* is never gonna happen." Linc's voice boomed from the garage door opposite the breakfast nook, startling both Jenna and Sam.

Sam grinned and she turned, her heartbeat stuttering as she

took in Linc's wind-ruffled hair and the heated concern in his eyes.

Though she hadn't been frightened since recognizing Sam, only now did she feel secure.

"I see you two have met." Linc closed the door and stepped into the kitchen.

"Most memorably," Sam muttered, glancing at the gun before returning his warm gaze to Jenna.

Linc's gaze lit on the gun, then slid to Jenna. He raised an eyebrow.

She shrugged, tamping down her irritation. She had been ready to shoot Sam and he was acting as if they'd met at a party! "I didn't know he was coming."

"I didn't, either." With loose-hipped grace, Linc strode over to the center island and stopped beside his brother.

Sam dragged his attention from Jenna, half turning toward Linc. The butt end of a gun protruded from the back waistband of his jeans. "Mace said you had to go to the hospital and he was concerned about Jenna being alone. I wasn't busy, so I told him I'd come out."

"Glad you did." Linc clapped his brother on the back, then walked around him to stand next to Jenna. "You okay?"

"Yes, now." She wasn't quite ready to forgive the youngest Garrett for scaring her out of her skin.

"I really am sorry for startling you like that."

She nodded, still regarding him warily. "It's all right. I'm just glad you're a friend."

Linc nodded and clasped his brother's hand. "Keep your charm to yourself. She's not interested."

"Says you." Sam grinned cockily, revealing dimples deeper than Mace's and Linc's. "Why does my serious, stuffy *older* brother get all the good-looking women? It's the medical degree, right?"

She found herself smiling at their banter. Sam *was* a charmer, she admitted, not feeling in the least threatened. Perhaps it was only because Linc had told her about Sam's recent losses, but Jenna thought his eyes seemed haunted behind that devilish glint.

Touched by the deep affection between the two men, the last of her tension drained away and she forgave Sam for scaring the life out of her.

A sudden urgency stormed through her. Watching Linc with his brother made her ache to be more than his patient, more than a woman he had helped because he owed her. He'd told her she was more than that to him, but how could she be more?

This sensual awareness, the thawing of her most feminine senses tempted her to accept Linc's challenge, to make love with him, but she couldn't forget the ugly reality that lurked just beyond his doors. Ramsey would never let her forget.

She drank in the sight of Linc's strong features, his fatigued smile as he spoke to his brother. With rising frustration and self-disgust, Jenna reminded herself she couldn't even find the courage to explore the physical attraction between them, the sense of completeness and belonging he stirred in her.

Again she remembered the fierce heat of his passion, the gentleness of his kiss and a bleak realization settled over her. For the first time, she couldn't imagine the rest of her life without Linc, but she had no right to him. She was still married to the past.

She tore her gaze from Linc and moved out of the kitchen. "I'll let you two talk."

Feeling his watchful gaze on her back, she headed for her bedroom. When this was all over, where would they be? Afraid to think the worst, not daring to hope for the best, she walked down the darkened hallway, torn between fierce longing and brutal experience.

Sam walked to the kitchen door, watching Jenna thoughtfully as she disappeared down the hallway leading to her room. He turned back to Linc. "Mace caught me up on what's going on. How's she doing?"

"Considering what Ramsey's doing to her, pretty good, I think." Linc took in his brother's dark, stubbled jaw, the red-rimmed blue eyes, the wrinkled T-shirt and grimy jeans. "How are *you* doing? You look terrible."

"Thanks," Sam replied, planting his palms flat on the counter tile of the center island. "I was going for that nineties grunge look."

"Really, Sam. Are you still seeing the department shrink?"

His brother shrugged in that all too familiar dismissive gesture that meant he'd rather talk about his sex life to their parents, Cliff and Bonnie. "I think I've come to terms with Brad's death."

"What about Dallas? Have you heard from her—"

"No." Sam's jaw snapped shut on the word, making it clear he didn't want to discuss his partner's widow, either.

Linc distinguished the pain beneath his brother's acid retort and wondered for the hundredth time what had happened to the heretofore good friendship between his brother and Dallas Kittridge. Whether it had been Brad's death or Dallas's leaving, something of Sam had gone, too. He had never told Linc or Mace.

Linc could respect that. He'd waited over two years before he'd told either of them about the baby.

Sam eyed Linc with lazy cunning. "Have you told Jenna about Michelle?"

Linc's gaze sliced to him. "Why would I—"

"It's obvious she's more than your patient." Sam cocked an eyebrow. "So, have you?"

Linc's gaze went thoughtfully to the empty doorway. "Yes."

"Is that right?" Sam's voice brimmed with pleased disbelief.

"Don't choke on those feathers in your mouth," Linc growled, slanting him a look.

"Well, you've never told anyone else."

"I know."

Sam's grin slipped slightly. "And you've told her about the baby?"

"Yes."

"Wow."

Strangely, Linc's thoughts of the baby didn't knife through him with their usual razor-edge. The pain had dulled and again he was glad he'd shared it with Jenna.

At Linc's admission, Sam turned serious. "You're really falling for her, aren't you?"

"Yeah." He exhaled loudly. "She's just not falling for me."

"Don't tell me you're losing your touch, big brother."

"I haven't had a 'touch' for years," Linc reminded sardonically.

"You're not the only one who's lost it," Sam muttered.

"What's that?" Linc looked closely at him.

His brother chuckled. "It'll come back to you. It's like sex—"

"Jenna's different."

"Yeah, I can tell." Sam nailed him with a steely look. "So, what are you going to do about it?"

Linc snorted. "What do you mean?"

"I mean, tell her. Don't screw around about it, either." Something like regret shaded Sam's voice. He sounded as if he knew from experience and Linc frowned.

Sam straightened, his eyes earnest. "Mace will get Ramsey, Linc. Don't wait until then to let her know how you feel."

Linc rubbed his neck, wondering exactly what his feelings were for Jenna. Oh, he knew he wanted her. And trusted her. But beyond that? "I'll be glad when the whole thing's over. I hate what he's doing to her."

Sam nodded, walked to the kitchen doorway and called out, "Goodbye, Jenna! It was nice to meet you."

"Goodbye." She appeared in the entryway, holding a

brush in her good hand, reminding Linc that they still needed to drop by her house and pick up a few things.

"I'm ready if you are," he said, then turned to Sam to explain their plan.

"Want me to come along?" Sam asked.

Linc slanted a glance at Jenna, taking in her composed features, her beautiful eyes. "Nah, we'll be fine."

She nodded imperceptibly, smiling at Sam. "Thanks, though."

"No problem." He grinned on his way out the door. "Hope to see you again soon."

Jenna didn't respond, but hope shot through Linc like a rocket flare. He didn't know exactly what he wanted, but he did know he wasn't ready for her to walk out of his life.

That cool logical side of his brain told him to wait until this was over before trying to pin her down about her feelings, but Linc had seen over the ten days how uncertain, how volatile life could be. Tomorrow couldn't be taken for granted, especially with someone as crazy as Ramsey thrown into the mix.

Linc didn't want to add to Jenna's pressures, but he wanted to know if she was at all interested in giving them a chance. Sam was right. It was time.

Indecision sawed at her and she toyed with the frayed hem of her denim shorts. What was she going to do? She could no longer deny the bond she and Linc shared. It was more than the pain of their separate traumas. It was a meeting of their hearts, their souls. And Jenna didn't want to turn away from that.

But how could she let herself believe in something that might never be? Ramsey's malice, his deliberate onslaught of her shriveled every hope of the future she had.

She slid a glance at Linc, wishing she could scoot across the bench seat and sit next to him. He'd been quiet for most of the drive, yet she sensed a restlessness in him. A couple of times she thought he'd been about to speak, but he hadn't.

The radio played softly in the background, and she found herself aching at the stroking melody of Conway Twitty's "Slow Hand." The chorus brought to mind Linc's patient treatment of her, the fragile web of seduction he'd slowly woven around her with his trust and gentleness and desire.

Thank goodness, Linc hadn't tried again to change her mind about being frigid. After that kiss last night, her body still thrummed with need, a low simmer that needed only a touch or a look from him to ignite the heat in her again. And tempt her to believe, to try, to risk.

She could no longer deny something strong and intense burned between them, but neither could she encourage it.

"Jenna?"

"Hmm?" She tried to pretend an interest in the passing landscape, the stop sign where Linc pulled up at Coltrane and Danforth, nearing her housing addition.

"I want a chance. For us." He spoke fervently, his eyes steely with intent. "When this is all over, I want a chance to convince you that things can work between us. That you can be different with me."

Her head whipped toward him. She should've guessed by his uneasiness, his nervousness that he was leading up to this, yet she hadn't. "Linc—"

"Say yes, Jenna. Say yes."

Not far away, a siren wailed. Behind them, a car honked and Linc turned right, heading south on Coltrane.

"Why won't you just let it go?" she asked tiredly, although a small finger of warmth worked through her at his determination. "When this is over, you'll want to be rid of me, move on with your life."

"When this is over, my life won't be the same and neither will yours." He reached over and squeezed her hand.

She couldn't deny that, nor could she seem to deny herself his touch.

As they neared the turn-in to her neighborhood, she glimpsed a billow of black smoke. Then the acrid odor filtered into the truck. "I don't know, Linc. I don't want to say no, but I don't see how I can say yes."

"Because of Ramsey?"

"Of course." The bitter odor of smoke grew stronger, tickling her throat.

"Is that all?" he asked tightly.

She gazed at him full on. "Are you asking if I still believe I'm frigid? I *am*, Linc."

"Well, I don't believe it." He slammed a palm against the steering wheel. "You couldn't have kissed me like that last night if—"

"Obviously, that's not the part I have trouble with," she said ruefully, her heart aching, wishing he would let the subject drop.

"You felt something." He hit the turn signal with force.

"You know I did." Her heart broke, not only for the frustration he must be feeling, but for the chance she was probably ruining right now. "Yes, I responded to your kiss, but what if that's all I can do? Even before the rape, I had no success with sex. I've never been that comfortable with it—"

"You *do* respond to me, Jenna. We can start there."

"But—"

"Give us a chance. When this is all over, let's try."

He turned down her street and the shrill scream of a siren startled both of them.

He spoke louder, slowing as they drove down her street. "I want the chance to convince you that this thing between us is stronger than the both of us, that together we can figure out how to make it work. I'm willing to take a chance if you are."

Astounded at his words, at the hope shining in his eyes, she looked at him for a long moment. Screeching horns and sirens clanged, deafeningly close, but she tried to keep her mind focused on Linc.

His fervent belief made her want to agree, to say whatever he wanted to hear and she found she couldn't deny him this time.

He squeezed her hand again, his eyes earnest. "Come on. What do you say?"

"It's not that I don't want to—" A puff of black smoke rolled across the hood and she turned, frowning out the windshield.

How close was that fire? The stench of smoke charred the air, overwhelming now. She stared in disbelief at the number of cars jammed onto her block. Fire engines, police cars, news vehicles from different local channels, and clots of people cluttered the street.

What was going on? What had— Dread hammered through her, aborting her thought. As Linc slowed the truck to a crawl, she had a perfect view between the corner of a fire truck and a news camera.

She couldn't breathe, wouldn't let herself think it, wouldn't even allow the possibility to skim through her mind. She completely forgot Linc's question, forgot everything.

Not my house. Please, not my house.

Hoses writhed, spewing water at the burning house. *Her* house. Yellow-coated firemen swarmed in *her* yard, flanking *her* house, wielding hoses like sabers, trying to battle the searing enemy at their head.

Linc choked out something in a harsh voice. He braked to a stop several houses away, as close as he could get. Jenna was out of the truck and running hard before he even killed the engine.

Moving on pure adrenaline, she elbowed her way through the crowd, smoke and heat stinging her eyes. Breaking free of the tight clump of bodies, she jumped the curb and tore across the yard, her shoes squishing in the muddy earth. She sprinted toward her house and straight into the arms of a husky fireman.

"No!" she screamed, struggling to escape his hold. "That's my house! That's my house!"

"I'm sorry, ma'am." He held her tight, his yellow coat smeared with grime, stinking of smoke. Dark compassionate eyes stared at her from behind a mask. "We're doing everything we can. It was blazing pretty good by the time we got here."

He moved her easily back to the curb and stood beside her, holding her by the arm. Riveted in horror, she couldn't tear her gaze away. Wicked flames spit and hurled out of her house, shattering glass, reaching out the windows to crawl like fingers across the walls, over the roof, curling paint and popping shingles as it moved.

Even from yards away, heat seared her cheeks, toasted her clothing. She was vaguely aware of water soaking through her shoes and she knew she stood in deep puddles of filthy hydrant water. Her nerves seared into numbness. Pressure, tight and hot, built in her chest.

"How?" she asked numbly.

The fireman shook his head. "We don't know yet."

But she knew. *She knew.*

A slight wind picked up and buffeted her body. She stood there, heedless of soot and dirty water flying around her, splattering her clothing, raining down on her pristine cast like drops of blood. It might as well be her blood, she thought dully.

Ramsey was drawing it out drop by agonizing drop, stripping her of everything, everyone.

"You got her?" the fireman said.

"Yes."

Linc. Jenna recognized his voice and turned blindly toward it. The fireman released her and she stepped on wooden legs toward Linc. She looked into agonized, enraged eyes. "He burned my house. He burned...my house," she repeated in flat monosyllables. "My house."

They seemed to be the only words she knew, the only words that made sense.

Fury crested on his features. Tears glittered in his eyes and he pulled her to him. The sobs tore free then, exploding through her chest, pouring out of her with savage intensity. She couldn't get a breath, could only sob helplessly against Linc's hard chest.

His arms closed tight around her and she latched on to his strength with frightened desperation. He pressed her face into his chest, buried his face in her neck, and stood with her, enduring, supporting, constant.

"First and ten, do it again. First and ten, do it again." Deke chanted the words in a measured, slow rhythm, each one accompanying the blows he struck against the big man's body.

From the back room of Jenna's clinic, dogs bayed and howled, putting up a good, futile fuss at his presence. Deke studied the man who now lay on the floor.

Blood oozed from the guy's ear, from several places on his back and shoulders, seeping through the fabric of his work shirt.

Deke felt only blind rage, fueling each blow. He narrowed his eyes at the doctor, remembering the little message he'd left for Jenna at her house. Someone would've become aware of that by now. A burning house was hard to miss. Satisfaction curled through him. He was eliminating her possessions, her friends, her protection, one by one. Just like she had done to him.

Deke let his gaze wander around the back room of her clinic. He had finally realized she would have someone looking after her patients. The dogs had a clear view of him from the back room and had started a ruckus as soon as he'd entered.

Now their barking turned to vicious snarls. They pawed frantically at the doors on their cages, clanging steel and metal in an effort to get at him.

Their constant, deafening barks swelled in his head, causing his concentration to falter. "Shut up," he screamed.

For an instant, the dogs quieted, one emitting a tiny whimper as the noise died. He smirked, raised the bat again to hit this lanky cowboy veterinarian. The dogs exploded in a frenzy of sound and motion, bucking in agitation, scratching at the cages, the steel doors clattering like rocks on metal, jumbling with their shrill piercing barks.

"Shut up! Shut up!" Deke narrowed his eyes at the doctor on the floor. Blood matted in the man's auburn hair, splattered on Jenna West's clean white tile.

One down, two to go. The guy was big and had put up a good fight. Deke fingered his swollen jaw and busted nose, thinking that the guy looked vaguely familiar. Deke had a sense that he'd known him long ago. Maybe in college? *Before* his whole life had been ruined by Jenna West.

The rage crested again, blocking out everything except the triumph, the calculation. Deke had eliminated one more layer of protection from the wall around Jenna West. All that remained was to get that policeman and the other guy. If he hadn't missed his aim at the cemetery, the cop would already be gone, but it didn't matter. Deke always sacked his opponents.

Now that there was no longer anyone here to care for her animals, she'd be back. He was more than ready.

When he got his hands on Jenna West—

He grew hard, sliding his blood-speckled hand to his crotch. He was going to make her suffer, just like she'd done him all these years. Ah, when he got ahold of her, he was going to tear her up. He was going to strip her naked and—

The crunch of gravel speared through his fantasy and his head snapped up. Gripping the bat, he stepped to the front door and peered out the glass. Damn! A woman with a poodle climbed out of a gray station wagon.

Deke whirled, leapt over the doctor's motionless body and sprinted through the back room. Dogs yelped and snarled as he passed, clawing at their cages to get out. But they couldn't catch him. No one had ever been as fast as he was.

Exiting through the back emergency door, he darted into the small stable at the back of the clinic, disappeared into the shadows. "Ready or not, slut. Here I come."

There was nothing left. Jenna knew it deep inside herself, but couldn't make herself accept it. Surely there had to be a scrap of clothing, a shoe, even a lone photograph that had escaped. But the firemen said there had been nothing. Nothing.

She couldn't feel her heart beat. She couldn't even see where the foundation of her house had been.

Linc said she had minor burns on her arm from falling ash and flame. He gently rubbed salve over them, but she couldn't feel it.

Couldn't feel anything.

Ramsey had destroyed her home. And he wouldn't stop until he got her. Jenna didn't think she would even care now if he did. She couldn't seem to dredge up a single emotion.

She rode in Linc's truck, staring blankly out the window at the passing trees, fence posts, the mall, a church. She knew they were going to Linc's, knew this road was supposed to be familiar, but she recognized nothing.

Ramsey would never stop, never stop, never stop. Just when her nerves had settled from seeing that death certificate, he'd burned her home.

His vindictive acts were escalating. Mace said it was because his fury over not being able to find her was growing. Jenna only knew that each day notched the tension higher, sharper, tighter. Terror and dread ate like acid at her stomach, thinning her nerves like a razor on a strap.

The one steady, *safe* constant was Linc.

She didn't know how long he stood in front of her with his hand out before she realized they had reached his house and he was waiting for her.

Her eyes burned from soot and tears. She didn't care, had no desire to rub them and ease the burning sensation. She wanted to feel something, *anything*—loss, pain, fear. She felt nothing.

Linc held her close, not speaking and she didn't care about that, either. He led her into the house, closed the door behind them and looked at her.

Late afternoon light streamed through the French doors, striping his shirt, the tiles on the entryway floor. He guided her into the living area and stopped, staring at her as if he were lost, as if he didn't know what to do next.

"I want to help you, Jenna. I don't know what to do."

She looked up at him, seeing the torture in his gray eyes and thinking she should try to reassure him, but she couldn't. "I think I'm hungry," she said dully.

He led her to the love seat and eased her down into it, kneeling in front of her. "Jenna, this was horrible. You need to get mad, cry, something."

"I cried." She had, hadn't she? She thought she recalled tears on her face, soaking Linc's shirt.

Misery pinched his features. "You can't shut down like this."

She heard him, but there was nothing left in her to say. Something unfamiliar and dark twisted deep inside her, then disappeared.

He took her good hand in both of his and pressed a soft kiss to her knuckles. "I'm going to call Mace. Do you want to come with me?"

She shook her head, trying to understand why he would call Mace. It didn't matter, did it? Nothing did.

Linc stared at her with frustration, pain and raw fury in his eyes. He rose, then bent and kissed her forehead. "I'll be right back."

He moved out of view and she heard him behind her. Again that darkness moved through her, stronger this time and searing. She straightened, surprised to feel something, uncertain about what it was, uncomfortable with the force of it.

Without even realizing she'd moved, she found herself in the kitchen, opening the refrigerator. Linc, using the kitchen phone, frowned. His gaze followed her as she pulled out turkey and mayonnaise and placed them on the counter.

He kept his voice low as he spoke to Mace, his words clipped, the conversation short.

She reached up and opened an overhead cabinet, pulling down a plate. She stared at the white ceramic thickness and that blackness moved through her again, burning, clawing to volatile speeds inside her. The plate fell, shattering on the tile floor.

Fury. She recognized it now. Fury discharged inside her like a lit stick of dynamite. Just like the uncontained power of the blaze at her house.

Spurred by the rage, she reached for another plate and threw it to the floor. At the crash, something broke free inside her. Ceramic chips flew over her shoes, under the counter, across the floor.

Following the sensation of release growing inside her, she reached for another one. She was ready to slam it against the counter when her vision cleared. As if she'd stepped out of a black fugue, she realized what she'd done and a sharp pain jabbed under her ribs.

Shaking uncontrollably, tears streaming down her face, she stood hostage to a rage like she'd never experienced. She gripped the ceramic plate tightly and her gaze rose to find Linc staring gravely, apprehensively at her from his place by the phone.

She trembled harder. He hung up the phone and walked carefully toward her. Her gaze fell to the plate, realizing she'd destroyed his property without even the slightest thought. Driven by the fury exploding inside her, she had simply reacted.

"Oh, Linc I'm so sorry—"

"Do it," he said in a thick strangled voice.

"What?" She blinked at him.

He reached into the cabinet for another one. "Break them. Break all of them."

To punctuate his hoarse command, he sent one crashing to the floor.

We've both lost it. The thought flashed through Jenna's mind, then she hurled her plate to the floor.

She broke one; he broke another.

"I've always hated these plates," he growled.

With tears streaming down her face, she flung one at the floor, gratified when jagged bits of pottery rained over her hands, joined the growing pile of remains on the floor.

Linc dropped one from above his head, grinning like an idiot when it shattered at his feet.

They reached for the last one at the same time.

"You go ahead," he offered.

The last crash satisfied some dark wildness in Jenna, something she couldn't even begin to explain, but at last it released that tightness in her chest. Anger, frustration, fear—she felt it all in the span of a heartbeat.

It steamrollered through her and she began to laugh. At first it was hysterical, fueled by fear, by the realization of what Ramsey had done, how he was slowly, systematically eliminating everything she cherished.

Then rage boiled up again. Her laughter grew deeper, choked, then tears poured down her cheeks. Silent sobs wrenched through her, slamming home the fact that Ramsey was winning.

She stepped over the shattered pottery and walked straight into Linc's arms. "I'm sorry about the plates," she sobbed.

His arms closed around her and he sank down to the floor, cradling her in his lap. "Shhh. Just let go, Jenna. Just let go."

The fear broke free, snatching her breath and she tried to fight back with the raw fury that had erupted in her a few minutes ago.

She sobbed out every nightmare, every threat Ramsey had ever made against her. Her good arm tightened around Linc's waist and she buried her face in his chest. Linc was her reality. He wouldn't let anything happen to her.

She was tired of being afraid, tired of running from Linc, tired of cowering at every noise, tired of hiding.

Linc rocked her, cradling her so that her injured arm was protected. Her sobs calmed; the fury abated and a bone deep relief washed through her, cleansing, renewing. Still a ragged weariness clung to her.

Linc held her, crooning soothing words to her over and over. His arms were strong and solid and familiar around her. When his lips brushed against her hair, she swallowed hard, aching at his gentleness.

His lips slid over her temple, pressing a butterfly kiss there, then on her nose. Soothing, so gentle. Jenna snuggled closer to him, lifted her face.

His lips touched hers, lingered, tasting, comforting for a split second. Then he jerked back. "Sorry," he whispered.

"No." She raised her hand and pulled him down to her.

He resisted. "Jenna—"

"I need it, Linc. I need *you*."

Need and surprise flared in his eyes.

"Please," she whispered, lifting her face for his kiss, aching to taste him.

His lips covered hers and she opened, wanting to focus only on the warmth infusing her soul, burning away the pain, the fear, filling her with gentleness.

Linc gently sipped at her lips, coaxing her tongue to stroke along his, giving her soft, languid, deep soul-kisses that knotted her belly in a sleek knot. An unfamiliar impatience ignited within her.

She wanted to give to him as he gave to her, wanted to touch him. The kiss grew more hungry, more desperate. Restraint vibrated in his body. His arms corded with leashed power, yet he held her as if she were the most delicate surgical instrument.

She wanted him to shed those inhibitions. A reckless hunger rose inside her, drove her on with a lash of desperation. She wanted to know all of him, be a part of all of him.

His arousal nudged her and excitement zipped through her. Giving herself over to the pure sensual energy sluicing through her, she met his kisses, hot, openmouthed, feeling a new kind of heat low in her belly.

Her fingers floated over his face, stroking the smooth skin of his cheek, the slight whisker stubble on his strong jaw. She wanted him to touch her, wanted to feel his hand on her breast, his mouth there.

"Touch me," she whispered against his mouth.

She felt his jolt of surprise and then his knuckles brushed the swell of her breast as he loosened the buttons on her shirt.

Anticipation coiled through her. *Yes, yes,* she urged silently, drowning out the old voice of doubt.

His hand closed over her, warm and strong and slightly callused. Heat turned to liquid between her legs and she shifted, pressing her breast into his hand, seeking more contact with him.

He pulled his mouth from hers, tilted her head as he rained kisses over the corners of her lips, her cheek, her ear. His tongue dipped inside and a streamer of fire tingled down her arm.

She urged him on hoarsely, savoring the brush of his shirt against her bare breasts. Her breasts grew heavy; anticipation quickened her blood. She wanted his mouth on her.

He nipped and laved his way down her throat to the swell of her breasts and…halted.

"Linc?" Her voice was raw, foreign. She opened her eyes.

Desire sharpened his features. His eyes had darkened to metal gray. "I can't stop this time, Jenna. I want to make love with you."

"I want that, too," she whispered. "I don't want you to stop."

His eyes widened, disbelief and hope dilating the gray depths. "Are you sure?"

His hand still rested on her breast and she looked down, marveling at the bronze darkness of his hand next to the lighter color of her skin. In answer to his question, she covered his hand with hers and squeezed.

Embarrassment flushed her body, but it was far outweighed by the pleasure of his flesh on hers.

Heat burned in his eyes. Dull color crept up his neck and she could feel the restraint in his body, in the taut corded muscles of his arm beneath her back, his thighs cradling her.

"I want you, Linc. I'm tired of running in fear. I'm sick of…hiding, coping, surviving. I want to *live*. And I want to start with you."

Pleasure flared in his eyes, a joy so profound that she felt her heart squeeze painfully.

"How?"

"I thought you knew," she teased gently.

"Not that." He grinned crookedly. "I mean, do you want to be here? Or in my bed?" His voice deepened, flowing over her like rough velvet and sparking a fluttery sensation between her legs.

"In your bed," she said quickly, wanting to give herself totally to this man and everything that was his. Despite the apprehension that niggled at her, she wasn't going to change her mind. She trusted Linc, knew he would be gentle.

She thrust away the nagging doubt, the enemy of her mind that said it would be a disaster. For tonight, she refused to listen, refused to be a victim to any more doubts.

Chapter 12

He carried her to the bedroom and laid her gently on the side of his bed closest to the door. His eyes blazed into hers.

"Anytime you want to stop, tell me. If you don't like what's happening, we quit."

She nodded, sharp need battling a surge of uncertainty.

"I'll pull the drapes—"

"No," she said quickly. "I want to see you. I want…to see everything." Though she flushed at her boldness, she didn't look away from him.

Hot sexual need flared in his eyes and he nodded, walking slowly toward her. He pulled his shirt over his head and dropped it to the floor.

She drank in the sight of his taut stomach, the broad lean chest. The scars of past experience twinged, but she pushed away the fear, focused on here, now, with Linc.

He eased down on the bed beside her, toed off his boots, then peeled off his socks. His gaze locked on hers. "We'll go as slow as you want."

She nodded, touched by his understanding. She felt clumsy

and inept and giddy with anticipation, as if it were her first time. In a way it was. She'd never shared a bond with anyone as deep and strong as the one she shared with Linc.

She licked her lips, nervous energy shooting through her. "I hope I can remember how."

"You will." He leaned forward to press a gentle kiss to her lips.

She met him eagerly, giving herself to the fire that flared between them. But when they drew apart, she was again assaulted by doubt. What if she froze up, just the way she had with Steve? What if, no matter how gently Linc touched her, she couldn't respond? She tensed.

Linc's gaze narrowed on her. He seemed to sense her nervousness, her uncertainty. "We only go where you want, Jenna."

"I want...to see you. Is that okay?"

"Yes." Desire darkened his eyes. He rose quickly, stacking several pillows against the headboard then he climbed onto the bed and lay back.

Slightly elevated, he stretched out on top of the comforter as if offering himself and folded his arms behind his head. His arousal bulged behind his zipper, setting off a flurry of sparks in her blood.

She sat at his hip, her profile to his face so she could touch him without the encumbrance of her cast. Anticipation eddied through her as she reached for him. She ran her palm over his flat stomach, loving the feel of warm, taut muscle beneath the smooth skin of her hand. A muscle quivered in his belly.

Excited at the response she'd provoked, Jenna trailed her fingers over his chest, rubbing at his flat brown nipples. He watched her with a heavy-lidded intensity, his breath steady, but growing more rapid.

He was so beautiful that her lungs hurt. She leaned down and pressed a kiss to his chest. His skin was warm and supple beneath her lips. Her tongue darted out and she tasted him— clean and salty with a hint of spice.

One of his hands moved to her waist, squeezed lightly. She smiled and leaned forward for a deep wet kiss. Her breasts felt heavy. Her nipples pearled and she ached between her legs, not the deep pain of the past, but a pleasant, needy ache.

Intoxicated by the dark scent of him, his heady warmth webbing around her, she slid her hand back down his torso and under the waistband of his jeans, her palm gliding over crisp hair and heated flesh until she touched the beginning swell of his arousal.

Her gaze shot to his and he nodded, his face flush, his features tight with desire and restraint. Her hands fumbled on the zipper, but he lifted his hips, helping her push away his jeans and underwear.

Suddenly uncertain about looking at him, *all of him,* Jenna bit her lip, trying to forge past the pain of the last time.

Then she shifted her gaze to his lean, muscular legs and finally the juncture of his thighs. For a long moment, she simply stared. His arousal was sleek and strong, throbbing almost imperceptibly with the beat of his pulse.

The pain of the rape flickered through her mind, dried her mouth. Her body tightened in memory at the way Ramsey had torn at her, violated her.

"It's okay, Jenna." Linc's voice, hoarse with need, soothed over her. "It's okay."

This was Linc, not Ramsey. Linc would never hurt her. Tentatively, she reached out and slid her finger along the velvet length of him.

His entire body went whipcord stiff. His erection grew and the muscles in his thighs bunched. She glanced up at him. His eyes were closed, his features creased as if in pain. She understood it came from pleasure and she understood he meant what he said. If at any time she wanted him to stop, it was over.

But she didn't want to stop. She wanted to fuse his body with hers, test that promise of passion between them, the beginning of a new life for her.

She looked up at him and before she could lose her nerve, she whispered, "I want you to touch me like this, too."

His eyes darkened and he sat up facing her, his knee resting against her leg. He framed her face with his hands and kissed her gently.

She gave herself up to the sweetness of it, gripping his bicep and feeling the power roll beneath his flesh.

He rose to his knees, smiling at her and she smiled, too.

Impatience pounded through her, but also wariness. It didn't matter how desperately she wanted this, it was still new, still threatening.

He undid the remaining buttons on her shirt and slipped it off her shoulders. She sat in front of him, naked from the waist up and his gaze riveted on her breasts.

She wanted to watch him, wanted to see if she brought him as much joy as he did her, but she couldn't. She closed her eyes, praying he wouldn't be disappointed.

He touched her cheek and she looked at him. In his eyes, she saw reverence, gentleness, desire.

With a dark male smile, he cupped her breasts. "Yes?"

Choked by a stabbing need, she could only nod. He fondled her with gentle hands, stirring a heat down low that made her squirm.

When he bent and tongued one nipple, she gasped in surprise, but slid her hand into his hair to anchor herself.

With each gentle caress of his mouth, he said everything she'd never heard. *You're beautiful. You're mine.*

His breath on her skin, his hands on her body, each touch of his tongue branded her his and melted a little more of her fear, her resistance. His touch filled her with a breathless expectancy. She could feel in him a leashed urgency, yet he didn't hurry.

When he pushed off her shorts, her legs reflexively squeezed together. He ran his palms soothingly up and down her back until she relaxed, until she was ready for more.

When she knelt naked in front of him, his gaze fastened

on her. Hunger and pleasure glittered in his eyes. He trailed
a finger over her hip, giving her time to adjust to him, time
to become accustomed to the heat raging through her body.

His hands covered her breasts, squeezing gently, kneading,
plucking at her nipples. An invisible wire snapped taut inside
her. She watched his hands on her and thought she'd never
seen anything more beautiful, more arousing, more sensual.

Liquid heat spread between her legs. He cupped her bottom, pulling her into him. She'd never been touched with
such reverence, such gentle awe. She'd never felt as if her
next breath might unravel her.

She looped her good arm around his neck and melted
against him. His arousal—thick, insistent, strong—strained
against her.

He looked into her eyes, murmuring encouragement to her,
telling her to feel what she did to him. Desire burned fiercely
in his eyes, but it was tempered with tenderness.

Moving his hands over her, he let her get used to the feel
of him. On her breasts, her belly, her hips, her back. Large
and broad and gentle, his hands cupped her rear and pressed
her gently into him.

She expected trepidation, a flare of panic. Instead she felt
only desire, an impatience to have him inside her. Could she
shed the last, most intimidating of her fears? Focusing on
Linc's gentleness, she reached down and wrapped her hand
carefully around him.

His eyes dilated and he froze. "Go ahead," he urged in a
strangled voice.

She dragged her hand the length of him and his breath
came out in a ragged moan. Liquid fire rained through her at
the sound, the knowledge that she could affect him as powerfully as he did her.

She stroked him again. He was steel and satin, pulsing
warm and heavy in her hand. She kissed him, begging entrance to his mouth with her tongue, following the wild urging

in her blood. His hand slipped between them, then grazed the nub between her legs.

For a second, she stiffened. Fear rushed back, knife-edged and cold. This was Linc. He wouldn't hurt her.

"Do you want to stop, Jenna?" he rasped at her temple, his body taut against hers.

She considered it. Then sweet fire trickled through her and she relaxed, following the call of her body. She leaned into him, loving the feel of her breasts against the tempered steel of his chest.

Gently, deliberately, he slid one finger inside her.

Terror flickered. She pushed it away, concentrated instead on the wickedly wonderful glide of his finger, the way her body melted around him. Sleek, delicious heat streamed through her and she sagged against him.

"Yes?" he whispered against her lips.

"Yes," she managed to reply, then caught her breath when he stroked that particularly sensitive spot again.

He laid her back on the bed, kissing her, his body half covering hers, giving her an easy escape if she chose. His muscular thigh nudged between her legs and she looked down, astonished at the difference between his hair-roughened leg and her smooth one. She couldn't believe she was actually doing this. And liking it. *Loving it.*

He murmured sweet words to her, nuzzled her neck, making her body go languorous and soft. Strong, gentle fingers stroked her breasts, rubbed at her nipples and all the while an urgency coiled inside her.

She stroked one hand along his hip, then moved back to his arousal. He was huge, heated velvet in her hand and she shifted toward him, craving more of him. He kissed her breasts, her belly, blew air kisses against that most secret part of her.

A white-hot core of need boiled within her, then spilled over. When he slid his fingers inside her, she was sleek and wet and hot.

"Still good, hon?" he panted against her, his eyes sharp with need.

She nodded, opening her legs slightly, unable to breathe. His hand laced with hers, then one finger stroked the inside of her palm. Tingles shot down her arm.

His fingers silhouetted hers, moved up and down each slender one, stroking, weaving in and out, making her ache to have his body joined to hers like that.

His gaze locked on hers. In the passion-dark depths, she read tenderness and fierce desire. Her throat tightened with emotion.

She realized he was careful to keep his weight off her and tears stung her eyes at his understanding, his unselfish passion.

His fingers strummed a desperate song inside her body. Need built, merged with that old anxiety, but she had come too far to stop now. "I'm ready, Linc." Her voice was rusty and hoarse. "I want to feel you inside me."

He swallowed hard and the muscles corded in his neck. Then he pulled her half on top of him. "You set the pace, call the shots."

"Really?"

He grazed a thumb across her bottom lip. "Really."

Taking courage from the desire flowing through her body, she lifted herself up and straddled him.

As the most vulnerable, intimate part of her brushed the heat and power of him, panic surged. She fought it. Keeping her gaze on his, she balanced herself with a hand on his shoulder. He steadied her with his hands on her hips, his arousal brushing the wet heat of her.

Fire licked at her. Though it didn't dim her anxiety, she concentrated instead on the tenderness in Linc's eyes, the leashed restraint in his body. He wouldn't hurt her. Wanting him, eager now to test herself, she slid down on him. Just a little at a time.

The struggle for control lashed his features. His legs and

arms trembled with restraint and she felt the coil of power in his body, surging up into hers.

His hips moved and he grimaced. "Sorry. Too soon."

That first stroke of his body snatched her breath. He pulsed within her, hot and heavy and foreign. For an instant, Jenna couldn't move, didn't know if she wanted to. Then reflexively her body pushed down on his.

Her tightness stretched to accept him fully and the sharp sensation in her body ebbed away. She stared into his eyes, victory and triumph and sheer joy coursing through her.

Then her body softened around him and she began to move, led by a force of passion she'd never experienced and now didn't question. Her gaze locked on his, she gave herself over to a world where nothing mattered but trust and intimacy and Linc gave her both.

Her rhythm was awkward at first, but he followed, his hands strong and gentle on her hips. When her rhythm turned slow and smooth, her breath escaped in a low moan. She felt new and undamaged. Linc encouraged her with whispered words.

Then his hands slid up, cupped her breasts and urged her forward so that she lay more fully atop him.

Her life changed with each long stroke of his body inside hers. She kissed him, long and deep, her tongue sliding against his, miming the way his body stroked hers. Desperation charged through her. She craved his touch everywhere.

His hands kneaded her breasts, plucked gently at her nipples. And when he firmly bracketed her hips, she began to move faster, driven by a fierce urgency she didn't understand. Locked in the scent and feel of Linc's body, all thoughts of the past, of denial, of unfulfillment shattered.

Operating on sheer sensation, she gave herself over to the magic of Linc's body inside hers. They moved together, faster and faster, stretching, reaching for something high and bright.

She heard his whispered encouragement. Her name spilled from his lips in a harsh cry and she climaxed. As shudders racked her body, she cried out in disbelief and triumph. He gripped her hips, thrust hard and deep and fast. Faster, faster, until finally he shuddered inside her.

Only the sound of their ragged breathing broke the silence. Sunlight filtered through the blinds on the window, gilding their bodies in liquid gold. Jenna floated on a cloud of sensation. Her breasts tingled and her skin seemed heated from within.

Her mind drifted as she savored the pleasant ache between her legs, the giddiness in her blood. Linc's sweat mingled with hers; his chest hair tickled her breast. His hands stroked her hips and his breath warmed her temple.

Realization unfolded within her. It hadn't been a disaster. Making love with Linc had been a perfect, eye-opening pleasure. In utter disbelief, she admitted their lovemaking had totally fulfilled her. She'd despaired of ever feeling such completeness again.

A tear slipped out, then another. She buried her head in Linc's shoulder.

"Hey, you okay?" His hands rose to her shoulders, caressing her. "Was it that bad?"

"It was wonderful," she sobbed.

He gently tugged her face up to his, kissing her lips, her tear-soaked lashes. "*You're* wonderful."

"Thank you," she whispered, stunned at what had just happened between them, at her total, unfettered response. "Thank you."

He shook his head. "Thank *you* for giving me what I thought I'd never find again."

"What's that?"

"My heart," he said simply.

Silent tears slipped down her cheeks and she pressed a gentle kiss on his lips. Triumph and gratitude and pleasure swelled inside her, filling her soul to painful fullness.

Linc stroked her back, wound a strand of her hair around

his finger. "It's never been like that for me, Jenna," he said quietly.

She lifted her head, searching his eyes. "Really?"

"Really." He kissed her long and deep, until she had no doubt.

She sighed and laid her head back on his chest.

He chuckled, the sound rumbling beneath her.

"What?" She lifted her head, swiping at her tears.

He grinned, unadulterated male satisfaction on his face. "Don't ever give me that frigid stuff again."

She laughed and soon he joined in, holding her close as the scent of intimacy settled around them. Warm and safe, Jenna had never felt such joy, such utter completeness.

She kissed him softly, then again, sighing contentedly when he deepened the kiss. She felt him grow hard inside her again and drew back, running her finger along his bottom lip. "Want to?"

"Yes—"

The phone shrilled.

She grimaced and he tightened his hold on her. "We'll just pretend not to hear it."

Their eyes locked, reality worming in to their idyll. Both of them knew it could be Mace with news.

The phone rang again and Linc snatched up the phone, snarling, "Yeah?"

His body tautened and his gaze sliced to Jenna. Fury darkened his eyes, slashed across his handsome features.

Dread unfurled within her and she gripped his hand as he replaced the receiver.

"It was Mace," she said, already knowing, wondering what now.

Linc nodded, compassion battling with the rage in his eyes.

"Ramsey's gotten to Steve."

Horror, uncertainty, panic swirled within her. As they drove, she held tight to Linc's hand in an effort to keep the panic at bay. Every moment of the ride scraped by, each moment pricking like a needle. Mace hadn't been able to tell them the severity of Steve's injuries. Jenna's chest hurt. She couldn't breathe.

They reached the hospital and she and Linc rushed through the halls to Steve's room. Mace's partner, O'Kelly, waited for them outside the door.

He smiled encouragingly at Jenna. "He's gonna make it, Dr. West."

Thank goodness. She nodded, her throat too tight to speak, and stepped into the hospital room. Mace rose from a chair in the corner, his gaze telegraphing concern and compassion.

Allie, Steve's fiancée, stood on the opposite side of the bed, holding his hand. Her eyes were red and swollen. "He's been asking for you."

Jenna heard the resentment beneath the soft words. She didn't blame Allie one bit. What had happened to Steve *was* Jenna's fault.

Jenna looked at him then, and what little relief she'd felt at O'Kelly's words evaporated.

Her friend lay on the bed, his face beaten so severely he was barely recognizable. But his eyes glittered at her and he weakly lifted a hand.

Jenna stuffed a knuckle in her mouth to keep from crying out. She took in his raw face, the bandage around his head, the cast on his left forearm and her knees wobbled.

Linc wrapped a steadying arm around her. "It's okay, hon."

For a heartbeat, Jenna let herself lean into him, absorb his strength, steady her nerves. Then she rushed to Steve, gently taking his hand, tears sliding down her cheeks. "I'm so sorry. So terribly sorry."

Through swollen lips, he mumbled, "Not…your…fault."

Allie looked away, wiping her cheeks.

"It is," Jenna whispered, struggling to keep from sobbing. "All because of me."

Beneath the revulsion she felt at what Ramsey had done, that dark energy twisted inside her. Her hand tightened on Steve's. "He won't get away with this. He won't."

"He already has," Allie said tightly, rage vibrating in her words.

Steve's gaze went to her and with an effort, he shook his head.

Her face crumpled and she looked down. After a few seconds, she took a deep breath, smiling at him. "I'm going to get you more ice chips, all right?"

He nodded, his eyes beseeching, trying to reassure her. It broke Jenna's heart. Allie grabbed up the plastic pitcher from the cart beside the bed and fled the room.

Jenna knew then what she had to do and she finally allowed an idea that had first horrified, then nagged her. Determination budded. She squared her shoulders and kissed Steve gently on the temple. "He will pay for this. I swear to you."

"What...are...you..." Steve dragged in a breath, his words mangled, his cheeks so swollen they looked stuffed with gauze "...doing?"

She smiled, taking strength and purpose from the fury that washed through her, cleansing, burning away the fear. "I'll be right back."

She moved toward the door, but Linc blocked her way.

"Let me have just a minute, please," she said.

His gaze, concerned and protesting, searched hers. Then he nodded.

She stepped outside. Closing the door behind her, she glanced at O'Kelly who stood several feet away. He smiled.

She lifted a hand in greeting, her attention going to the woman who stood at the opposite wall. Allie's shoulders were braced against the plaster and she looked so drained, so fragile that Jenna suspected the wall, and not her own energy, was what kept her on her feet.

Jenna took the few steps that separated them and pressed her own back to the wall, staring straight ahead. "I'm so sorry. I know this is my fault." Her voice cracked, but she plowed on, "I promise Ramsey will pay for this."

Allie stood quietly, the pitcher dangling limply from her hand. Blue eyes, red-rimmed and dull with trauma, finally met Jenna's. "I know I shouldn't blame you, but I do."

"If I were in your shoes, I'd feel the same." Jenna struggled to keep her voice even against the rage and horror tearing through her.

"It's not *really* your fault. I know that. Nothing could've kept Steve from helping you." She gave a broken laugh. "If he could, he'd get out of that bed right now and go back for more."

Misery razored through Jenna. She didn't know how to respond. There were no words to ease Allie's pain or resentment.

The blonde slid a sideways glance at her, bitterness lacing her voice. "You know, I've never been exactly jealous of you, but you always seemed to know Steve so much better than I did. You always seemed to have a part of him I couldn't reach. Then he told me about the rape and for the first time, I understood just how deep the friendship between you two is. And why."

"I'm glad he finally told you." Jenna wiped at her eyes. "The idiot thought he was protecting me."

Allie smiled then, a calm serenity spreading across her delicate features. "I feel like you're responsible, in some part, for what a wonderful man he is."

Jenna's eyes burned and she shook her head vehemently. "No, he got that way all on his own."

"You *are* responsible for one thing, Jenna."

"I know—" Her heart clenched. How could she ever make this up to Steve? Allie would never forgive her and Jenna didn't blame her. "If it hadn't been for me, Ramsey could never have gotten to him—"

"No, that's not what I meant. Your friendship with Steve, the things the two of you have shared, have made him the kind, caring man he is. He's told me that many times and I believe he's right.''

''I feel the same about him,'' Jenna admitted, the pressure in her chest finally easing.

Allie took a deep breath and turned to look at her. ''I want to thank you for that. Steve will be fine. I know he will. I was scared to death when I first saw him, but I know him well enough to know that he was where he wanted to be, doing what he wanted. He'll protect you with everything in him.''

''He'll do that for you, too.''

''I know that now.'' A tremulous smile spread across her face, turning her eyes the vibrant blue of washed sapphires. ''And I wish you the very best. I know this has been hell on you.''

''Thanks.'' Jenna leaned back against the wall, feeling drained and energized at the same time.

Steve's door opened and Linc stepped outside, relief flashing through his eyes when he saw her. His gaze shot to Allie, then back to her. ''Everything okay?''

''Yes.''

Mace stepped out behind him, closing the door softly.

Allie pushed away from the wall, moving back toward Steve's room.

Linc's gaze locked on Jenna. She wanted to go to him, let him hold her, just feel his strength against her and as if he read her mind, he walked over and stood beside her.

Shoulder to thigh, his body silhouetted hers and his unspoken support wrapped around her like the first warmth of spring, promising and sure. It was that support which allowed her to say the words she'd been thinking since she'd watched her house crumble into a pile of embers.

An image of Steve's battered face, Allie's pinched features, flashed through her mind.

Jenna looked at Mace, leaning haggard and worn against

the wall, rubbing his eyes. "Detective, I'm going back to work."

Allie, her hand on the doorknob, whipped around, her eyes wide with shock.

"What!" Beside her, Linc jerked and snagged her elbow, as if to keep her beside him.

Mace slowly straightened, his eyes narrowed as if he weren't quite sure what he'd heard.

She plowed ahead, knowing she had to speak now or she never would. Linc had given her more than her sexuality. He'd imbued her with a longing for a life with him and she wasn't going to let Ramsey simply take away that chance, like he'd done everything else.

Jenna had known Linc would hate the idea, but she had to do something. "Ramsey knows Steve can't handle my patients now. I'm going back."

How did she keep her teeth from chattering? Just the thought of facing Ramsey turned her spine to liquid.

"Jenna, you should think real hard about this." Mace stepped toward her, his gaze shifting between her and Linc. "Ramsey will know exactly where you are."

"That's the whole point. I'm ready to face him. I *want* him to find me. I want to draw him out, set him up, just like he's done me."

For the space of two heartbeats, the hallway was silent. Then everyone spoke at once.

"It's insane!"

"You're not doing it!"

"You can't!"

She kept her gaze on Mace, afraid if she looked away she would lose her nerve. "You can help me, right? What do I do?"

He cocked his head, measuring her, looking more like Linc than she'd ever noticed before. "We might be able to work this. We could wire you."

"Yes." She shifted, feeling as if her skin crawled with ants. "That way you can hear when I need you—"

"You can't do this, Jenna!" Linc still held her elbow and now spun her toward him. "This is crazy."

"Well, he *is* crazy, Linc, and if I don't do it, he'll never leave me alone. Or you. He's already gotten to Wilbur, to Steve, harassed my parents. You'll be next. I can't let it go that far."

"Steve won't like this, either," Allie interjected from the doorway.

"There's no other way," Jenna insisted, surprised at the growing admiration in Allie's eyes. "I should've done something before now."

"You've been in no shape to do anything, thanks to that bastard!" Linc snarled. "Certainly not anything like this."

"It could work, Jenna." Mace's voice was low and thoughtful. "We'd have to be careful, but it could work."

Linc glared at his brother. "You're not helping here."

"I know you don't like it, Linc, but this may be the only way we're going to get Ramsey in the open. Or at least get a chance at him. Jenna's right. He wants her. Let him come get her. We can rig it so she's protected, so we're there for backup."

"You're just handing her over to the bastard!" Linc's hand tightened on Jenna's arm. "Use a policewoman!"

"No, it has to be me," Jenna said quietly, turning to Linc, trying to soothe the anger and apprehension that rolled from him, though she felt the same things herself. He had to understand that only she could kill the demon of her past. "I have to do this. I have to end it."

"No!"

"Linc, listen to me." She tugged him a few feet away so they could speak in semiprivacy. Keeping her voice low, she looked into his eyes. "It's time. After we made love, I realized what we had, how special it was. Ramsey could still take that from me and I'm not going to let him do it."

"This isn't the way. If something happens—"

"You heard Mace. He'll be with me."

"She'll be wearing a wire," Mace suggested, making it obvious that everyone could hear their conversation.

But Jenna wasn't embarrassed about revealing what she'd shared with Linc.

He closed his eyes briefly, pain and reluctance and protest creasing his features.

"I can't live like this anymore, Linc. And I can't ask you to, either. Ramsey's not going to stop until he has me. Let's just end it now. Let's bait him. If we do this, we'll have *some* control. He won't call all the shots." Her gaze locked on his, drawing strength from him. "I'm tired. I want it finished."

In his eyes, she saw the struggle to understand, to accept.

"I don't like it. I don't like you being in the same country with him, let alone the same room."

"I don't like it, either." She squeezed his hand. "But I'm not going to live like this the rest of my life. I'm not."

Disapproval radiated from him, but finally he nodded. "I hate every bit of this."

"So do I," she whispered. "But it will work. It will."

"It better, or there will be nowhere he can hide that I won't find him."

She gave him a shaky smile and turned to Mace. "All right, what do we do?"

"I'm going with her," Linc announced, his hand still tight on hers.

"No!" Jenna turned to look at him. "No—"

"It's not up for debate," he said flatly, a savage light in his eyes that she'd never seen. Before she could renew her protests or Mace could add his own, Linc continued, "If I don't go, Ramsey will know something's up. After what he did to Steve, you would be foolish to go anywhere alone. He'll be suspicious if you do."

"He's got a point, Jenna," Mace said grudgingly.

Allie watched silently, her eyes filled with concern.

Everything in Jenna protested at putting Linc in such danger. "I don't want you to risk it. I don't like—"

"Then we're even," he said. "Because I don't like the thought of you going in there, either."

She stared at him, knowing further protests would be futile.

"This way, we'll be together," he added quietly, running his knuckles along her cheek. "No matter what happens."

Perhaps it was selfish for Jenna to want Linc with her, but she drew strength from knowing they would fight Ramsey together. That Linc would lay his life on the line for her humbled her, terrified her, and she prayed fervently that he wouldn't have to give that ultimate sacrifice. That none of them would.

Chapter 13

She sat next to him in the truck, her hand on his thigh, her head on his shoulder. All during the ride from the hospital, frustration seethed inside Linc. He'd tried again to change her mind about facing Ramsey, but she'd begged him tearfully to understand, to support her.

The problem was he did understand and that challenged every protective instinct he had. He knew how it felt to be reduced from competent and confident to powerless and uncertain. How could he ask her to walk away from a chance to end this and get on with her life, to get Ramsey?

He couldn't. And even though he hated it with everything in him, he wouldn't allow her to face it alone. Linc had to trust that Mace would make it as safe as possible.

Jenna had come to mean a lot to him. He'd fight with his life for her and realized that tomorrow, he would do exactly that. In a flash of insight, he realized she was doing the same. Trying for a future on her terms. Fighting for a chance. She hadn't said she was doing it for them, only for herself, but how could he not support her?

Tension sliced through him like newly whetted steel and a sense of urgency built. He wanted to do everything he'd ever left undone, attempt to right every regret. He was glad he'd told Jenna about the baby, but he wanted her to also know how she'd changed his life, reopened his heart. He wanted her to know before they faced Ramsey.

Tonight might be the only chance he had for that and he didn't want to delay.

She was quiet during supper. In an effort to keep her mind from the upcoming confrontation, he told her about him and his brothers as boys, hunting with their dad, fishing in the summers.

At one point, she said wistfully, "I'd like to meet your dad, both your parents."

"You will." He said the words because he wanted them to be true, because he believed them, but he couldn't erase the dark doubt that clung to every reassurance. Because the flat truth was he didn't know if either of them would survive what was coming.

Jenna became more withdrawn, more thoughtful, the mood between them more unsettled. After dinner, she excused herself to go call the hospital, then her parents and sister.

Linc ached as she walked away. He wanted to hold her, make love to her, and wondered if she would allow it. After he'd cleaned up the dishes, she still hadn't returned so he decided to shower. The scent of their joined bodies—delicate with a hint of his muskiness—still lingered on his skin and when he stepped into the stall, the sweet heady scent rose around him.

Reluctant to wash off the reminder of their lovemaking, he recalled her trusting surrender, her giddy disbelief when they'd made love. And the need to be with her, to protect her returned.

He stepped out of the shower and grabbed a towel, quickly drying off. Steam misted the bathroom, freshly scented with soap and shampoo he'd used. After knotting the towel around his hips, he rubbed at his hair with another towel.

As he walked toward the vanity for his comb, he noticed words forming out of the steam on the mirror. He smiled and his pulse kicked up.

Meet me in the barn.

He ran a comb through his hair, then dressed rapidly in a pair of knit shorts and tennis shoes, forgoing a shirt. What was Jenna doing in the barn?

Once outside, Linc saw the dogs loping around the perimeter of the barn. He reached the doorway and found Jenna leaning against the jamb, staring out at the beginning sunset.

"Hey, there," he said softly, admiring the soft golden light on her face, the sun-warmed brilliance of her eyes.

"Hi." She smiled at him, a combination of desire and reserve. Her arms were crossed, her lean fingers resting on the new cast Linc had given her at the hospital since her arm wasn't quite healed.

He eased up beside her, taking in the gleaming auburn hair that fell softly thick and luxuriant to the top of her shoulders. His gaze trailed over the thrust of her breasts beneath his shirt, the sleek length of her legs. "Everything okay?"

"Everything's fine." She reached for his hand, tugging him closer. "You got my message."

He nodded, curious, enjoying the sight of her. She'd showered, too, and the fresh citrus of her shampoo floated to him, mingled with the clean air and the heavy perfume of grass.

She'd changed into denim shorts and another of his shirts, this one a plain teal that shimmered in her eyes.

She squeezed his hand, then stepped away to tug one of the barn doors shut. "Good."

When she reached for the other door, he pushed her aside and began to close it, anticipation tapping at him.

The dogs raced up to the door, tongues lolling as they started inside.

"You boys stay outside."

At Jenna's command, all three animals plopped down on their haunches, watching her expectantly. She patted each of them on the head, then slid the door completely shut.

Soft darkness closed around them. The barn was dim and pleasantly cool. Lingering sunlight filtered through the slats of the barn wall in a soft amber glow.

Linc's heart turned over. He wanted this woman in his life, his bed. A slow burn inched under his skin.

"Come with me." She laced her fingers with his and led him toward the back of the barn, to one of the empty feed bins.

He looked inside, eyes widening in surprise. At his grin, she smiled shyly and stepped up into the small, contained room.

She had spread a thick floor of hay then covered it with two blankets. In the corner sat his portable CD player, which normally rested on a small table by the barn phone up front. The soft aching strains of Céline Dion floated out, transforming the spot into a secluded hideaway.

Jenna turned to him, her gaze softly inviting.

Heat and restlessness steepled inside him. In a low voice, he asked, "Did you bring me out here to seduce me, Dr. West?"

"Would I be able to?"

"No doubt." His body tightened. Just looking at her made him itch to touch, to taste.

"Maybe you could return the favor," she said huskily, her eyes glowing provocatively. She held out her hand and he took it, stepping up into the feed bin.

His thumb stroked the curve of her cheek. "I want you, Jenna. I've never wanted another woman the way I want you."

"Show me." Longing and fierce desperation ached in her voice. Tears glittered in her eyes as she covered his hand with hers. Raw need etched her features, but there was also apprehension.

"I won't let Ramsey hurt you. I'll kill him first—"

"Shhh." She pressed a kiss to his lips, lacing her fingers with his. "Let tonight be only for you and me. No past, no future, no threats. Only us."

Unmistakable desire burned in her eyes along with a plea and his throat tightened.

"Make love with me?" she whispered.

Want deepened her voice, but Linc also heard an edge there, felt her desperate attempt to hold on to now, put off tomorrow.

"Please?"

He couldn't deny her, wouldn't deny either of them what might be their last night together. Need and profound caring welled inside him and his hands shook as he gently framed her face. "Yes."

A tremulous smile radiated on her face and she moved into his arms, whispering, "Lock out the world for me, Linc. Just for tonight."

He fitted her body to his, cool air shifting through his still damp hair, lifting the scent of Jenna's clean citrus to his nostrils.

Her head rested on his shoulder. Her body draped his like a silken shadow. His thigh moved between hers and she put her good arm around his neck, laying her head on his chest. Full breasts pressed against his bare chest and her nipples burned his skin through the shirt she wore. They swayed slowly to the throbbing strains of Dion's "Seduces Me."

A slow fire unfurled in him. He wanted this night to last forever, to delay the inevitable—

He cut off the thought. She was right. Tonight was for them, no thoughts of Ramsey, no uncertainty, no fear about tomorrow, only now. Narrowing his senses, he gave himself over to the brush of her thighs against his, the soft caress of her breasts against him, the languid way her body contoured his.

"Jenna?"

"Hmm?"

"Why here?"

Her breath tickled his neck. "This is where you touched me for the first time."

"I scared the hell out of you!"

"Not anymore," she said in a sultry tone.

Linc's arms tightened around her. Her tongue touched the pulse in his neck, igniting streamers of fire through his body. He bent, taking her mouth with his.

At first he kissed her languorously, gently, savoring the want that drummed through his body. He tried to curb his hunger, his impatience to go faster.

But she returned the kiss, sighing into his mouth, then gripping his arm, silently imploring. He wanted to go slow, savor every inch of her, make it last, but she had other ideas.

She pulled her mouth from his, breathing raggedly. Her eyes glowed with sensual purpose and anticipation. She raked her nails over the hard muscle of his chest, through the crisp dusting of hair, and down the tautness of his belly.

"I love the way you touch me, the way you feel," he rasped, trying to rein in the savage fire that tore through him.

Pleasure and need darkened her eyes to black in the barn shadows. A secret smile lit her face and she cupped his erection, already straining against the soft fabric of his shorts. A ragged breath shuddered out of him and he pressed himself into her hand. Her gaze locked with his as she gently rubbed and molded his rigid flesh to her hot palm.

Pleasure stabbed through him, sharp and merciless. Music played, but he could distinguish no words, only the arousing sob of the music, moving through his body with the pressure of Jenna's hands.

Hungry to taste her, he pulled her to him and drove his tongue into her mouth. She met him, her hand still stroking, firm and rhythmic and wicked, destroying every ounce of restraint.

A dark ferocity charged through him. Struggling to resist

the wildness, he fumbled open the buttons of her blouse. She tore her mouth from his to unbutton her shorts and step out of them.

Soft golden light painted her body. Her breasts were small, but full, the rose tips crowned and pouting for him.

"How can you be so perfect?" he whispered in awe, bending his head.

She slid her hand up his arm, clutching his shoulder as he bent and took her in his mouth. She gasped, her nipple rasping against his tongue and he shook with need.

His hands framed her hips, then cupped her bottom. His tongue stroked the creamy velvet of her breasts, the light skein of veins beneath the flesh. She tasted of soap and mystery.

Fire lashed him, stinging like a hot wind and unleashing a violent impatience. Lost in the feel of her, the slide of her skin under his tongue, he suckled her, raked his teeth gently across the velvet peak of her nipple.

Jenna pressed his head to her breasts, her fingers warm and insistent on his scalp. She moaned deep in her throat.

The sound shattered something hard, buried inside him.

Teeth nipping at his neck, she delved her hand beneath his waistband to touch the straining flesh there. "You're driving me crazy," she panted.

"The feeling's mutual," he gasped. He lifted his head and kissed her. The taste of her mingled on their joined tongues and drove a spear of heat straight through him.

With one hand, he pushed his shorts over his hips, stepped out of them at the same time he stepped out of his shoes. He pulled her into him, his hands cupping her rear. Covering her lips with his, his tongue slipped inside her mouth, coaxing, seeking. She flattened herself against him, snapping his last line to sanity.

He stopped suddenly, dragging his lips from hers. "Am I going too fast?"

"No." She reached for his mouth again. "Do it, Linc. Do anything. I trust you."

Her words caused his chest to tighten painfully and his throat burned. Her belly met his, soft and warm and bare. Then her hand wrapped around his throbbing arousal.

She molded him like perfection, as if she'd been carved from silk and smoke specifically for his body. He couldn't get close enough, couldn't touch her the way his heart needed.

One arm anchored around her bottom. His other hand moved between their bodies and his finger slid deftly between her legs.

She melted around him, silken rain and heat. "Yes, yes, yes," she whispered, moving against his hand, her hip stroking his arousal with each movement.

She nibbled at his lips, his jaw, his cheekbone, kissed his eyes before she said in a throaty moan, "I want you inside me, Linc. Now."

He very nearly lost it right then. He shook so hard he didn't know if he could move without falling down, but somehow he managed to get them to the blankets.

The music echoed around them, dimmed by the demanding storm of their bodies. Taking her lips in a deep kiss, he settled over her, savoring the feel of her beneath him, her hand on his back, then his face, her thighs cradling him.

Power surged through him, unbridled desire. He wanted to drive into her hard and fast and—

He tore his lips from hers, realizing that he'd probably frightened her.

"Linc?" Confusion flashed through her passion-clouded eyes.

He started to roll to his back, move her atop him. "I'm sorry."

"No." With shaking hands, she held him in place. "Here. Like this."

His weight settled on her, and he couldn't decide if it was pain or pleasure that creased her features.

"I'm not afraid. Not of you. Or your strength."

He bent his forehead to hers for a brief moment, relieved and amazed. How could he ever give her up? When he braced his elbows on either side of her, she opened her legs to him. At her total surrender, her stark vulnerability, his throat burned.

He kissed her long and deep and hard. His hand skimmed over the curve of her waist, the flare of her hip, then slid beneath her. He lifted her to him, settling himself fully between her legs.

His gaze locked with hers. No doubt shadowed her eyes, only acute need, possession.

"Yes," she whispered. "It's all right."

He pushed inside her gently and her body arched to meet him. Her breasts nudged his chest. Her good hand went around his waist, splayed low on his back, urging, inviting.

"Oh," she breathed, closing her eyes. Pleasure tightened her features and Linc thought she'd never looked more beautiful.

Then she opened her eyes, locking her gaze on his. She shifted, pulling him deeper into her body. His breath jammed in his lungs and he began to move. Slow, steady strokes, staring into her eyes, not wanting to miss a beat of her reaction.

Tenderness welled up inside him. With every thrust, every stroke of his body inside hers, he silently gave what he had of himself.

She kissed him, letting her desperation, her need speak through the fervor of her kiss, the abandoned response of her body. Her inner muscles clenched around him and he trembled with the effort not to anticipate her.

Then she climaxed and sweet, hot silk flowed over him. He threw back his head and drove into her, faster, stronger, deeper.

She called out, his name ragged on her lips, and held on to him fiercely. When he finally shuddered his last, she wrapped her arm around his neck, kissing his cheek, his ear, his forehead.

"Thank you, Linc. Thank you."

He raised his head, tenderness and desperation crowning inside him. Tears welled in her eyes and she kissed him again.

He rolled to his back then, bringing her with him. She settled her head in the crook of his neck and he stared up at the barn ceiling, the shadows of night now culling away the amber light of sunset.

She sighed contentedly against him, her breath misting his skin. The sweet scent of sex tickled the air and her belly was slick against his. He still pulsed inside her.

When this was all over, what would he do without her? Linc ached to declare his love, bare his soul, but he couldn't. Despite caring about Jenna, he didn't know if he was capable of love again, of giving all of himself to a woman. He hoped that, after tomorrow, he would have a chance to find out.

Jenna lay atop him, refusing to think past this moment. She savored the supple feel of his skin next to hers, his heat wrapping around her, his fullness ebbing inside her.

She was grateful that Linc hadn't insisted on voicing his feelings. She was too raw, too edgy to handle declarations. Showing her faith in this most elemental, primal way had been the only way to tell Linc how she felt. So much more powerful than words could ever convey.

He had given her back a sense of femininity, a sexual drive, and now, in this bid to have a future with him, she could lose it all.

But she'd had almost two weeks with him and they had changed her life. *He* had changed her life, the deepest core of her, her perception of herself. Linc had imbued her spartan, staid existence with texture and color and sensation.

He left her in no doubt that she'd thoroughly satisfied him as well and he made her feel more a woman than she ever had, a sexual, vibrant, responsive woman. He had given her a precious gift, helping her at last to conquer the cripple she had become after the rape.

Linc made her feel beautiful and sensual, but above all, he made her *feel*. And Jenna didn't want to lose that part of herself again.

Her feelings for Linc were about more than her sexuality. They seemed to key into a core part of her, fleshing out a vague shadow that had existed only to remind her that she was less a woman.

She was sick of Ramsey, sick of his games, sick of his hold over her past. With Linc's help, she could beat him. She believed that, and yet Ramsey's nightmarish legacy haunted her, flashing images through her mind—of the rape, Wilbur's death, Steve's battered face, her home burned to cinders.

Old doubts rose up, nicking at her determination, her new confidence. But she refused to back down. No matter what the risk, she was breaking free of Ramsey's hold tomorrow.

"Get to your office at eight sharp," Mace said the next morning just after sunrise. "We checked it out last night. It's all clear."

He stood just outside the kitchen with Linc, his back turned as a policewoman taped a body wire to Jenna's naked torso.

"All right."

Linc heard the uncertainty in Jenna's quiet voice, the shaky thread of anxiety.

He glanced over his shoulder at her, his heart clenching at her wide, troubled eyes. The policewoman helped her slip on another of his shirts and Jenna met his gaze over the woman's head, her beautiful eyes holding the secrets of their time together.

She pressed her lips together, but otherwise gave no sign of the apprehension he knew she felt, that same apprehension that sawed through him.

He wanted to protest, to whisk her out of there and drive out of the country. But he knew she had to go, had to do this.

She was right. Running from Ramsey, looking over her shoulder was no kind of life. Linc just didn't know if he could outlast this tension that blistered his insides like burning coals.

The policewoman straightened Jenna's collar and turned toward the doorway. "All right, Detective. She's ready."

Linc pivoted, his gaze fastening on Jenna's, offering silent reassurance.

Mace nodded and stepped into the kitchen, his voice brisk and efficient. "There will be a county truck just up the road from your clinic and several ditch diggers working on a trench just feet from your office. We'll position ourselves so that we'll be able to see you and hear everything from that distance."

"We?"

"Yeah." He grinned. "Captain Price said if I don't catch Ramsey today, I can just keep that ditch-digging job."

At his attempt to ease the suffocating anxiety, Jenna smiled slightly.

He sobered. "We'll be able to see him when he comes in and we'll be on him."

She nodded, her injured arm pressed close to her side as she slid her other palm down her jeans.

Sweat slicked Linc's palms, too. Tension arced in the room, plucking at his need to do something, the impatience to end this thing.

He watched Jenna, seeing the same dread in the rigid set of her shoulders, the shadows in her eyes. Regret rose up in him for what he hadn't been able to say to her, but he was grateful for the memory of last night. For always, the image of her trusting abandon would brand his soul.

He wasn't about to lose her. If today was the end, they would go together.

She swallowed hard, her gaze steady on him.

Linc turned to Mace. "We're ready. I'm taking the .38."

"Good." Mace turned to Jenna. "Do you know how to use a gun?"

"Yes—"

"Ask Sam." Linc looked at Jenna, sharing a small secret smile with her.

Mace glanced from one to the other of them, then shrugged. He picked up the phone and called Captain Price, telling her they were ready to move.

Linc didn't remember much about the ride there, only that Jenna's hand gripped his with desperate fervor.

He pulled into the parking lot of her clinic, gravel crunching beneath his tires, and killed the engine. For a long second, they stared at the brick building in front of them.

Jenna looked at him. "I'm ready."

He bit back a protest and squeezed her hand. Together, they climbed out of the truck. At the front door, her hand trembled on the handle. The keys shook, clanging against the glass, rubbing metal against metal, scraping across raw nerves.

Linc covered her hand with his. There was nothing he could say, nothing he could promise, but he was here.

She looked at him, took a deep breath, and her trembling eased somewhat.

His gaze traced her features, taking in the strong cheekbones, the full lips, the fear-fringed courage in those gorgeous eyes. He brushed a quick kiss across her lips.

Her eyes glowed at him, then she squared her shoulders and turned the key. The lock clicked. She pushed the door open, allowing him to enter first.

Despite the flow of sunlight through the partially open blinds, Linc flipped on the overhead light. The files were as they'd left them. Even the chairs appeared slightly out of alignment with each other, just as they had when he and Jenna had sat here after finding the death certificate.

Everything appeared undisturbed since their last visit and Linc was relieved to see that no signs of Steve's blood remained on the floor. He silently thanked whoever had cleaned it up. In the back room, the dogs stirred, a couple of them baying in welcome. The cages creaked as the animals moved about.

He glanced at her, noting how she bit her lip, the white of her knuckles as her fist closed tightly over the keys.

"I guess we just wait for him?" she asked in a thin voice.

"I guess." Tension closed over the room like a giant fist, cutting the air, suffocating him, knotting his shoulders.

Linc wanted to pull Jenna to him, protect her from what was about to happen, but he knew she didn't want that.

"If I just sit here, I'll go crazy. We can feed and water the dogs."

"Good idea. Why don't you let me—"

"Linc, I need to do something," she said sharply, then gentled her voice, an apology in her eyes. "I can't just sit around here."

He nodded, wishing he could protect her from all of this and knowing he couldn't. Just being with her would have to be enough, no matter how he hated the feeling of helplessness.

He stepped toward the steel door that led to the exam room. "You get the water. I'll get the food—"

A noise clattered beyond the door, loud enough to excite the dogs even further.

His gaze snapped to Jenna's. Dread pinched her features. Her lips flattened in a grim line.

Linc stepped toward the door. "Stay here. Let me check it out."

"It was probably one of the dogs. Mace said he'd already checked out the place."

"Right. I'll just take a look."

Foreboding stabbed at her. "I don't think you should go back there by yourself."

"Mace is right outside," Linc reminded. "If something happens, get the hell out of here."

"I won't leave you." Despite the misgiving in her eyes, her voice was firm, stubborn.

"Jenna, please."

"I won't."

He knew there was no sense arguing with her and hoped it was a moot point. "I'll be right back."

She stepped toward him, as if she might go.

"Please, stay here." He leveled a look at her until she nodded reluctantly.

He opened the door, his gaze taking in the pristine exam tables, the dull silver gleam of the refrigerator on the far wall.

Looking into the shadows beyond, he saw the sheen of metal cages. The stringent odor of antiseptic cleanser hung in the room, underlaid by the faint scents of animals and urine.

Something else, something vile and rotten, floated beneath the surface of the other scents, something Linc couldn't identify.

He stepped further into the room. "See, it *was* just the dogs—"

Pain exploded in his head and he registered that he had been hit. Jenna spoke, her voice faint, drifting away. He staggered forward, tried to turn, tried to see who had hit him.

Another vicious blow slammed against his head. He looked back and this time his gaze connected with the man standing behind the door.

A warning screamed in his head. Horror clawed through him as Linc saw the raised bat, the cold rage gathered on broad, handsome features. It was Ramsey. Ramsey was already inside.

"Jenna, run—" Linc pitched forward, the words strangled in his throat. Darkness devoured him.

Chapter 14

Linc's choked warning stabbed straight through Jenna.

Reflexively, she moved forward, his name on her lips, but before she could speak, a wide-shouldered silhouette filled the doorway.

"I knew you'd come."

The nightmare of the rape, of the last assault crashed in on her. *Ramsey.*

The windowless front room pressed in on her. Mace's photo had captured the familiar features, the short, dark hair, the cold soulless eyes, and the raw scar that slashed from his ear to his collarbone. But once again face-to-face with him, she shuddered in the wake of uncontained fury that girdled him like poisonous fog.

The dogs whimpered, the sound playing through her mind like a distant echo. The rancid stench of fear burned the air. Her heart hammered against her ribs. Nausea climbed up her throat.

She backed toward the front door, trying in a split second to gauge his moves, to determine which way to run. Her gaze skipped around the room, searching for something, *anything* to use as a weapon.

She saw only files, chairs, a phone, a pen.

The dull *smack smack smack* of a wooden baseball bat against Ramsey's palm filled her head. The overdeveloped muscles of his shoulders and arms strained the seams of a light blue T-shirt. Thick thighs rippled as he stepped toward her. Dark scarlet stains streaked the light, polished wood of the bat and Jenna knew those stains must be Linc's blood.

Dread knotted her stomach. "Wh-what have you done to Linc?"

"If I were you, I'd be more concerned about myself than lover boy." He stepped toward her, heavy work boots squeaking on the tile. Twisted desire gleamed in his eyes. "Oh, I've waited a long time for this, you slut. A long time."

Talons of panic ripped at her and she fought to keep her wits. The dogs barked in an uneven, agitated staccato. Try to talk to him, she told herself. She was wearing the wire. Mace would hear. He was on his way. She attempted to speak past the knot in her throat, but she couldn't.

"Now, it's just you and me." He edged toward her, moving with unusual grace for such a muscle-bound man. "I've thought about this for eight long years. We've got a lot of catching up to do."

"You're sick." Her voice shook. Maybe she shouldn't antagonize him, but her nerves were talking now. Fury at his stalking of her, at the way he'd harmed her loved ones rose up in her, battling with the fear. She edged around the desk, trying to keep space between them.

She thought she heard the rush of footsteps on the gravel and prayed it was Mace with his men.

Ramsey advanced, miming her steps. He drew even with the front door and reached out, flipping the lock.

The heavy *click* knifed through her. She would have to get to the back door. If she could make it into the exam room, she could lock the thick steel door between them.

His eyes narrowed as he advanced, copying her steps with his own careful, precise ones as he followed her around the desk. "Remember what I told you that night in the parking lot?"

She remembered every frightening word, but she wasn't about to admit it.

He snarled, baring his teeth at her. "I'm going to kill you. But before I do, I'm going to rip those clothes off, tear some of that delicious flesh off your body."

Nausea roiled through her and she shuddered. *Think,* she ordered. *Think.* Where was Mace? How was Linc? With shaking, slippery hands, she groped her way around the desk, feeling its edge, using it to guide her steps.

Ramsey tracked her and she rounded the corner, backing toward the exam room door, careful not to look at it. Cold sweat slicked her palms, between her breasts. Her legs trembled so badly she could barely stand.

"You won't get away this time, bitch. You're going to pay for everything you did to me, everything you took!"

"You deserved every day you spent in prison!" The sound of her shrill voice, spewing such hate and fear, shocked her.

She wanted to glance behind her, measure the distance to the open exam door, but she couldn't afford to look away from Ramsey for a second.

Then she heard the glorious, unmistakable sound of footsteps thundering up to the door. Shadows arched into the room. She opened her mouth to scream a warning.

At the same instant, Ramsey exploded into motion, leaping atop the desk and over it in one powerfully fluid motion. The bat clattered hollowly to the floor. She whirled to run and he caught her midstride.

Brute fingers bit into her good arm. He whipped her around as if she weighed no more than a feather pillow. Her head snapped back and she reached for the wall, the door, something to steady herself.

Black horror rose up inside her, jamming her breath, suffocating her.

"You're going to pay," he roared, grabbing her between the legs and shoving her into the exam room. He slammed the door and locked it in one vicious fluid motion.

Fear clawed at her. His hands, hot and brutal between her thighs, detonated a charge of panic. She yanked away, slapping at him, hysterical.

He knocked her to the floor and as she scrambled to her feet, he lunged across her, knocking her down again. Pain shot up her hip, burned in her broken arm.

Ramsey grabbed her solid steel autoclave and hefted the sterilization equipment. Muscles popped out in his neck, his arms and he staggered to the door, dropping the piece and effectively blocking any entrance or exit.

Fear tore at her. Winded from his blow, she struggled to breathe and gain her footing. She scrambled up, turning at the same time.

"No, you don't!" he screamed, snagging the collar of her shirt, spinning her toward him.

She heard the explosion of a gunshot, shouted voices. The police trying to force their way through the front door.

Jenna screamed, "Go to the back! Go—"

Ramsey slammed a hand over her mouth, shoving the words back down her throat. He tasted of sweat and dirt and blood. Bile rose in her throat and she fought against his hold.

He slammed her against the wall behind the door, only feet from an unmoving Linc. Ramsey's meaty hand fisted in the neckline of her cotton shirt and ripped.

Two buttons flew across the room. She screamed behind his hand, fighting frantically. She kicked him viciously, almost senselessly, over and over. He would not rape her again. She would die first.

Heavy fists pounded against the door. Unfamiliar voices rang in Jenna's ears. "Open the door, Ramsey! You're surrounded!"

A tattered strip of her shirt hung down the middle of her chest, exposing the beginning swell of her breast. And the slim wire she wore.

Ramsey saw it and roared with fury, his face contorting into lines of terrifying malevolence. He held her to the door with one hand, reached for the wire with the other.

She fought, kicking him in the shin, the knee, the ankle. Her one good fist struck a blow at his throat, knowing a punch against his massive chest would be futile.

Breathing hard, his handsome features strained and vicious, he shoved her up against the door and pinned her there with his body. Solid muscle nailed her to the steel, crushing her ribs. Her broken arm twisted at a painful angle.

"No! No! No!" With her good hand, she raked at his face, tearing skin on his neck. Her nails scored his lip, and he tried to bite her.

She screamed again, bucking wildly, her mind focused solely on survival, her breath-to-breath effort to escape death, elude for one more heartbeat his brutal hands tearing at her body, violating her.

He cursed and reached between them, squeezing her breast. Pain shot through her, radiated up her arm.

Fatigue washed through her and the sensation sent a new surge of panic through her. She couldn't stop fighting. She couldn't. She had to get away.

She thought he would throw her to the floor, try to subdue her, but instead he reached inside her shirt, ripping the wire from her body. In the wake of ice-edged terror, she barely felt the sting of tape as it was yanked from her flesh.

He wrapped his fingers around her throat, then lifted his other hand and spoke into the microphone he'd torn from her body. "Hello, you pigs. You're signing off."

With that, he dropped the bug and crushed it beneath his heavy boot.

For an instant, fear paralyzed her. He smiled, so purely evil that she couldn't even breathe. Cruel deliberation contorted his features.

She wondered if she should try to talk to him, or stop fighting him. If she pretended to be submissive, would he relax his guard? But when he grabbed her jaw and lifted her off the floor, forcing her head back against the door, she knew she couldn't pretend anything. If she died, she would die fighting.

"Now," he breathed, twisted satisfaction glittering in his eyes. "We're all alone." He bent his head, biting her neck hard enough to make it sting.

Moving on instinct, she kicked him. He grunted as she connected with his knee. His breath blew hot and heavy on her neck.

He bit her again, harder. "Oh, it's gonna be good this time. So much better than last. You're gonna cry for me, bitch, and you're gonna beg me to end it. You're gonna beg, just like I begged you all those years ago not to ruin me. You shoulda listened. You shoulda listened."

Tears streamed down her face, burning her cheeks. *Where was Mace? Linc?* A sense of hopelessness gripped her, weakening her knees. It beckoned her to slip into a dark void of peace. To cross over the line where her mind parted from reality.

She wanted to give in to the blackness reaching for her, descend into the silent buffered world of her mind where she would feel nothing, hear nothing, know nothing. Oblivion.

His teeth raked her collarbone, and his hand tightened around her throat.

Feeling abandoned and helpless, she sobbed, still struggling, barely able to breathe past the crushing pressure of his body. She just wanted it to be over, wanted to surrender to the darkness, to the place inside herself where she would feel nothing.

"Beg me to stop," he panted against her skin, his breathing ragged. "Beg me."

Sickened at his arousal, she saw then how perverse he was, how he orchestrated this whole sick game to some evil music in his mind. She thought of Linc's gentle strength, his unwavering support and love. A small bud of strength sprouted inside her.

She would never beg, never give in until her last breath. Before she let Ramsey rape her again, he would have to kill her. Especially after what she had shared last night with Linc.

"No!" she screamed, renewing her struggles, her body slamming into his as she fought to get away.

She bit, kicked, scratched. Every movement drove his fingers harder, deeper into her throat, choking her. Black spots danced before her eyes. The door rattled from the force of banging fists.

Her cast banged the wall, jarring her arm. Without even thinking, she twisted and slammed the plaster into the side of Ramsey's head as hard as she could.

The blow knocked his head away from her chest and she did it again, catching him in the face before he drew back. Bone crunched and she hoped it wasn't her arm, breaking again.

Blood spurted from his nose. He howled, grabbing at her, but she hit him again, this time catching him in the chin. He flinched and it gave her enough time to scramble away from the body-and-muscle box he'd erected around her. He spun, grabbing for her, but she eluded him.

If only she could get to the back emergency exit! She could escape. Mace could get in.

She darted away, torn between staying with Linc and going for help. But she was their only chance for rescue. She zigzagged through the room, moving into the back half where the lights were still off, her gaze searching around the wall extension for the blinking red light that marked the exit. She forced herself to keep running, praying with everything in her that Ramsey followed her.

He did. He hurdled Linc's inert body and kept coming.

Panting, struggling to keep from unraveling, her gaze darted around for a weapon. Anything at all. She scanned the tops of dog cages, then the small lab area across the room.

Ramsey's heavy footsteps thundered behind her, menacing, imminent, resurrecting all the horror of the past. Her tennis shoes slipped on the slick tile, but she didn't fall.

The dogs were hysterical, barking and snarling and throwing themselves against the cage doors. Sheer instinct guided her to the cages, though it brought her within feet of Ramsey.

She slammed her palm against the latch on the first cage.

The door sprang open and Rollo, a Scottish terrier, sprang out, barking wildly and heading straight for Ramsey.

She prayed the little dog wouldn't get hurt. She'd only been trying to buy some time, put some distance between her and the maniac chasing her.

She hit the next latch and the next, releasing a Labrador, a rottweiler and a Doberman, a beagle. She could barely breathe. Couldn't think. Desperate and frantic, she ran. Tears burned her eyes.

Glancing over her shoulder, she saw the dogs crowd together and charge toward Ramsey as a pack. Her throat tightened on a sob. The rottweiler planted himself in front of Ramsey, baring his teeth, growling viciously.

She rounded the wall that separated the kennel area from the stainless steel tub used for bathing and dipping. Now, she could see the red exit light. Freedom. Escape.

Behind her, Jenna heard a meaty thud, then a dog's whimper. As she neared the door, she looked back again, biting off a scream.

The beagle and the labrador yelped and skidded across the waxy floor, sliding into Ramsey and knocking him off balance.

Jenna sprinted past the stainless steel tub and, on an impulse, snatched up a bag of powdered flea dip without breaking stride.

Ramsey's harsh curses punctuated the dogs' fevered barking. One of the animals yelped and Ramsey's footsteps resumed pounding after her.

"Jenna!"

Her heartbeat stuttered and she nearly stopped. That was Linc's voice! Faint, but definitely him.

She wanted to go back, but she was here, at the exit. She skidded into the door, heart thundering, adrenaline blistering her veins. Gulping in air, sobbing, she struggled with the door, but it wouldn't give. Then she understood and cried out in horror.

A lead pipe was jammed beneath the door handle that stretched across the metal frame, effectively bolting her inside. Locking the police out.

She switched the flea powder to her injured hand and grabbed for the bar with her left. Her hand, slick with sweat, slipped on the steel as she tried to wrest it free.

She could hear Ramsey behind her, nearing. Frantic, choked by panic, she struggled to work the pipe out from under the push handle.

Voices yelled from the other side. "Get away from the door! We're going to shoot."

"No, don't!" Tears coursed down her cheeks. Desperate, she wrestled with the pipe. "It's me, Jenna. Don't shoot."

"Jenna, are you all right?"

Mace!

Ramsey's hand clamped her arm like a meat hook.

"No!" she screamed.

He spun her around and slammed her against the door.

The bar ground painfully into her hips. Dull pain arrowed up her arm. At her back, the door vibrated from the powerful pounding on the other side.

Ramsey was breathing hard, virulent hatred blazing in his eyes. Despite the trembling that worked through her body, Jenna noted with satisfaction that blood trickled from his lip, his ear, a vicious scratch on his neck. Then fear surged back, more crippling than before. How could she escape him this time?

Sweat trickled down his temple, melded with a streak of blood. Bitter rage shook him. "You never shoulda done that."

Reading death in his eyes, her thoughts raced desperately. *Linc, Mace, somebody!*

A low vicious growl sounded behind Ramsey. Jenna gasped. Ramsey's eyes widened in surprise, then pain creased his features.

"Owww!" he bellowed, his grip cutting tighter into her arm.

He flinched and she realized that one of the dogs had bitten him. Before she barely had time to process the information, he screamed in pain again and jerked back.

His hold on her loosened and Jenna took her chance. Pushing at his chest, she wrenched free. In a breath, she registered the fact that both the Doberman and the rottweiler had sunk their teeth into Ramsey's leg. She ripped open the flea powder and hurled the bag at him.

Gray-white powder covered his face. He screamed, first in fury, then in pain. Bitter, metallic chemicals seared Jenna's lungs.

Frantic to escape, to let the police in, Jenna bolted, scrambling around the cages, registering that the other dogs had crowded under the foremost exam table and barked ferociously.

Then she saw Linc. He moved, touching his head, trying to push up on his elbow.

"Linc! Linc!" Her knees wobbled in relief that he was conscious, but she forced herself to move past him, to the door.

The steel shook in a steady, ponderous rhythm as if the police now used their bodies instead of their fists.

She pushed with all her might to move the heavy autoclave away from the door, but it wouldn't budge. Sobbing now, her fingers slick with sweat and fear, she pushed harder. She couldn't believe how easily Ramsey moved it.

"Jenna, the gun." Linc's voice was faint, but insistent. "Get the gun."

She turned, saw Ramsey rounding the corner, heading straight for them. In her desperation, she'd forgotten all about Linc's .38. She slid down beside him, tears streaming down her cheeks.

"Where? Where?"

Ramsey's weight rattled the floor.

"Here," Linc panted, trying to reach for the gun himself, his handsome features twisted in agony.

Ramsey bore down on her. He shook off the Doberman, flinging the lean muscular dog across the room to slam into the wall.

She reached behind Linc, pulled the gun free of his waist-band. Jenna turned toward Ramsey, knowing she had to shoot or he would kill both her and Linc. Her fingers fumbled on the safety, but she managed to flip it off.

Linc struggled to sit up. She aimed the gun at Ramsey, who charged toward her like an enraged animal. He neared, only feet away. The distance narrowed.

Her hand shook. Tears blurred her vision. She couldn't steady the weapon. She shifted the gun to her right hand and tried to squeeze the trigger, but her hand was too weak.

"You're dead, you bitch! Dead!" Ramsey lunged, going for her throat.

At the same instant, Linc grabbed for her. His hand closed over hers. He squeezed the trigger.

Just as Ramsey's hand closed around her throat, a gunshot cracked the air.

Jenna recoiled from the force. Smoke burned her nostrils.

The dogs yelped, dove into the corner by the cabinet and whimpered into silence.

Stunned, trembling uncontrollably, she could barely register the scene. She stared into Ramsey's face, waiting for the choking, mind-numbing pressure of his hand around her neck.

Surprised disbelief registered in his eyes, shifted into hatred, then abruptly expired into emptiness. His hand around her throat loosened, then fell. He toppled to the floor only inches from her.

Jenna stared, her mind trying to catch up. Her breath ripped through her body in a desperate attempt to reach her lungs. Linc murmured a prayer behind her.

He pushed himself up and leaned over to feel for a pulse. Pain and relief roughened his voice. "He's dead."

Her teeth chattered.

His arm went around her, held on tight. "Jenna, honey, give me the gun." He took it gently from her. "You're safe, Jenna. Safe."

In a daze, she looked at him. "You're all right. You're alive."

"Yes." He pressed a wobbly kiss to her lips.

She raised an unsteady hand to his face, her vision blurred by tears.

The sound of hammering fists pierced her consciousness. Linc glanced at the door. "We've got to let them in."

"We're all right," Jenna called out. "Ramsey's dead."

"What's in front of the door?" an officer shouted.

"The autoclave." Jenna turned to Linc. "I can't move that thing and neither can you." Her teeth chattered on the words as reaction streamed through her body. "There's a pipe jammed in the back door. That's why I couldn't get it open."

"We'll go there."

She rose, helping him to his feet, her good arm strong around his waist. Cold ached in her hands, her feet, but she focused on Linc. They were both safe. Both alive.

Fists pounded on the back door. Mace's voice, strident with alarm, boomed through the metal. "Are you all right? Jenna, what's going on? Finch, get this damn door open!"

"Don't shoot anything," Linc yelled, then winced as pain pulled his features taut.

"It's jammed," Jenna called, limping to a stop with Linc in front of the door. "We're okay."

Linc leaned weakly against the wall and together they worked the pipe free. Jenna pushed open the door, sagging in relief as fresh air rolled inside.

Mace and two other officers rushed in, weapons drawn.

Linc gestured weakly toward the front. "He's up there. He's dead."

"You two okay?" Mace's gaze was sharp and dangerous, his voice husky.

She nodded, dragging in clean air, gripping Linc's hand tightly.

The other officer returned. "Yep, Ramsey's a goner, Mace."

"Thank goodness," Mace said roughly, looking at Linc with a combination of relief and concern.

Jenna turned to Linc and whispered against his lips. "Thank *you*."

Still shaking, but finally believing Ramsey was dead, Jenna led Linc back to the waiting area. The autoclave had been moved and she helped him through the doorway, settling him gently in a chair close by.

He agreed to let her look at his head only after she kissed him. Stroking his face gently, she blinked back more tears and went to one of the cabinets in the exam room, returning with sutures and alcohol.

Linc eyed her warily. "What are you doing?"

"Stitching you up."

"You're a vet, for crying out loud—ouch!" He winced, gingerly touching the back of his head. "All right."

Mace moved into the doorway. "I've called the paramedics. They can stitch it."

"No, Jenna can do it." Linc smiled up at her, love shining in his pain-ravaged eyes.

Mace shrugged and turned away to confer with another officer. The other officers milled about, taking notes, herding dogs into cages. Someone covered Ramsey's body with a disposable sterile cloth from her cabinet.

She eased down beside Linc, her hands still shaking. For just a moment, she sat there, clutching his hands tightly. Slowly his strength seeped into her.

She knew how close she and Linc had come to death, knew a more severe reaction might set in later, but right now she was giddy with relief and gratitude and security. Ramsey could never hurt her again.

She rose to her knees and turned toward Linc. "Okay, let me look at your head."

"I'd feel a lot better if you'd just kiss me again."

She did, then gently turned his head away so she could examine the cut on the back of his head. The wound was about an inch long, but deep. "You're going to have a big bump."

"How many stitches?" He nibbled on her neck, his breath tickling her skin.

"Stop that." She drew back to look at him, smiling softly. "Probably seven or eight."

"They can wait then."

"No—"

"Jenna." Linc winced slightly, but didn't stop. "I've got some things to say and this time, you're going to let me say them."

"He hit you really hard, Linc." She lifted an alcohol-soaked cotton pad to his head. "I think you should let me clean it up."

His fingers circled her wrist and he lowered her hand back to his lap, lacing his fingers with hers. "Sam told me not to screw this up and I'm not going to."

"Sam?" She frowned. "What does Sam have to do with this?"

"I was about to ask that myself," Mace drawled from his position in the doorway.

"Mind your own business, bro," Linc commanded, keeping his gaze on Jenna. "Last night in the barn, I committed myself to you. *All* of myself. I didn't even realize it."

Wonder shone in his eyes and his hand tightened on hers. "I thought I was still protecting myself, maybe even protecting you, but now I see I had already given you my heart. I didn't even know I was capable. You found my heart again, Jenna. You made me not only believe in love, but want to take a chance."

Tears burned her eyes, but she smiled, lowering her voice for Linc only. "Do you know what you did for me?" Emotion choked her voice. "What you gave me?"

Tenderness and male satisfaction gleamed in his eyes. "It *was* pretty good," he admitted smugly.

"Not just the sex, but yes, it was great. It's more than that. You…fixed me. You really did. You restored a piece of myself that I thought damaged forever."

Tears welled up and this time she couldn't stop them.

Linc placed a tender kiss on her lips, thumbing away her tears. "I love you. You have to know that. I want to spend the rest of my life with you."

Joy swelled in her chest, stretching almost painfully across her lungs. "Oh, Linc."

He smiled crookedly. "That's not exactly the response I was hoping for."

"I love you, too," she whispered.

Heat flared in his eyes. "Enough to marry me?"

Mace snapped to attention, squinting at him, "*How* hard were you hit?"

Linc glared at his brother, then turned back to Jenna. "Well, how about it? We belong together and you know it. There's no way I'm letting you walk away."

One corner of her lip lifted in a smile. He was offering her a life of stability, of trust, of *passion*.

"You can't use the excuse of your past anymore," he growled. "And neither can I."

She laughed softly, caressing his beautiful face. "I wasn't planning to."

"Then what? Tell me. I can get rid of every excuse—"

"You really think you can fix everything, don't you, Dr. Garrett?" she said smartly.

"Damn right."

"Well, this time you're right."

His eyes widened. "Does that mean yes?"

"Yes," she whispered, leaning into him for a long, deep kiss.

A small smattering of applause broke out and Jenna pulled away, her face heating as she smiled sheepishly at the officers who now crowded the doorway with Mace.

Mace shook his head, planting a fist on his hip. "Sam is never gonna believe this. And I owe Devon big time."

"For what?" Linc hugged Jenna to him.

Mace grinned. "When I told her about Jenna, she bet me two months' kitchen duty that you were in love with her."

"You should never bet against love, big brother." Linc smiled down at Jenna, the promise of the future shining in his eyes. "I love you, Jenna West."

"I know, Linc." Love ached in her heart, thawing the last frozen piece of her past, healing the scar that had caused her to nearly lose the one man who had found her soul, guided her back to passion. "That's why it's so wonderful. *Because I know.*"

*   *   *   *   *

Has the charmer met his match? Watch for Sam's story coming in December, 1998!

The World's Most Eligible Bachelors are about to be named! And Silhouette Books brings them to you in an all-new, original series....

World's Most Eligible Bachelors

Twelve of the sexiest, most sought-after men share every intimate detail of their lives in twelve never-before-published novels by the genre's top authors.

Don't miss these unforgettable stories by:

Dixie Browning

MARIE FERRARELLA

Jackie Merritt

Tracy Sinclair

BJ James

RACHEL LEE   Suzanne Carey

Gina Wilkins

VICTORIA PADE

MAGGIE SHAYNE   Anne McAllister

Susan Mallery

Look for one new book each month in the
World's Most Eligible Bachelors series beginning
September 1998 from Silhouette Books.

Silhouette ®

Available at your favorite retail outlet.

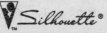

PAULA DETMER RIGGS

Continues the twelve-book series— 36 Hours—in May 1998 with Book Eleven

THE PARENT PLAN

Cassidy and Karen Sloane's marriage was on the rocks—and had been since their little girl spent one lonely, stormy night trapped in a cave. And it would take their daughter's wisdom and love to convince the stubborn rancher and the proud doctor that they had better things to do than clash over their careers, because their most important job was being Mom and Dad—and husband and wife.

For Cassidy and Karen and *all* the residents of Grand Springs, Colorado, the storm-induced blackout was just the beginning of 36 Hours that changed *everything!* You won't want to miss a single book.

Available at your favorite retail outlet.